HOTT MOTORS

BY

JULIO ORTIZ

ISBN 978-1-956010-66-4 (paperback)
ISBN 978-1-956010-67-1 (digital)

"Hott Motors" by Julio Ortiz
Julio82ortiz@att.net
Julio82ortiz@gmail.com
Instagram JUELZ828486

Rushmore Press LLC
1 800 460 9188
www.rushmorepress.com

Printed in the United States of America

"Dedicated to all the people in all extents of the auto industry all around the world. Thank you for your influence."

—Julio Ortiz

CHAPTER 1

"Take it on the other side."

It was a cold day with a huge bright sun in the sky, the first Saturday in March. A 20-year-old Garrett Lee was attending visitation at Menard Correction Facility in a small southern Illinois town of Chester, not too far from the Mississippi River. Garrett patiently waited in his chair for his name to be called, watching other people and wondering who it was they were there to visit—a brother, a friend, a cousin, an uncle, or a father like him? Garretts's father was a gentleman named Warren Lee who had been an inmate at Menard for 13 years. He was now convicted as a collaborator in several crimes being a contractor to a mafia that had once held a strong grip on Chicago. It was a time when most of the progress in town occurred through their knowledge. You help them out, they help you out. And if you keep your nose clean, you never see a day behind bars. Warren almost made it. He could have ratted out his handlers but that wasn't his style. It wasn't in him to blame someone else for his actions. He believed he deserved to be there. Garrett the son was a lengthy, light-complected Caucasian male with dark brown hair. He was a simple, easy-going kind of guy, not a follower of trends trying to act and dress like everybody else nor the kind of guy who goes along with the crowd. He grew up in small circles and learned to always follow and be himself. Garrett wore dark red work boots and a pair of jeans with the ends rolled just at his ankles, sporting a bright red buffalo flannel also with the sleeves rolled up despite the cool temperatures outside. He was a true midwestern kid. His hair was gelled back and his face had just a bit of fuzz piling up on his chin along with stubs, making out a patchy beard on the lower part of his cheeks. All and all, he was a handsome young man, still a sponge looking for his own way in life.

Garrett had an added characteristic to him. He possessed the aura of a tough guy—this kind of snare you might find from a retired boxer and a gentle calmness where he didn't care if you attacked him verbally or physically. Maybe he just didn't know how bad things could be. He hadn't bled enough yet or maybe it was arrogance due to visiting a prison with the privilege of being able to leave that afternoon. He had that neighborhood look but had not paid his due to the streets. He didn't have to. His father was respected enough in town that nobody before had ever messed with Garrett and Garrett didn't have a reason to mess with anyone. But his time would soon come. There are things a man must learn to do all on his own. When a boy wants to be with a girl, he needs to become a man. There is no boy anymore in doing men's things. Being with a woman, he was no molester or joker. Guys did things "for real!" and "forever." There was no halfway play! There were no "maybes" and "takebacks," yet all of these things were what Warren hadn't been able to teach his son. He did the best he could. He looked out for his friends and hoped they would look out for Garrett as they did. Garrett grew up in Chicago. He never played sports, so he wasn't much of an athlete, but he had a fair build, although not like an underwear model. Perhaps, he could have easily been mistaken for a football quarterback. In school, Garrett was a decent student but he didn't believe college was an option for him. He knew there was another line of work out there for him, but he hadn't found it yet. He was the kind of guy who enjoyed working with his hands and being productive. His dreams were mostly spent daydreaming about being a professional race car driver, but for a ghetto kid from Chicago where there were no racetracks nor kart tracks, it didn't seem like it was a dream worth talking about. Impossible, he thought. Maybe he would stumble into a trade and just stay there forever? It was the best thing that could happen to him, he thought.

Garrett was in his early twenties. These once-a-month visits helped him a lot. He got to bond with his father and hear him out. He valued these visits and paid attention to every word he said. Garrett read about everything related to Menard. He read about guys being sentenced to long stays and other guys dying before being released from prison. It was in the back of his mind that he may never get to see his dad released again. It was his biggest fear. Warren Lee had once been associated with the good Ol' Chicago Outfit, a ring of organized crime primarily functioning from Illinois that had been around since the days of Al "Scarface" Capone, rumored to have ties today all around the world. Warren's family had been in Chicago a long time. He studied to be a mechanical engineer but turned it all down to stay in town and marry his high school sweetheart Clarissa, Garrett's mother. Maybe it was a sign to the wise guys. Warren had a sleeve that could be pulled on. He wanted to give her all the nice things he was destined for from a prosperous education, so he began doing jobs for the mob just to make a few extra bucks. His wife never suspected a thing since that is what is passed down through the generations in the Lee household: "You do what you have to and never look for fame or fortune." Garrett had heard it from his dad several times before, so much so he was beginning to doubt the moniker, especially the way the world was going with social media, overnight sensations, and all. Garrett at times even doubted that this kind of evil still lived in the world today. He kept his distance and had yet no way of knowing if it still existed or not. Some of the things his father told or hinted at to him just seemed like tall tales. Garrett didn't want to believe in organized crimes or that he could be blackmailed. He didn't think of himself as being worthy of having anything of value that anyone would risk breaking the law to take from him. His father would answer him by saying, "If that trash can over there could come to life and make me one dollar! Just one dollar in all its life, it would have served its purpose." Garrett would say, "Dad, there's more to life than money," to which Warren would say, "If that garbage were a person and it stole one dollar from you, does it matter?" Garrett back then shrugged his shoulders, then Warren said, "What if that garbage can make a choice that keeps you alive or takes your life? Does that matter?" Garrett said, "Of course, it matters, but that can't happen, dad. Other people don't make decisions that affect me." Warren replied, "You're wrong. Everything is tied together! Always! Be the silent cog, be you. I'll help you whenever I can. Take care."

Garrett always thought of his father as being wise. At times, he felt cheated that he wasn't able to grow up with him every day, but he just lived with it and moved on. The old-timers called Warren "Motors" because ever since he was a kid, he always worked on motors of all kinds, big and small. He was always curious and taking them apart, learning how they worked and thinking of ways to improve them. Around the neighborhood, a lot of the wise guys cheered him on when he left to go to college in Michigan. They hoped he would find his own way, a better way, but even Motors was not strong enough mentally to put Chicago away. What brought him back was his heart. Garrett also groomed himself to be mechanically inclined. It became something else he and his father had in common, although Garrett secretly felt like he would much rather be a race car driver than a repair tech. Maybe if his father was not in prison, he could have been. Garrett worked at an NTB. He started parttime while still in school and worked his way up from the bottom with just a set of craftsmen tools that cost him no more than $100 bucks. Today, just 3 years later, he owned a double bay toolbox loaded with the best type of modern tools available, developing the skill to wield them. Garrett was still a single guy and the young car enthusiast rarely even communicated with anybody, much less a woman that interested him. There was a woman he liked a lot. Garrett kept a second job to feed his personal ambitions at a bar where he would see her every few days bartending, but he could never muster enough courage to go and invite her out. He was still too young and lacked confidence.

Warren's heart brought him back to town. His love for Clarissa was too great it weakened Warren, but he never saw it as a weakness. He saw it as him pursuing something so true and grand that it was beyond him or Garrett's mother. The Outfit played a key role in Warren's life from his return and onward. They facilitated several things for the two of them to be married. Once the other guys in town heard Warren was interested in Clarissa, they all knew she was "off the table." Warren would also be kept busy as to keep him from wandering his eyes. Although he was so in love, he did not need help. Warren and Clarissa were married in the fall of 1995. Sam Loutessi himself made a good contribution to the event and attended, praising the young couple. All the while, the Outfit always reminded Warren as to who was helping him. Warren was not known for being ungrateful. As time went by, his duties just grew in commitment. He was trusted around higher figures and since he had more to lose, they trusted him to keep himself disciplined.

Things in Warren Lee's life were doing well back then. When Garrett was born, he was a happy man, then before he even had a chance to notice, he found himself always leaving his happy home to complete jobs for the Chicago Outfit. Motors became their go-to guy for fixing damaged or bullet-wounded cars for them, changing VIN plates, and modifying cars that needed to be made to look different before they got rid of them. At the time crime in Chicago was near an all-time high, the cars he worked on kept having longer and longer rap sheets attached to them. The police were all but too far away. Other factions saw defects in the Outfit which also led to wars among the streets and thick steel plates being welded into the doors which could be traced from the manufacturer to the shop where Warren worked. Multiple locations need to be used. The downside was when Warren was forced to use the facilities at his day job to fix the Outfit's cars. In a single week, it would all come crumbling down for him. The Outfit was backpedaling. A new location was in the work to be occupied by them, but Warren would never get a chance to use it from his job at a dealership. Cars from the Outfit would arrive dripping blood on the lot to being driven away in pristine conditions. Motors was doing everything he could but working until 1 AM even in a busy city like Chicago was not being so subtle. A rival gang member would work out a deal and turn the CPD on to the dealership. A day later, an investigation on the dealers' service department happened. Several people attempting to save their own beacon began talking and all of them mentioned Warren Lee. There was a wave of new police officers taking charge in town. They were wise to the way things worked. A young officer named Juan Vega was among those leading the charge against the Outfit. With so many groups taking aim, the Outfit didn't stand a chance. There was a bullseye exactly over it. The Chicago Outfit was losing allies in the city hall, precincts, and mid- to large-level business partners. The chaos was slowly being tamed. The Chicago Outfit found themselves without a choice but to backpedal. Diminishing in numbers one by one, they were dying or getting arrested. They would lose their stronghold in town that year. Well, most of it. Small independent gangs would take advantage of the Outfit. Being no more, they cradled turf and paid no one but themselves. Large international groups which had previously been negotiated with at the gate now made all their way to the living room and kicked their feet up the ottoman, laughing at the downfall of the once-great Chicago Outfit. Motors could see the writing on the wall. He talked very deeply with his wife and said, "It's time to leave town." The following day, a call came in telling Motors there was going to be a raid of the dealership the following morning and he had to go to the shop at the dealer to dispose of the evidence tying Mr. Loutessi to the shop. Warren had no choice but to go. He knew he was up against a double-edged sword but he feared the Outfit the most and in the back of his mind, he was just as guilty as any of the men who claimed to be taking care of him. His bed was already made. Garrett remembers the day it happened very well. His parents devised a plan where they could evade the police and leave town before the raid took place. Clarissa kept Garrett from kindergarten that day which he did not want to miss. She packed several suitcases, then they loaded them onto their car. She was to pick up Warren at the dealership before it opened where they would drive away, never to return. When they arrived at the dealership, Clarissa began crying. She saw from half a block away that she was too late. The police had already arrested Warren in front of the dealership. Garrett and his mother saw his father being escorted to the back of a squad car handcuffed. He motioned with his mouth as if to say, "I'm sorry." His mother was in tears the entire time. Warren touched the side of his head to the door glass, always looking toward them and his lips motioned as if to say, "I love you." Warren got rid of the evidence but was caught himself red-handed. Although he kept Mr. Loutessi from being arrested, it was just a matter of time for his freedom to be numbered.

Garrett grew up resenting cops from that day on. They always rubbed him off as being different people. For him, they are cold-blooded and cruel, but as he grew up, it was the words of his own father that taught him to let go of his hatred toward them. His father made Garrett understand that he was guilty, and they had all the agreed-upon rights to do the things which they did that day. Warren would say, "The best way to avoid them coming for you is don't give them a reason to." Garrett understood what his father told him that day. He vowed to himself to always be as best a straight shooter as he could and try to never put himself in the position of being arrested—a high bar to give oneself especially in the place where Garrett grew up. Too bad, not all people shared the same point of view. Most looked forward to doing things illegally because the traditional legal world seemed too far out of reach for them. As if that world didn't mean to them. Taking what one wanted was the only way to get ahead in life.

Today, Warren lived with the guys who also grew up taking what they wanted until the world decided to take something back. They all claimed to be friends and family, but the truth is their sentence was the only thing they had in common. They learned to make the best of their situation together. They would sit around together telling each other the same old war stories over and over.

They would play cards and build on their old code in the Outfit, sharing privileges and skills with each other. Warren had ignited his curiosity and learned how to use the internet. Warren completed his degree in Mechanical Engineering from behind a prison wall. Garrett joked with his dad about that often. He joked how he himself was on the outside and couldn't afford to attend school, nor could he find time to have that comradery or friendship with anyone about how blessed his father was. Garrett seemed to downplay his life when he would tell his father how he drove the same beaten sedan since he was 17, or how he still lived in his mother's attic in a makeshift room his stepdad had built for him. Warren would laugh and say to Garrett, "Maybe one day, things will get better for you."

A guard interrupted Garrett's train of thought. He yelled at him saying, "Garrett Lee, window 8!"

Garrett got up from his chair and made his way to window number 8. He sat down on a cold stainless-steel stool in front of a counter next to a sheet of glass where his father was being signaled to sit on its opposing side. Warren was wearing an orange pullover and green pants along with white socks and plain white sneakers. Physically, Warren looked great. His shoulders were broad, his biceps swollen, his hands clean, and his nails well-groomed. He had a bounce to his step and a subtle smile due to his guest on the other side of the glass. Warren may have been working in the garden recently. He had a pinkish hue in his forehead, his cheeks, his nose, even on his forearms. He wore glasses and was in his late 40s. His hair was thinning but still looked full and healthy. It was jelled down loosely, forming a hump toward the front. He kept a light mustache. Warren continued adding to his arm tattoos. By now, he had multiple images of cars, wrenches, pistons, women, and flaming skulls all over. He had a demeanor like he was still young, cool, and calm, yet he sounded like a college professor.

Garrett was smiling. He grabbed the phone off the wall and waited until Warren did the same, then he said, "What's up, Pops?"

Warren said, "Hey there, young man. Same stuff, different day."

Garrett said, "Yeah, so how have you been in here?"

Warren said, "As good as I've ever been. Well, let me tell you this. There's a good chance of me getting paroled this month. Could you believe it? I've been putting in some real work, studying, and building privileges. I asked to be reviewed for parole and the warden said yes. So maybe on the 24th, you might be able to come by and pick me up?"

Garrett said, "That's great, Pops, then you will work as an engineer?"

Warren said, "I'd like that. That'd be really nice. But a bit too much for an old guy like me. I have a friend named Charles who got out a few years back. I hear he owns a restoration shop in San Anton that might be a little more along the route of a former con."

The two of them shared a smile then carried on talking for a while having a great time. Garrett suspected the 15 minutes were coming to an end. Warren was warned he only had a few minutes left. He began saying his goodbye for the day and said, "Well, keep learning the web. I'll be looking for your emails and yeah, I'll come by to pick you this month. We'll leave town, whatever. Just make it happen."

Warren said, "I'd like that. I will. kid."

The guard behind Warren said, "Times up, Motors."

They held out one last stare at each other for that day from across the glass then walked apart. The guys who were watching couldn't help but be jealous that Motors and his kid had such a good relationship. Most of the inmates had bad relationships with their families on the outside. People usually went to visit them out of need or necessity. When the other inmates heard the news about Motors being in the warden's good graces, it raised a lot of eyebrows. Several guys did not like it, not one bit. They turned and stared at him, but he was not one to be intimidated by looks. He got in line and walked down to his cell block like nothing had been said.

Garrett left the visiting area. He walked down the corridor and made his way across the front door. He made his way to his car.

Garrett was excited. The thought of being able to walk out that same doorway with his father by his side was thrilling to him and it just so happened his best upbeat song came on over the radio as soon as he started his car. On the long drive home, he thought about all the kinds of things they could do together like open a repair shop or ride motorcycles across the great Midwest. His father could use his degree and go work for a big manufacturer as an engineer but his idea of moving to San Antonio would be pretty neat, too, he thought. He was curious now about the Alamo and wondered about the Riverwalk. It'd be cool to live there.

Garrett spent the following few days trying to get back to normal, keeping his nose clean, learning as much as he could about cars, and trying to talk to women. His boss at a local NTB and the senior techs alongside him did a good job passing on their knowledge to him. Usually, as the situation presented itself, they would help him solve it. Although NTB isn't known for working on high-performance cars, he usually got to see his fair share of tuner enthusiasts coming through the shop. He would go over and just be present when the hood came up to try and absorb as much as he could. Garrett would attend car shows and ask the guys there about their battery maintenance, which usually lead him to such comments as, "You can bring it to NTB."

Those cars would occasionally stop by, taking him up on his offer. Garrett loved doing all the simple things such as battery inspections, tire inspections, or alignments. He learned all about how modifications affected the factory specs and adjusted his equipment accordingly. His boss liked Garrett. He was a hard worker, always on time, showed up in a fresh, clean uniform ready to get going every day. Garrett promptly purchased all the specialty tools required for the job. He never threw a fit like some other mechanics when they had to deal with rusty bolt and seized calipers even if it meant losing his ass on some of those tougher jobs. Garrett would occasionally be tasked with diagnosing cars even if he wasn't the greatest at it, all makes and all models. Garrett was usually comfortable just getting the trust and learning experience. He would only receive one labor hour upfront while some of the veteran techs usually wanted more time. If he did on a car, meaning, he spent longer than 2 hours with no leads. There wasn't a lot of pressure on him to persuade the customer into higher fees, or ask for more time, nor did it change his demeanor to solve the problem. He always kept a cool head and didn't stop until he found the root of the problem, a trait he also used in real life. Garrett maintained a night job. The owner was a friend of his mother and had hired him to work there since he was 18 due to him wanting to have his own money. He worked at a local pub washing dishes and taking out the garbage. It didn't pay him much but on certain nights, it would become the place to be, socially speaking, but nobody ever seemed to notice Garrett was even there. He didn't say much nor command a crowd. Even his crush who worked there, Dayana, rarely ever had a single word with the guy. The pub was a standalone building off of a major road just off the expressway in Addison named "Black Door."

Garrett was a young guy. He didn't mind being bossed around or taken as dope or screwup. He enjoyed just being there some nights. He enjoyed staying up late even if he was cleaning vomit off of chairs with a dirty rag or mopping and picking glass one piece at a time from under tables. His drive was to build enough money to live on his own and release himself from this child mentality. No one but himself can influence his decisions on where to go from there. Truth is, his day job at NTB alone is a great job to have. But he didn't see it like that. He wanted more out of life. He felt like he was meant for more and was determined to risk everything when that opportunity presented itself to him. He would dive headfirst. Money was necessary for everything—from buying a fast car to being able to afford a garage of his own where he could build a race car, then he drowned himself wondering what would be next. Well, he would need to buy a trailer and pay the entrance fees to be able to haul and drive it on racetracks all across the country, but how? There's a reason racing is not popular in the ghetto, he thought to himself, then he would mutter, "Maybe I should street race my sedan?"

In the upcoming days, Garrett's boss at the pub encouraged his staff members to be more friendly to one another, to try and set a tone for the environment, and not be so gloomy toward each one. He specifically picked on Garrett and said, "That means you, Gare, be a little bit more smiling please!" Everyone turned to look at Garrett who was turning all different shades of pink and red. As he was standing there, Dayana noticed how shy he was and made it her personal goal to interact with Garrett more often. She was one of the good ones. Garrett tried to remain the same as he always had been but his co-workers didn't. They tried to get him involved and became a little bit more cheerful. They would walk near him and high-five him. Most of them didn't even know his name before, but now, everybody called him "Gare." His duties at Black Door evolved into longer hours, more days, and tougher tasks. He was seen more often in the guest area stocking the bar, lifting dishes from tables, and even dispatching a couple of lagers by himself once or twice. He even cracked a smile. Lucky for him it was in the direction of Dayana who happened to be smiling back. Dayana was just a walking source of positive energy. She was constantly being hit on by guys who came into the bar and she knew exactly how to handle them, protecting her own interest, of course. Garrett would be hurt sometimes seeing how she handled these guys. They were better-looking, with more money, have bigger muscles, and own nicer cars than him. He slowly went back to try to be invisible, repenting of his ambition to be with Dayana. It's not that Garrett wasn't as good as these guys, but he lacked that confidence that these guys had—the kind where they know they are good enough even without the money, cars, or muscles. They trust themselves. Garrett didn't trust himself so he held back and looked for opportunities that he could control, make one-on-one conversation in the quiet parking lot, or maybe confess his intentions toward Dayana through a third party where the rejection would be less hurtful. Garrett had no idea what being a man was all about. How could he? His stepdad was a loner with the motto, "Fuck 'em all. Look after number 1! Always!" How about Warren, his dad? Garrett has it understood that his dad was the most popular guy in school. Besides his arrest, he had never heard anyone say anything bad about him, nor was there any evidence of him ever being a coward. Garrett would make attempt to break the ice with her. The little he knew about love was that it is weird. It's either there or it isn't. People can tell right away if they are going to date someone or not, so there was a lot of pressure on him to be perfect to her from the first conversation and onward. From what Garrett saw, he noticed most girls always seemed to prefer the risk-takers or rebels, the guys who just didn't give a shit about anything. But if he acted like that, he would be lying to himself as to who he really was. "Could Dayana be interested in a guy like that?" he thought. Garrett tried to pick up on trends or features that some of the guys would do when they talked to Dayana. He noticed a lot of them talked down to her or made her less. But why would she even put up with a guy like that? he thought. When he asked his mother about it, she told him, "Too many women have been hurt by the sweet guy. It's like saying 'I'm sorry for being a pig so here's some flowers or a box of chocolates to cover it up.' So, most women prefer the cold hard truth. Just be yourself, Gare, always, and if she isn't for you, then she isn't for you." Garrett couldn't find it in himself to talk down to her. He couldn't grow a beard. He couldn't afford a flashy car and didn't have time to lift weights. Ultimately, he gave up. He saw her start to date one guy and then break up with him. *How could she stay positive and cheerful after having her feelings go through an emotional roller coaster?* he thought. *She must be the strongest woman in the whole wide world and I want her.* Garrett wanted a girlfriend so bad it didn't have to be Dayana. But every night before he went to bed, she was the last thing on his mind, as if the universe could hear what he wanted even without him asking for her, hoping that she would keep him.

CHAPTER 2

"Trying to catch me riding dirty."

At Menard Correction Facility, the Chicago Outfit found out about Motors' parole hearing coming up later that month. The current leader of the Outfit, a guy named Joeblas Juerta who they call El Bambino, decided to confront Motors. He asked a guy to tell Motors to accompany him at a table in front of his cell, which Motors did. El Bambino explained how the Outfit was changing and if he accepted, there would be high rewards coming his way. Warren had nothing left to prove even before El Bambino asked. He already knew he would turn the offer down. He was out. El Bambino was a lifelong mobster since the late 70s. He was always a tough kid able to take beatings and dish them out just as well. It would be pretty hard to disagree with a guy like that, but that's exactly what Warren did. Sam Loutessi was also at Menard but had passed a little over a year ago, solidifying the 'age of El Bambino.' The Outfit had morphed in the last 10 years. It became more of cybercrime with secret international dealings and offshore fake and real businesses. El Bambino was a recent addition to Menard but very easily the most important mobster in Warren's cell block. He had his own private 5-star hotel in his cell and was known for being the brains of the organization. Several people speculated he came to Menard because it was safer for him to be in here than out there where even all the money in the world couldn't defend him against these other powerful people he was terrorizing. El Bambino was a very clever guy, a Northwestern grad. Recruited by the Outfit for his business talents, he then helped sprawl them into the modern era. He was bringing back the Outfit, devising schemes involving new ways of debt collecting, commercial theft, drug smuggling, people smuggling, buying politicians, blackmailing billionaires, and prolonging the threat of violence. Some would say he was meant to take the reins. The Outfit did everything to make El Bambino comfortable. He was different from everybody and they knew it, but his work was considered legendary. He was revolutionizing Cosa Nostra, bringing it to the modern-age boys who were once again given the opportunity to be men. Nobody gained more than the Chicago Outfit. El Bambino had never met Don Sal. He was exercising a plan to have more loyal inmates released, creating sleeping agents from the prison into the real world who could follow only his specific instructions. Several members were eager for the opportunity. There was also cooperation from other gangs to join as Bambino agents. They facilitated introductions to the other parts of the world— Mexico, Cuba, Russia, Laos, Kenya, and Nigeria. Warren felt as if he owed the organization for his well-being but that his loyalties died when the man who once ran the Entire Midwest passed the year earlier. Warren remembered what Mr. Loutessi told him a few days before he got sick. He said, "If you ever get out, Motors, be your own man and seek things you can do for yourself."

El Bambino wrapped up his intro then made the question to Warren. He paused and said, "So what do you want to do?" Warren was still seated at a table in front of El Bambino's cell. Next to him were a few of the hardest guys he had ever known—cold-blooded killers. Warren cleared his throat and replied, "No, I'm done. I'm done with the Outfit. If I get out, I'm leaving town and starting fresh."

El Bambino half-smiled then leaned forward and said, "I take pride in not begging nor repeating myself. I admire you, Motors. If you want to pass up on the job of your life, who am I to judge? I wish you the best."

El Bambino stood up and shook his hand, then with his left hand, gave Warren a pat on the back, then turned around and walked off to his cell. His bodyguards stayed there looking at Warren in disappointment. They heard Motors' response and were shocked by what they had heard. They took it nearly as an insult, as if Motors was now saying he was too good for them, the family, the organization. As Motors began to walk back to his cell, one of them peeked into El Bambino's cell and said, "Bambino, do you want us to take care of him?"

El Bambino said, "No. More gravy for us, let him go."

Sitting nearby in the common area listening to every single word being said was a Mexican guy who was involved with an Illinois gang called Los Setenta Y Cincos or the 75s in English. His name was Cruz Santiago. He was outnumbered, so he usually kept a low profile. He had no intention of folding and joining the Chicago Outfit. He once had heavy ties to people in Sinaloa and he believed he could run Chicago better than El Bambino ever could. That moment, he thought of a plan he could use to hurt the Chicago Outfit. He would use everybody's doubt against them. The Outfit will buckle once again. Cruz went to a computer and sent an email to a person he knew on the outside who was an independent contractor in the underworld, a guy who had many names but went by El Diablo. He tested the will of boys and sometimes, those boys evolved into men. Other times, they became demons to do El Diablo's bidding but since he believed himself to be doing a righteous service to mankind, he usually caused more harm than kindness. He was just right to tempt the son of Warren Lee. Warren would have no choice but rejoin the Outfit or bury himself trying to help his son without them and his son would be forced to be a hood like everyone else or kill El Diablo and be liberated. Cruz smiled. It was the vengeance he had been waiting for his entire life. Either way, whatever happened, he couldn't lose. All he had to do was put the cards in motion and watch them fall from afar. He went into a classroom then began typing away on a computer to a supposed psychiatric doctor he had access to. It reads:

Dear Dr. Joseph,

I've had a little headache that needs your help; I'm worried it could turn into a big disaster like a full-grown virus. Somebody needs to tempt this pain. My friend Motors said it's nothing. I don't believe him! He said his son knows more than he does. Maybe we all need Motors on our ground to tame the snakes. Thanks, Doc.

The recipient of the email was an independent guy who, when he began mentoring ex-gang members, only had the best intentions in mind. He was an acquaintance of Cruz Santiago and all it took was for one ex-con to see them together, then all of the 75s believed El Diablo was the leader. More and more hoods began to seek him out to advance their dangerous career. Little did they know what they were up against. It would be a battle against their own will to see if they deserved to be in God's good graces by being tempted by the devil or as his demons knew him as, the highest ranking leader of the 75s. He was born Agusto Reyes, a savvy businessman who had made several mistakes of his own throughout his life but managed to understand a higher meaning to life. Now, all he wanted to do was educate those less fortunate than him to find their own light. People believed he held all the contacts in his hands like strings ready for him to pull them whenever he wanted to, so he did. A one-time street hustler selling anything he could to make ends meet, in and out of jail since 14, he finally did a stint that held him until he was 19—probably the best thing that ever happened to him—he finally walked in the light. He was broken no more. He developed enough willpower to avoid falling into evil ways. He understood the teachings of the bible, giving him the strength to heal all wounds then new strength to go to places farther than any man like him had gone before. As Agusto grew older, he attended school, completed a GED, then decided to go all the way and attend college. He had met Cruz Santiago while in jail. They became friends, but secretly, neither wished they ever see one another ever again. However, fate had different plans. Agusto graduated then started his own business of garbage service where he handpicked garbage himself, disassemble components, and break down all of the metals and rare materials. Eventually, he rented space then hired employees. There were big companies that seek out his recycled material and bought it from him at a wholesale price. Everybody won. Agusto found that his strength was in mentoring and helping people but he couldn't find enough employees to mentor. He would have to change his occupation and as a work sent from God, a major recycling company gave him a hefty sum to buy him out of his business. Agusto accepted. He would sell his business and use his wealth to help those that turned Satan away. It was a hard task to do and the rest is history. Agusto and Cruz would cross paths several times in Chicago, always on opposite sides. One of them claimed to be good sending them off to hell and the other pretended to be Satan trying to guide them into the light. Everyone chose for themselves.

Agusto received the email he picked up on what Cruz was trying to tell him and immediately searched all the inmates at Menard associated with the name Motors. He found Warren Lee and within minutes, was able to find out everything about him. He came across Garrett Lee, his personal details, and random social pictures. He made a note from one of the pictures which indicated he worked at an NTB. Also, it looked like he was a busboy at a pub. Agusto found the place to be Black Door. He deciphered the photo to find it to be the one in Addison. He figured a hundred ways to infiltrate Garrett's life. If indeed the kid was in the dark, it was time to bring him to the light. He needed to become a man just like everybody else if he had it in him. Motors was none of his concern as far as Agusto knew. The Outfit kept him in check, but the kid didn't seem like Outfit material. The best way to know was to bring him in. If he was Outfit, he would soon join them. Agusto heard rumors of the Chicago Outfit trying to rebuild but he hoped that people could be strong enough to make a stand against an organized crime and it would never pick up steam if it were true. Agusto had met El Bambino. He was one of the reasons why he went into hiding but not once did he underestimate him. Agusto knew it would be very difficult. He said to himself, "A stab at the Outfit? If it's meant to be, it'll be."

Agusto smirked then sent Cruz Santiago a correspondence:

Dear patient Cruz Santiago,

My diagnosis of your symptom is a minor migraine common among inmates. Please get some rest. Don't frustrate yourself any further. I will complete my follow-up. In time, we will eradicate the migraine. Thank you.

El Diablo got to work immediately. He went to a tracking system which he forced all of his demons to use and had different members of the 75s trailing young Garrett Lee. All of his demons regardless of race or affiliation, if they fell to him and he could blackmail them with their own deed, El Diablo tracked them. They were only out if they straightened their evil ways and believed they were out. If they believed they were his minions, then they were. El Diablo heard of all crimes that went down. It was a way to entice them in the first place, then he would attempt to drown them even further. They could refuse anytime but what he noticed is that many of them enjoyed burying themselves even deeper—a mentality that he himself could understand. Garrett would be difficult to crack. He was very clean, no crimes, had no vices, no mistakes, and not even had a pair of tits in his life to help him lose an angle. Difficult but not impossible, Agusto said to himself in his study, "If he has no vices, let's find one and give it to him. Then we sit back and see what happens."

Garrett was currently working at Black Door. Several 75s were already regular patrons but now had the task of keeping tabs on Garrett and take note as to what he liked. What bothered him? One of the guys began flirting with Dayana right in front of Garrett. She showed interest, but the guys were focused on the bus boy's reaction. He was discomforted and seemed irritated. "Bingo," one of the guys said. Somebody else sent his reaction to a group chat that Agusto had set up for them. The text was going wild. Everyone wanted to join in to break this guy just as everyone had been involved when they broke them. The teasers were requesting a picture of her. Someone at Black Door took a picture of her then the chat room was bombarded with catcalls pouring in. Agusto joined in on the chat then typed, "I think she's just right for our guy. Be friendly. His name is Garrett. Lure him in. Bring him home." The catcalls stopped. The best they could do without arousing his suspicion was leave a big tip for the guy and hand it to him personally so that's what most of them did. Toward the end of the night, Garrett was clearing mugs and bottles from the bar and one of the 75s there made a comment toward him, "She's real cute huh?"

Garrett said, "Who?"

The guy said, "The bartender."

Garrett said, "Aw . . . yup."

Then the guy said, "How well do you know her?"

Garrett said, "Well, we've been working together for over a year now."

The guy said, "You ever asked her out? She looks like she's single and you're probably her type."

Garrett said, "Yeah, I asked her out once. Well, it was more like I went over to help her change a tire on her sister's car once, but her dad ended up doing it for her."

The guy said, "Damn, struck out, huh."

Garrett grinned at the floor then went back to work. The guy texted onto the chat, "Garrett is possibly gay. I don't think he can get this hood rat at the bar." Several guys began posting memes for laughs.

Agusto sent a message, "Silence! None of you are as strong as he is. He's 20 and never even gotten a traffic stop. He just doesn't know how to turn the key but he will. That's enough for today."

The 75s left the pub. Others kept their distance following him all the way home. Around 8 a.m., Garrett again left the house. They knew he would be going to work at a local NTB but one of the demons noticed a member of the 75s who also worked there. He was involved but still not at the stage where he could be fully trusted—a guy named Pablo Gutierrez. Pablo Gutierrez was held on a leash because he had that "boss in the making" demeanor about himself. He was too strong to be included often. Pablo was the kind of guy that could flip the table on you while you were having a 3-course meal, always looking out for himself and clever enough to make it happen. Pablo worked with Garrett, and from what the guys outside could see, the 2 guys greeted each other and somewhat got along. He was the best guy for the job of bringing in Garrett but capable of stabbing the hand that would help him. The call was made, then after a long pause, Agusto said, "Yeah, let's make it work."

Pablo knew of the work the demons did, but the thing is, if you wish to do the demon's work, you don't get to do it. Pablo was bitter. They let him see behind the curtain then kept him out of all the fun stuff. He learned all the code and all the lingo then as expected, he used it to his advantage. Pablo was a passionate womanizer. He constantly fought his will and surrendered it to one beautiful woman until he gained hers then he withdrew his interest and found someone else to vest it in. Dragging with him the good name of anyone associated with him, he could not be cracked. He could leave any possession that was given to him and this worried Agusto because it reminded him of him. There really might be no person capable of matching wits with this guy. If he started the war of wills, this guy might be able to beat them all. He knew the rules and tweaked them to his advantage. Money and women came easy to him, all without his help. Pablo had suffered low points in his life and he blamed certain people for the downfall. He believed El Diablo had lured him or tricked him into it. Pablo acknowledged the mistake and moved on not even wanting the devil's help, yet he wanted to be free to do mischief on his own. It didn't work like that and since he was outnumbered, he went along with the flow and pledged himself to the 75s. He followed the rules and broke some whenever he wanted to. He owned his will. Demons would pressure Pablo into fighting, usually tempting him to uphold his love toward a girl he had loved or by threatening his livelihood, but Pablo never broke. He would smile, shake the hand of his tempter, and walk away. He didn't care, but there was a woman with whom he wanted to raise the bar with. She was so high up his chain of command he hadn't dated her yet and already, he had feelings for her. No one knew how he felt for her and thankfully for him, she lived more than a thousand miles away. He could not easily be tempted by her but he could tell the pressure was rising. He may actually lose himself for her one day. Pablo was mostly cool and calm yet possessed decisiveness and spontaneous capabilities. He could be aggressive whenever he wanted to pursue a true wild card.

Pablo was older than Garrett, maybe by 3 or 4 years. He was also the more experienced tech and he knew how to handle people when the text came in masked through a fellow 75s asking him to get dirt on Garrett to bring him in. Pablo knew exactly what he was talking about. He knew he was just a pawn as well but he wanted to cooperate. Maybe he could learn something. Pablo knew Garrett had a thing for racing and he knew exactly how to press his buttons before the guy's shift was over. Pablo went over to Garrett, joked around with him, and said, "Man, this is taking you too long. Did you, like, forget how to work on cars?"

Garrett said, "Naw, just got some stuff on my mind."

Pablo replied, "Like what? A girl."

Garrett said, "C'mon, am I that easy?"

They both smirked a little. It was time to go home. Pablo walked away to get ready to leave. He waited for Garrett in the parking lot next to his tricked-out Mitsubishi Evo. As expected, Garrett went over and decided to be a little more friendly. Garrett said, "Nice car."

Pablo answered, "Thanks. Which one's yours?"

Garrett nodded in the direction of a worn-down sedan and said, "There she is, my pride and joy."

Pablo already knew the sedan was his, but he was drawing conversation with him and said, "Are you kidding me?"

Garrett stood there and with a wholesome charm, Pablo told him, "How about I let you drive a real car? Wanna come?"

Garrett said, "What? Drive your Evo?"

Pablo opened the driver's door and said, "Yeah."

Garrett was feeling adventurous and tempted to do something fun with his friend, even if it was out of his norm. Garrett nodded his head and said, "Ok, let's go."

Garrett walked to the door smiling which was rare because he rarely smiled. He sat in the driver's chair. It was a comfortable racing seat, sturdy like a glove. He put his left hand on the leather steering wheel and his right hand on the titanium shifter knob. It felt amazing. Pablo sat in the passenger seat. He closed the door and pointed forward saying, "Let's go."

Garrett stepped on the clutch pedal with his left foot, then pressed the keyless start switch. They heard the starter engaging and turning the flywheel, cranking over the engine to generate compression followed by the nicely tuned sound of the exhaust rumbling behind the car. Garrett stepped on the accelerator. He heard the turbocharger spooling up, then when he released the pedal, the suction noise leftover inside the intake. Garrett helped Pablo install the new Evolution X Turbo boosting a hundred more horsepower than it already had. He had been looking forward to this day for a long time. Pablo's music started playing with low volume. He reached the dial and cranked it up higher shaking the rearview mirror with the excess bass from the subwoofer in the back. The scrolling name of the artist on his custom display screen said the artist's name was Chaos. Garrett moved the shifter sideways verifying it was in neutral.

He withdrew his right foot from the brake pedal and removed his left foot from the clutch. Garrett pressed the handbrake downward. The car was facing the parking lot. There was no need to reverse. He glanced at Pablo who simply said, "Go for it."

Garrett flashed his left foot on the clutch pedal again this time engaging the shifter into first gear and simultaneously pressing firmly on the accelerator pedal with his right foot all the way down. The car squatted low and squealed all 4 tires briefly before gripping then speeding forward. Garrett enjoyed how powerful and balanced the car felt, giving him the confidence he lacked before. Now, he was complete, fully embodied with the car as one. The end of the parking lot came up a lot sooner than Garrett thought. He pressed in the clutch and the brake pedal at the same time. He rolled onto the busy street well above 40MPH. He shifted into second, released the clutch, and hammered on the gas. The Evo screamed down the street pressing both men deep into their chairs. Garrett continued flying down the street. Weaving in and out of traffic, he constantly shifted gears and punched the accelerator. They were all smiles flying down the road. A police car passed them going in the opposite direction. It stopped quickly then turned around in the middle of the road chasing them. The squad car turned on its red and blue lights. Garrett felt sick. He knew his fun had come to an end. He had done the crime and now he needed to do the time, just like his father. Garrett slowed down and pulled off to the side of the road coming to a full stop. Garrett lived by a code and although he usually said it to himself alone this time, he had an audience, but he said it aloud anyway. He said, "Whatever happens, happens."

Then Pablo said, "Dude, what are you doing?"

Garrett said, "I'm getting pulled over."

Pablo said, "No way, dude, gun it!"

Garrett said, "What? No! I'll take the fine. It's all good."

Pablo wanted the guy to lose his edge. He knew if he was to meet with El Diablo soon, he needed to walk with God and the best way to do that is to fear him—to find God because if he goes before

Diablo without peace and that sense of confidence knowing he can do good without Diablo, he feared he would fall much worse than reckless driving. Pablo wanted Garrett to go to jail and find God the hard way just like everybody else usually does. Pablo thought fast to make Garrett drive off, so he lied to him saying, "I got four keys in the trunk! You need to drive!"

Garrett thought about the conversation he would have explaining the drugs in the trunk, about how he would say to the police officer, "I swear, Officer, it's not mine, I swear."

Then the officer would reply, "That's what they all say. C'mon, let's go."

Garrett thought he was done for. Just like that, he was going to be put away in prison. He thought about his father being incarcerated for the last 13 years and now, he would likely suffer the same fate just 3 weeks before his father would be paroled. Garrett was furious at Pablo. He was contemplating about breaking the law and driving away, something that 30 minutes ago didn't even exist. The officer's car pulled up behind them. The door opened and the officer stepped out quickly, angered. Garrett thought it was not going to go well. Garrett squeezed the steering wheel with both hands then looked forward and yelled, "Shit!"

He pressed the clutch, dropped the shifter into first gear, then stomped the accelerator and popped out the clutch pedal letting the four tires again squeal before releasing the car forward. The Evo roared in front of the cop then just like that, it was gone. The officer went for his sidearm, but a second patrolman sped past him already in pursuit.

Garrett continued shifting gears so perfectly, matching the gearing to the road speed. The EVO moved effortlessly. Garrett raced northbound on Swift Rd., ripping in and out of traffic just missing various vehicles along the way. When he reached Army Trail Rd., there was heavy traffic. He stopped at a red light, slowed down, and took a long look in his rear-view mirror. There were no squad cars in sight. He moved eastbound on Army Trail Rd. looking to take the ramp onto I-55 South but before he reached the ramp, he spotted two patrol cars charging toward him. One of them skidded to a stop near the ramp as if to barricade Garrett from taking it. Garrett was forced not to take the ramp southbound. Instead, he would maneuver around traffic and take the following direction to the left northbound. He swerved to the left, but the second police car lunged to pinch him off, causing a collision with a citizen driving. Garrett punched in front of another citizen in the far-left lane using nothing but pure speed. He braved against oncoming traffic cutting in all directions reaching the northbound ramp. There was a line of slow-moving vehicles ahead of him. Maybe one of them would notice what was happening and attempt to help the police. Garrett needed to hurry before they did. He took the fading shoulder and accelerated heavily to pass all traffic. There was a semi-truck with a 53-foot trailer in the lead of the slow traffic. Garrett needed to pass him before he ran out of his shoulder. The guard rail was quickly shrinking and coming closer to the EVO. It could fall off the side of the ramp onto houses below. Garrett held the 4th gear and stepped on the accelerator as hard as he could to push the Evo ahead. Pablo grimaced and held his breath as they sped alongside the trailer's cab. The turbo was screaming as it spooled loudly. The front end was raising. Suddenly, Garrett saw the front bumper of the semi-truck and squeezed alongside it. He looked for a last moment at the entrance and forced the car to take it cutting the steering wheel to the left of the car quickly. He did it. The EVO took the position in front of the semi-truck then before long, cleared a lot of space in front of it. The driver got scared when he noticed the car pop out of nowhere and hit the brakes, causing congestion on the ramp.

Garrett had made it. They were in the clear. They soon passed Lake St Garrett and eased on the speed attempting to blend in, but it scared him when he took a turn onto expressway 290. A speed camera flashed at him. Pablo was not the kind of guy to be caught off guard. He convinced Garrett to hide out for a while. He said there were some older homes in a nearby area where they may be able to let the heat pass for a few hours. The men approached the area. Garrett drove through several allies looking for an open or unlocked garage where they could hide out. It didn't take long to find one. Garrett sped the Evo into the garage, pulled the handbrake, then quickly jumped out to check the trunk, but Pablo reached for the garage door to lower it then said, "Dude, that was amazing, you can drive! Woooo!"

Garrett raised the trunk lid and looked inside. There was nothing there. Pablo slowly made his way to the trunk then met him to say, "Guess what? You're a 75 now."

Garrett said, "No. I can't be. What? You're a 75? No, not me, besides I don't want to be one. I thought that was a Mexican thing."

Pablo said, "Naw, we don't discriminate. We got white boys and black people too. Here, give me your phone."

Garrett pulled out his phone which was doing some weird stuff. Pablo took it from his hand and said, "Here, I can get you into this secret chat, and basically, you do what it says, or you go to jail for driving like a douche."

Garrett said, "For what, reckless driving? I can take that it's probably a month at most."

Pablo said, "Oh, you don't want to go to jail, trust me, not even for a single day. Besides, with pictures of you and this car, they could get you for anything they want. Maybe use it in a robbery? Or in a murder? Trust me, bro, they got chu."

Garrett went to the steering wheel attempting to wipe down as much evidence of himself as he could. Pablo walked over and said, "There's no getting around this. Only God can save you. Heck, maybe not even him. What you do next is solely on you, my friend. Think wisely."

Garrett said, "The mob doesn't scare me. I've done no murder. The truth will set me free."

Pablo said, "After how long? There are a lot of crimes out there that you potentially can commit. Do you think you can clear all of them? Look, do what you're told, behave, 'n you'll be ok."

Garrett said, "Why me?"

Pablo said, "We all go through this, Gare. Some people don't mind God watching over them all the time. Others stop caring and misbehave on purpose. You ever heard about the Diablo being real? Maybe you're meant to do something."

Garrett said, "Diablo? Me? For what?"

Pablo's phone went off. An alert had come in. He looked at his phone, then he said, "Apparently, I need to drive off and leave you here to walk home. I'll see you at work tomorrow."

Garrett half-grinned then said, "Sure."

Pablo grabbed a sweater from the backseat, opened the garage door, made his way to the driver's seat, then said, "That's the spirit. I knew you belong here. Laters, bro."

Garrett began walking by himself. It was maybe 3 or 4 miles to the NTB shop where his sedan was parked but he was young, so it was not as difficult as one would think. The worst part was how far his mind was wandering. His father had always told him to stay away from all gang members, keep his nose clean, and do the right thing. He felt bad because he failed. He wanted to turn himself in, but he did fear Satan, the real one. He went to church. He knew there was something more to this world. But a person going by El Diablo was nothing more than a man. He knew nothing else about him. It took him under an hour to reach his car. It was almost 6 PM now. He thought about a time his father mentioned a guy that goes by "El Diablo" but ruled him out as being a quack. Garrett didn't know which way to think but something inside him clicked. He knew the only way to figure it out would be judging for himself by confronting and getting to know him. Maybe then, he could find out why El Diablo wanted him in the first place. He considered himself a poor, lonely, white boy who had nothing to offer anybody. Why would El Diablo want him? Suddenly, his phone rang. It scared him. It was his boss Edgar from Black Door. Garrett answered it and said, "Hello."

Edgar said, "Oh, hey, Garrett, how's it going, buddy? Just wanted to let you know I heard of having your car troubled and wanted to tell you it's ok. If you can't make it in tonight, we can manage."

Garrett said, "Ugh . . . Ok."

Edgar continued, "Oh and hey, Dayana asked me about you. She wanted to know if you were with anyone. You should make your move on her, bro."

Garrett said, "Ugh . . . Sure. I mean of course, yeah."

Edgar said, "That's the spirit. I'll see you tomorrow."

Garrett hung up the phone call but noticed there was a picture on the screen. It was a picture of a guy wearing a Halloween costume. Some kind of a cheap cartoony red devil got up. Then, his phone began to act up. An address flashed on his screen multiple times. It read, "11311 Dearborn Ave. Aurora @9 PM."

Then just like that, the image disappeared. His phone went back to normal. Garrett searched his phone attempting to reopen the image, but it was gone. It was go time. Garrett had a decision to make. He could ignore the invite or take a chance and see where this goes. There was adventure inside him. He had just outdriven the police, been granted privileges, and scored points with Dayana. He was riding very high on cloud nine; he had to go. Garrett picked up his steps. The time was 6:56 PM. He was confident he could make it there in time. The street address was already burned into his mind. He believed Dayana was interested in him. He would drive a thousand miles to see if it was true. Luckily, he just needed to go 25 miles in the opposite direction. Garrett reached his car. He opened the door and jumped in, then he replied, "Whatever happens, happens."

CHAPTER 3

"Welcome to the jungle."

Garrett had an edge to himself when he was behind the steering wheel. He loved it. Driving Pablo's EVO was illegal but it felt right. He had that aggressiveness to himself that most guys have when they know they can win at something. Garrett further convinced himself that he belonged behind a steering wheel. He now knew he had an extraordinary talent to drive a car in any way he wanted. He even pressed his sedan aggressively on the expressway to Aurora on I-88 and loved it. When Garrett reached the address, it was still before 8:45 PM. The place was an old-looking warehouse on the poor side of the town close to a junkyard and the train tracks, not too far from a residential neighborhood. Garrett had been to Aurora before, once or twice, but never to this part of town. He drove into the property by a gated fence that was open in the front. He passed several project cars and trucks and big diesel covered with a tarp. Garrett parked his car close to a tall garage door that was open. He could hear music playing but couldn't find anyone in sight. Garrett dared to walk inside. What he saw was just more of what was on the outside—project cars and trucks being worked on. Garrett peeked in a doorway. On the other side, he found a very elegant and modern office with a large desk which held different monitors on it. The walls were covered in diplomas and pictures of different events.

There, he found someone behind all of those screens playing music softly. Garrett knocked on the desk and said, "Hello?"

The guy looked clean-cut. He had glasses on and wore jeans, along with a shirt that looked like a "bowling" tee and a pair of sandals, not exactly someone who Garrett would think of as El Diablo. The guy lowered the music even more on a screen, then he said, "Come in and welcome to my shop. My name is Agusto Reyes. I've been expecting you."

Garrett said, "Are you El Diablo?"

Agusto said, "My friends have made several names for me throughout the years. For now, just Agusto or Mr. Reyes will do. How about that?"

Garrett said, "Ugh, that's fine. What am I doing here?"

Agusto walked into the shop with Garrett following him. He picked a freshly machined part near a CNC machine that looked like the main component for building a gun. He brushed it and stared down the top as if to check for straightness, then he said, "Why do you think you are here?"

Garrett answered, "I don't know. Maybe you like my driving."

Agusto said, "You do have skills. Not a scratch on that car, huh."

Garrett smiled, already friendly with Agusto, and he said, "Yup."

Agusto put down the freshly cut block then walked to another area. He asked, "Did you get your kicks breaking the law? Being reckless?"

Garrett snapped back saying, "I was in control the whole time!"

Agusto picked up a finished revolver and loaded a single bullet from his pocket into a chamber then he said, "Are you in control now? There's another gun on the counter. Go ahead and pick it up. Let's see what happens when you do what you're not supposed to."

Garrett looked at the bench. He could see the bright nickel-plating gleaming with a reflection of light. Garrett said, "Maybe not."

Agusto said, "Good for you."

Agusto walked back into his office placing the weapon inside one of the drawers of his desk. He signaled Garrett to be seated in front of him, then he began saying, "The whole world is messed up. Wouldn't you agree?" Garrett nodded from across his desk, then Agusto went on, "Since the beginning of time, man has been hurting his fellow man, but how much can a man take? How much pain can a guy handle and still be with God? You do believe in God, don't you?" Garrett again just nodded from across his desk agreeing with him. Agusto went on, "I know who your father is. News has traveled to me. I know your father is no longer with Chicago Outfit and I know that he's up for parole this month. Now, if he's released, he's going to need protection no matter what team he bats for. That's where I come in. My friends can oversee things, so your father is safe. All you have to do is work for me and do my bidding. Maybe once he's released, if he gets released, things can change, so what do you say, sport? Do it for the great city of Chicago. C'mon."

Garrett was looking at pictures where Agusto comes out next to the Police Commissioner and the Kane County Sherriff. Garrett believed to be on opposite sides with Agusto, so he fiercely said, "We don't need your help. We can take care of ourselves."

Agusto answered, "Ha, you're wrong. I'm here to help. Hmm, maybe I can help you achieve something else, something you want?"

Garrett answered, "Like what?"

Agusto said, "Well, there are some guys I know who love street racing. I keep them on the streets, and I can help you to race with them."

Garrett said, "Why?"

Agusto said, "Because they work with me. It's the least I can do for them."

Garrett said, "I can beat them with a 3-car lane head start!"

Agusto said, "Whoa, whoa! Be careful about what you say." Agusto looked all around his office as if someone else was there, then he said, "Everything gets heard, even your thoughts."

Garrett looked all around. He was not buying anything this guy was saying. His dad was right; this guy is a quack. He wanted to leave so he said, "I'm done. I'm out of here." Garrett stood up and made his way to the door. Agusto said, "You ever do time before, Garrett? No, right, I have. You're being watched all the time, yet violent acts constantly happen and even if you are secretive and pick the darkest area possible, everybody always knows exactly what went down and why. There are no accidents! There are no coincidences! Just like you were meant to be in this room at this exact time tonight, Garrett, because it is time for you to grow."

Agusto stood up and met Garrett squarely by the doorway and said, "The real world is a prison. If you think it is."

Agusto gave Garrett a few seconds waiting for him to leave but he didn't, then Agusto began again and said, "Words have power, Garrett. People get hurt all the time and I fear you're not someone who pays attention to everything that is said. Ironically, the best way to take away the spear from these threatening words is to stop caring about it, not letting it affect you or having enough willpower to rise above the spear, not letting it penetrate your soul. Can you do that, Garrett? Are you a master of your domain? The things I can teach you, Garrett."

Garrett said, "I'm not signing up for this. I don't want you to teach me anything."

Agusto said, "Precisely what a guy who doesn't know any better would say. Let me ask you this, how do I keep these racers from racing?"

Garrett asked, "If you don't want to hurt them, why not take their money? Or throw them in jail?"

Agusto smiled and said, "They don't have money, and jail, well, they could do time, then they would be out within a month. Do you think they would have learned their lesson?"

Garrett remembered he said something similar to Pablo when they were in the car earlier that afternoon. Garrett's mind got a nudge because the pieces were mixing together. Garrett weakly said, "You run the 75s?".

Agusto said, "A tale for another day. You took a chance on me now. I'm going to take a chance on you. Come with me."

The two men walked through the warehouse, then Agusto said, "I want you to race against these racers on my behalf. I will vouch for you and get you good with them. Heck, I'll even give you a car to drive."

Garrett said, "Which car?"

Agusto stopped in front of a car. He pulled off the dirty tarp away from over it and there before them was a sporty 2-door German coupe. Agusto said, "It's a 2000 M3, modified. It has a monster supercharger, high compression pistons, new camshaft, tuned ECM, Bilstein's all around. If you don't win in this car, you have no business racing. Ever."

Garrett was thrilled. El Diablo had found his weak spot. Garrett said, "Alright, alright. We can do this."

Agusto said, "Alright, we'll see what you're made of. Keys are inside. She's all yours. Oh, and it should go without saying that if you lose or get arrested, we never met!"

Garrett said, "Ok."

Garrett was too busy thinking about driving this car in front of him to realize he had just agreed to do something on the devil's behalf. A cell phone rang. Agusto reached into his pocket and pulled it out. A guy on the other end called Agusto "Lucifer."

Agusto walked away to further talk with the guy on the phone. He told Garrett, "Fire it up. I'll meet you by the door."

Garrett maneuvered the car toward the door where Agusto told him. Agusto opened the door, signaled him to go, and said, "Can you move your car to the far side? And don't worry, we'll be in touch."

I guess every man has his price and Garrett's was a flashy coupe and a chance to race in Chicago's underground. Garrett did as he was told. He parked his sedan to an isolated spot then inspected the coupe with a small flashlight from his car. Garrett was all smiles as he sped off the lot and turned left toward Farnsworth Ave. He drove the car hard the entire way punishing the suspension as it pivoted around every turn as if it were gripping into the floor. Garrett was a natural behind the steering wheel, displaying himself very calmly, accelerating perfectly at the top of the apex, and exploding forward from the height of every turn. The vision and comfort inside the vehicle were very accommodating. The gauges were so easy to read. He loved the car. Garrett kept wondering of things he could do to it in the next few days to push the car even further. Garrett thought the car had too much torque on the low end. He also felt like it was missing something above 5000RPMs. He figured it needed a turbo to take it to that next level of speed. The plumbing and the cooling system for the big turbo he had in mind would have to be MIG welded from bare aluminum. In his mind, all the pieces were coming together perfectly. Garrett had his work cut out for him.

On the following morning, Garrett drove the coupe to work when he arrived. He noticed Pablo got to work in a different car, an Impreza STI. However, it was the same color as his EVO. Garrett smirked and held his lip curled in his direction which Pablo noticed. When he got out of his car, he tapped the hood of Garrett's coupe and said, "C'mon, we're on the same side." Pablo walked into work like nothing had happened last night, as if Garrett was still driving his beat-up sedan. Garrett was upset at Pablo for setting him up, but he just let it go and got to work. Garrett was kept very busy throughout the day, mostly with maintenance work that he enjoyed doing. He would almost forget about the German coupe waiting for him outside and that he would be involved in a race just 4 days away. It took a few minutes before his shift was over for him to remember that he needed to get started on the coupe. He purchased the additional fittings and plastic tubes he would need to complete his project, special order. A fellow technician had an EVO8 turbo for sale. Garrett asked if he could borrow it from him and return it after the race. His friend agreed. Garrett wasn't ready to begin working on his race car, but he did have to go to his second job. Plus, there was an added bonus—Dayana would be there.

Dayana's shift usually started at 4 so she was always at Black Door before him. Today, when he arrived, Garrett was surprised to find out Dayana was not there yet. Garrett got to work. There weren't a lot of people so he found himself looking at the door randomly throughout the night hoping his esteemed friend Dayana would walk in. Edgar wanted Garrett to be more cheerful and more willing to learn new things. He could do it at the pub by participating more in the kitchen as well as attending to customers regularly. He got Garrett set up on a register. Garrett was not impressed with his new duties. He had thoughts of quitting but then everything changed once the door opened, revealing a golden sunset behind a silhouette of a young female strolling inward. It was Dayana. Garrett took a mental snapshot of her. As she walked toward him behind the bar, she cracked a large smile that pierced him all the way through to his spine. She moved her hip radiant with neon-colored clothing and walked behind the counter. Garrett still frozen faced the incoming door. She punched him on his arm and said, "Hey, buddy, moving on up?"

Garrett eventually said, "Oh yeah, you're right, good one."

He looked over at Edgar who was smiling at him from the hallway in front of his office, then when he saw Garrett looking at him, he walked inside.

At Menard Correction Facility, Warren was having dinner but his friends from the Outfit were asked to no longer associate themselves with him. Warren didn't really care; he just kept on eating. Warren still had more than 2 weeks before he would go in front of a parole committee. This rejection brought the outside world just a little bit closer. Maybe it was a good thing. A guy from another table took the liberty of sitting close to Motors. He snuck in his tray when the guards weren't looking, hoping they wouldn't say anything. They didn't. Shortly after that, the guy began small talk with Motors. Warren didn't really care so he went along and talked to the guy. His name was Enrique but amongst his Mexican buddies, they called him Loro. Warren didn't know what a "Loro" was. He mistook it as "lloro" that he somehow understood as "cry" in Spanish. He assumed the guy was a cry baby. The bigger guys were always beating on him. Warren didn't care, so he went along with Loro. It was rumored the guy once had deep connections to the Sinaloa Cartel but when his gang went to war with another group, he flipped and fled Mexico. He was caught just before St. Louis, only fitting he would end up in Menard. If Loro ever gets out of Menard, he better apply for citizenship in Brazil because Canada doesn't take cons. *Must be a sick feeling,* Motors thought, *when they don't want you here, and don't want you there, not belonging to your home nor your adoptive home. Fuck!* Loro made a comment to Warren, something he was persuaded to say to him. He said, "Hey, Motors, I heard something that you might want to know."

Warren smirked and said, "Naw, man, I'm done with all this prison shit. There's nothing you know that I would be concerned about."

Loro said, "It's about your son. I heard he's a 75."

Warren stopped chewing and looked at Loro then said, "What the fuck are you talking about?"

Loro said, "Man, I was visiting with my attorney today and there were two cops at a table close to mines talking with a con, a 75. They asked him about a driver in a heist and the guy talked. He clearly said, 'Yeah, I know him, yeah, he's a 75. That's Garrett Lee from Franklin Park.' I was like, holy shit, man, that's Motors' kid. What would the Outfit do if they found out?"

Warren leaned forward and hung his head over his tray uneasy then he said, "Is that what they said? Are you sure?"

Loro said, "On my abuelita carnal."

Warren said, "It can't be. My son would never do something like that. I know him."

Loro said, "Really? How well can you know him being locked up in here?"

Warren was deeply affected. The remainder of the afternoon, the information triggered something inside Warren a shock he had no way of dealing with because he never imagined something like this happening. Warren got a deep sense of failure inside himself. He punished himself mentally for not being able to be there for his son.

A hard depression followed that kept him awake all night. Warren remembered how cons often lied to each other to lure them out of their money for protection. He convinced himself that is what it was. The cons messing with him, there's no way Garrett could have done what Loro said. It was early in the morning when Warren convinced himself to disregard the news and write it off. Motors had a connection on the outside, a guy who was his cellmate briefly at Menard, a young guy who he mentored and helped out once or twice from fighting in the yard. His name was Jake Eldridge. Jake was a natural earner, but he got pinched over a deal that went south. However, the Outfit was able to damage his partner, giving Jake higher credibility. Thus, he would go free to keep earning. El Bambino liked him. Jake was from the old neighborhood and he was willing to play ball together. They came up with several money-making schemes and from what Motors heard, they all worked very well. Before Jake left Menard, Motors made a deal with him. He set up Jake with a friend of his in El Paso. In exchange, he asked Jake to look after his son Garrett who at the time was 15 years old. Jake agreed. In the morning, Warren would have access to the classroom, which meant he could use the computer and email Jake to ask him over his son. When Jake replied, he simply said, "Sorry, bro, I'll check in with him and let you know."

That reply wasn't good enough for Warren. He wondered if the Outfit had told Jake to abandon all communication with Motors. He was overthinking. El Bambino didn't know nor did he care if Warren had asked one of his associates to babysit his kid. Jake was a straight shooter, besides being a criminal, but the Outfit making a comeback kept him busy. Things were going to be bigger than ever. Jake was a Caucasian guy in his late 20s with greased-down hair and a clean-cut, a boss in his own right, but he knew everywhere he went, eyes were on him all the time, especially now that he was backed by the Outfit. He did periodically go and check up on Garrett. He had personally left and knocked on the kid's door asking to be around him more but when his mother found out he was also a member of the Outfit, she prohibited Jake from contacting or grooming Garrett.

She said, "You come to me, I'll tell you how he is," and shut the door on him. About every 6 months, Warren would remind Jake to make his visits to Clarissa, and every time, it was the same answer, "He's fine!" followed by the door slamming on his face.

Jake warned the hoods and hustlers near Franklin Park that Garrett was off-limits. He figured that would be the easy thing to do instead of getting a door slammed on his nose twice a year. Warren tried to have a good day, but he was angry and bothersome. He was very sleepy and couldn't think and when he did, it was always about him kicking himself for his failure. It bothered him a lot to think his son would join the 75s. The few Warren had met were like crazed animals, tattooed grunts, or psychopaths with no mind, like zombies unable to think for themselves, but was he so different? Warren exhausted his patience. He snuck back into the classroom to send his son an email, asking Garrett to go and visit him ASAP. Then Warren heard, "Mr. Lee, what are you doing? Motors, get off that computer right now, sir!" *Damn,* Warren thought. He was caught on a computer without permission and was about to lose privileges.

Garrett received the email. He usually drove to Menard once a month. The soonest he could go and visit his father would be on Sunday the 12th. The 75s kept a keen eye on Garrett. At the same time, Cruz sent Agusto an email in which he told him, "Everything was healing just as planned." Pablo wanted to test Garrett that night. He purposely invited him out to a strip club on a Tuesday night claiming it would be the "best party you've ever been to!" But Garrett declined. He was interested in Dayana. Besides, he assumed it would turn into a drunk feast with a strange woman he didn't care about having anything with. It would be a waste of time. Garrett was off Tuesday night but he pulled in the German coupe and began tearing it down so he could make measurements to construct all the ducts and plumbing for his massive turbo he was adding. Garrett would work all night.

On Wednesday afternoon, Garrett's parts came in. He would be welding all night and he was so confident in hitting all of his deadlines flawlessly that he planned to take Saturday off so he could get the car tuned on a dyno. His boss said, "That's fine." Pablo was hungover Wednesday but promised to stay late the remainder of the week to help him work on his car. Garrett agreed. Garrett had to go in to work at Black Door on Wednesday and Thursday. All he thought about was how much more he would rather be working on his race car. He thought so much of his car that he even neglected Dayana who was working alongside him, although it would end up being a positive thing. It forced her to talk more to him. It was slow those days, without a lot of customers, so she found herself usually walking over to Garrett and saying, "What cha doing?" To which Garrett replied, "Stocking the fridge? What's up?" She spontaneously laughed and said, "You're cute when you're foolish." Garrett's palms were dripping in sweat. He was nervous, but this was that small little ray of light peaking from behind the doorway. He wanted to walk through and see her on the other side so bad. Garrett found himself taking steps in her direction as if he was being guided from above, then he was right behind her and out of nowhere, he said, "Hey, Dayana, can I get your number?". She turned around and said, "What? You want my number?" Garrett turned the look at the lone guy sitting at the bar, a rough-looking 60-something-year-old guy drinking an old style. Garrett was blushing, but he was standing precisely in a dark spot away from the hanging lamps for anyone to notice. Garrett repeated, "Um, yeah." She suddenly perked up and said, "Of course, you can have my number. We're friends. Here you go." Then, she read off the numbers as Garrett input them into his cell phone. Then he pressed the dial button. Once her phone lit up, he said, "There you go, that's my number." Dayana said, "Cool. I'll call you," then they both got back to work. It was the single greatest feeling in Garrett's life up to that point.

Between Garrett, Pablo, his boss Chuck, and 2 other techs who stayed late on Friday, they all rushed to complete the final assembling on his car. The big thing would be adding all of the fluids and trying to start it with a fixed modified ECM programming they had downloaded using the scan tool. It was late when they got ready to fire it up. The car cranked quickly then fired up, with no leaks in the exhaust. The turbo spooled perfectly. Upon a test drive, the car ran quick but Garrett was convinced that through tuning, he could get more out of that big turbo. The boost gauge pegged at a 20PSI boost. He knew the engine was getting more than 20PSI. It was 9 PM Friday night when Garrett locked up his toolbox to go home. He had asked for Friday and Saturday off and by a small miracle, he had received them. Garrett looked at his cell phone and noticed he had missed a text message. It was from Dayana and read, "Too good for work? Rich guy!" He grinned and texted her back, but she was working and replied at random times. Garrett was so tired to stay up but managed to stay up until her shift was over just texting silly one-liners and short questions to her with a lot of emojis.

The following morning, Garrett's boss expected him to finish at the dyno then go to work. The owner of the speed shop was a friend of his and was charging Garrett a discounted rate. Garrett was already outside the speed shop before it opened. The place was called Ortiz Motors. They specialized mostly in diesel engine rebuilding, did custom fabrication, and had a large torque dynamometer built into the ground. The owner opened the door and greeted him. He then instructed Garrett to tie the car down and set up the fans while he scanned the van and took some specs from the tires, rear end, and transmission to input into the computer. Within a few moments, they were ready to go. Garrett walked into the office area behind a large glass to check what else needed to be done, then the owner said, "We're all set. Here, take a walkie-talkie, jump inside, get the tires warmed up, and I'll tell you when to punch it to 6k." Garrett sprinted out to the shop. He mounted the car and accelerated it just as the owner asked him to. There was a screen outside where Garrett could see the readings on the screen. The owner was modifying fuel trims and lying to the secondary throttle plates, so they opened up sooner and longer. The two men worked on the car vigorously trying to get the results Garrett was looking for. A thick and continuous power band that stays up for longer RPMs and that's what he got—a lot more power in the higher RPM range without losing anything in the midrange. Garrett was thrilled.

Once completed, Garrett untied his coupe, paid the guy for his service, and drove off in his flashy German coupe. He was driving aggressively the entire way back to NTB when a guy in a V10 Dodge Ram pulled up alongside Garrett and said, "Hey, kid, I bet you $100 my truck can beat that shitcan!"

Garrett said, "You're on!"

The two vehicles were stopped at a red light. The truck had some serious street wheels, but Garrett was one with the car. He knew he could not lose. Garrett saw the lamp on the intersecting street turn yellow. It seemed to last an eternity, then it went red. He looked up at the streetlight and counted "One Mississippi," then the light turned green. Garrett popped the clutch and slammed on the accelerator. Both vehicles got a little squiggly off the line. Garrett could hear the driver of the Ram come off the throttle due to having a lot more torque to the rear wheels than his coupe did, and even so, the truck was faster off the line. The exhaust from the Ram drowned out the noise from his import. He concentrated on his shifts. Every time the turbo spooled up, the front end wanted to lift up and point to the sky. Garrett looked down to his gauges. He was doing 90MPH in 5th gear, neck and neck with the big V10 Ram. His foot was firmly on the accelerator. The next streetlamp was coming up fast. Garrett was now in the lead. The car was still accelerating and pulling away from the Dodge Ram. He was now out in front by a lot even though he could still hear the guy pushing his truck as hard as it would go. Garrett passed the streetlamp which turned yellow. The guy in the truck stuck out his middle finger then turned to the left avoiding the payment which he owed Garrett. Garrett had a really big smile on his face and said, "What an asshole."

Garrett's phone was going off after having received an alert. It read, "Amber Alert: Red Sedan on 290 Expressway License plate Illinois GRS 9555: Alert."

Garrett said, "Ok, ok, I'll just take it easy."

Garrett couldn't wait for the big race that night. He was riding a huge high which hadn't been seen in him for days. Pablo was nearby and did not think the same. To him, El Diablo was a very real threat and if Garrett didn't focus, he could end up losing his life as he had seen happen to other guys who mess around with the devil. Pablo began thinking to himself how somebody ought to make El Diablo pay for all the harm he has done. Maybe, just maybe, if he ever got a chance to be in front of him again, he would punish him. What Pablo didn't know is that he was just much more disciplined than all of those guys who lost against El Diablo. He had the kind of self-confidence and willpower El Diablo just couldn't break. Pablo wanted to help Garrett, so he went up to him and told him, "Hey, man, focus, save all that positive energy for the race."

Elsewhere that afternoon, a phone call was made to a young Chicago PD detective named Julissa Reyes. She was sitting inside an unmarked black SUV on the passenger chair. Julissa was in her early 30s. She was niece to Agusto Reyes. However, she had no idea her uncle was the man known as El Diablo. Members of the 75s used untraceable methods to tip her off to intercept certain criminals from time to time. Her uncle always looked after her. She was family and although he begged her several times not to be a police officer, she couldn't see herself doing anything differently. She believed she was born for it. Agusto did the best he could to keep her safe, always never allowing her to discover how far his youth mentoring duties extended. She knew he was a public speaker at the Juvenile Detention Center and that was it. In the driver's chair was her partner and commanding officer, a veteran of the police force named Sargent Juan Vega. Sgt. Vega was around 50 years old with thinning hair, built like a linebacker, a natural-born leader with the thorough vision of a jungle predator. He suspected several things about what really went on in Chicago but as long as the innocent stayed innocent, he was willing to look away. Julissa answered her phone, then someone groaned out some words in a low tone. They said, "There will be a race tonight starting at Ashland and Archer to 64 to I-90."

Julissa said, "Got it," then the caller hung up. She looked on her phone and saw it came from "no caller ID."

Sgt. Vega said, "You got something?"

She said, "Street racing tonight. We're going to need the Viper."

Sgt Vega said, "The bird could come in handy."

She said, "Naw, bunch of low-level guys. Probably it won't be necessary."

Sgt. Vega said, "The fear of God always helps."

She replied, "They should fear me. C'mon, let's go."

El Diablo took his meeting with Garrett word for word. Garrett wanted to arrest all the racers to keep them from racing illegally again so, tonight, it would be so. The 75s asked several racers to come out for the race but gave them every opportunity not to run in it. Their greed couldn't keep them away. The buy-in was the highest. It had been a long time for a $1000 buy-in. A lot of races were conducted illegally. A lot of money was traded hands-on as long as discretion was maintained. It could go on forever; no racer would ever have another racer arrested. That is until Garrett suggested it. Tonight, Agusto would live up to his role as El Diablo. The pot would be nearly $20,000 for a 20-minute race, but the host knew nobody was going to cross the finish line. The notification went out just one hour before the race, "Meetup at the parking lot on Archer and Ashland." El Diablo had no remorse for what he was doing, but the birthday surely had to be there. He verified his location and noticed Garrett was still at his house. He called Garrett personally at 9:15 PM asking him if he was showing to the race. Garrett was running all over the place and said, "Yeah, I'll be right there." As he passed the living room, his mother yelled at him saying, "Dammit, Gare, you've been out late every night. Can't you just stay in tonight?"

Garrett said, "I have this thing to go to. I won't be late. Bye."

Garrett jumped in his car and fired up the ignition. The thrill rushed through him. He checked his phone then headed to the meet-up spot. When he got there, he was in awe. This was where he was meant to be his whole life. It was blissful. Most of the other racers were also young people, 18-25. There were a lot of Mustangs or Camaros, a few cool imports. Most of them were regular street cars with a few mods. Garrett felt good about his chances. The 75s were all over the place. They acted like security for the event, collecting buy-ins, organizing bets, and directing the traffic. A lot of them had taken positions along the route to live stream the race. As the racers went by, everyone could see the entire action. Garrett was now convinced Agusto was the best friend he could ever have, and he was pretty sure Agusto was someone very powerful.

CHAPTER 4

"Some of them want to use you."

El Diablo invited Pablo, but he chose not to go. Instead, he stayed at home and sent flirtatious messages to a woman he liked in Texas, Karina. Pablo didn't mind not attending. He was comfortable at his house. He was hosting a small party with his close friends and they had access to the feed being recorded by the 75s. They wouldn't miss a thing. The conversation from everyone attending Pablo's party sounded like none of them liked Agusto. They hated him for twisting the minds of everyone who came around him, but he couldn't be caught. Agusto never went to jail, no matter how many hardened criminals he hung out with would catch serious cases. As a matter of fact, Agusto would disappear and abandon guys who they believed to be his own crew. *What's Agusto really doing?* they thought. Pablo walked into the room and said, "He's a hustler! El Diablo is going to make a lot of money off this! Just watch."

In reality, Agusto believed he was helping humanity. He was mentoring everyone to treat others the way they would want to be treated, but tonight, he would thin the herd. He was not betting on anyone to finish the race. But you never know he thought that maybe one of them really has skill in driving. There were a lot of racers gathered. It was common to set up races for a few hundred bucks just to keep the guys with burger money, but tonight had been made into a main event. More and more guys came out to join in. If they only knew it was a trap. Tonight, Agusto was embodying a real-life diablo. He knew that the police would be occupied that night with the race. There would be parts of the city left out of reach giving an advantage to common thieves. With 30 minutes to go, he had several petty or "wanna-be" cat burglars contacted and offered them a window to get their feet wet, "at a price of course!" It was another way of making these people grow up, something to hold over them should they fail to get with the program and if Agusto made any money in the deal, he always distributed it among those that had learned to keep their mouth shut.

Garrett knew nothing about what was "really" going on in town. He wanted to cruise around the parking lot in his borrowed coupe so he could see and be seen by everybody. Members of the 75s were whistling to Garrett signaling him to a certain open parking spot for him to park. As he approached, people began moving out of the way for him. The car looked and sounded great. Garrett stayed late at work applying a fresh coat of wax. The hood was carbon fiber which looked great with the headlamps' LED halos. The night was cool and brisk. The Chicago skyline peaked up from behind the adjacent buildings, cutting through a glowing background sky. Some of the other gatherers felt threatened by Garrett. They walked over and began asking him about his car. Garrett told them everything. He was eager to make friends. Little did he know he was pissing them off by showing them up. The chat was asking for the last call to register for the race. The total number of drivers at that point was 35. El Diablo swore to double the purse to anyone who could win the race and he offered a purse for second and third place to get more people involved. Potentially $70,000 for a $1000 entry fee, it was very tempting. A few guys in the crowd brought their money together and several more cars signed up. Members of the 75s talked Garrett into not talking to other racers. He was told politely, "Hey, get back inside the car and shut up."

Garrett agreed but just as he had settled inside his car, a guy walked up to him and said, "Well, well, well, looks like Satan found another sinner."

Garrett turned to face the guy. A member of the 75s checked his phone then stayed nearby. He asked the guest racer to get back to his car, saying the race was about to start, but he kept tormenting Garrett. The guest racer said, "Damn, Agusto must hate you. What'd you do to be set up in this piece?"

More 75s came over and attempted to push the guy away from Garrett. The guest racer said, "Hey, hey! Don't touch me, bro! Me 'n the Outfit want to see this fresh meat. Hey, whiteboy! Let's get a side bet going. What you think?"

Garrett didn't have any money. It was entirely out of the question. Besides, he noticed the guy walking back to a blue and gold RX7 just being parked. The car looked fast. It intimidated him. The guest racer kept talking. He said, "That's right. El Diablo doesn't like the direct game, does he? Let's do this. I know he can hear me $5Grand! C'mon!"

Garrett told one of the 75s standing near him, "Why don't I put my fist in his face!"

The loudmouth guy heard him and said, "There it is. He can't control himself. He's not a real driver, probably not even a real man. Diablo, he can't beat me, he can't beat me!"

Agusto was aware of what was being said. He needed to show a vow of confidence in his driver, so he sent a message to one of the guys there. The 75 saw the message then said, "$10Gs and we're in."

The loudmouth guest racer wanted to comply, but he had to check with someone else, and there, with one leg folded up against a beautiful custom Ford Mach1, was Jake, the breadwinner of the Chicago Outfit. He used his index finger to lower his shades to the tip of his nose allowing him to get a better look at who was inside the German coupe. He saw it was Garrett. He very calmly raised his shades back to where they were, then nodded a yes. It was on. The guest racer laughed and pointed at Garrett to keep his attention, then he waved his hand across his own neck signaling to Garrett, "You're done!" A new text message came into everyone. It was time to start the race. Unknown to them, there were over 40 police cars roaming the area near North Avenue and the I-90 expressway waiting for them. The location was where the racers would be forced to slow near hairpin and turn back south. Sgt. Vega and Detective Reyes were sitting in an SUV. They had wide vehicles to block escape routes, several barricades, and fasted police car in the state of Illinois, a Viper Interceptor. Inside, the voice on the scanners began coming up with a lot of activity saying:

"Two one one reported on south Halsted."

"Four five nine Alpha at Evergreen Plaza South Western."

"Four one seven reported at Southgate market canal and Roosevelt requesting units."

"Five Zero Three requesting units on Elston Avenue."

Julissa and Sgt. Vega turned and looked at one another. It was unusually high activity at precisely the worst time. Several squad cars left the ambush to go and assist throughout the city. Sgt. Vega wondered if someone was playing them. Julissa herself grew impatient. More calls came over the radio. Sgt. Vega could take no more sitting there. He pulled up next to the officer inside the Viper and said, "Fred, stay here and direct the ambush. You know what to do."

Officer Fred agreed with Sgt. Vega. He replied, "10-4."

Sgt. Vega flipped a switch on the ceiling and mounted an instrument panel. A row of blue and red LEDs began to flicker on and off on the front and rear of the vehicle. The Blazer sped away from their own ambush. Julissa was deep in thought. She wondered why they had left. She looked out of the passenger side window then spoke up, "What are you doing?" Sgt. Vega said, "We're being played. Your inside guy fed us long enough to get us involved. Tonight, he's cashing in. We're going to have to look into your source." They looked at each other, then Sgt. Vega said, "I have a good idea where to start."

Julissa said, "Really? Where?"

Sgt. Vega said, "Your uncle might know a thing or two."

Julissa snapped and said, "He coaches troubled youths. What would he know?"

Sgt. Vega was showing a lack of confidence in her. He knew it would bother her. There was a side to Sgt. Vega that drifted to possible outcomes. He had long since evaluated possible conclusions and kind of figured things out but never confirmed it. Once before, he himself would try new detectives in a similar strategy. He even tempted Julissa, but she passed every situation and always did the right thing. It was in her naturally, although she was the niece to Agusto Reyes, a guy who always seemed to have ties with people up to the point where they became criminals to law enforcement. It was true. He was a life coach for disadvantaged youths. But Sgt. Vega always knew there was more to it. There were petty thugs coming up big then losing it all in fast swoops. It always looked like self-destruction, but who was fanning the flames? Agusto was the only common denominator among them, but there was nothing they could do, nothing they could prove. Even the guys in the know didn't know anything. Everybody always spoke highly of Agusto. Once a long time ago, Sgt. Vega crossed paths with Agusto Reyes when he investigated a guy for theft, which would later become a cop killer. Ironically, a week before the guy snapped, they were staking out the guys house when Agusto Reyes came out from the inside. They stopped him, questioned him, and searched his car. Agusto had different types of surveillance gear in his trunk which he claimed was to bolster security in his garage. Sgt. Vega later discovered it to be more like an industrial museum. Despite being a troubled youth himself and all the doubts, everything always checked out. The guy had not committed any new crimes, but Sgt. Vega always paid attention to him. They would cross paths several more times. Agusto has always been on his radar.

It could be said that things were always meant for Agusto to be who he had grown to become, El Diablo. Cruz Santiago, on the other hand, serves no one but himself. Cruz was once a known Chicago

Outfit foot soldier who abandoned the claim. Once they all started getting arrested, he pulled his family together and built a new gang based on the street they all lived near 75th street. Although Cruz and Agusto knew each other, there were several families and 75 members who Agusto was trying to educate just before the height of Cruz's power and wealth among street gangs. After Cruz would sacrifice a very ambitious expansion and fail at it ending in a shootout with FBI and DEA agents, Agusto was the only other guy the 75s trusted. El Diablo was born. He would inherit sole possession of the 75s and to this day, continue recruiting. Not everybody ends up badly after confronting El Diablo. He makes a note as to the first day he meets them and gives them 40 days to avoid him, to have enough willpower to not fall into temptation or false desires. For many, 40 days is not enough, but slowly wandering the wilderness with him, a small number of people reached the promised land and began to count on themselves to expand their own horizons. Agusto Reyes was the type of person who could will himself to be better than anyone else. He is a relentless learner, but if someone reaches to have more willpower than him, he could beat him. What made it hard was how advanced he was. Agusto had a college degree. He would have lunch with the mayor, attend meetings with the city council, knew judges and police officers firsthand, and everybody spoke good things about him, except Sgt. Juan Vega. To him, it was a trick of God himself when Agusto's own niece would end up applying for a spot in his investigation unit and further yet, receiving it.

On Ashland facing northbound, 25 cars clogged up all the lanes behind a spray-painted yellow line on the floor. People were all around the intersection and everyone was recording everything. Throughout Chicago, people in the know were also watching the broadcast on their phones and tablets including Dayana. Over at Black Door, the race was being displayed on a projector screen. She cheered him on and sent him a warming text message. Garrett was somewhere in the first row toward the left side of the street. There may have been 10 cars jam-packed on the yellow line with another

10 cars behind them with the bumpers touching. There were more cars behind them making up the third row. Some had their lights flickering and their sound systems blasting. Everyone was excited, except for the regular citizens who were stopped from entering the intersection. The streetlamp was still operating, then the 75s began yelling out, "Ok, ok, this is it! Everybody, when that light goes green, you go!"

Everyone hurried off to the side of the street. Garrett was one with the car. He trusted himself. He looked into the rear-view mirror looking at himself and said, "Whatever happens, happens."

He read the text message on his phone. He got all warm and cozy. He sent her a daring message back where he asked her for a kiss when he won. She quickly replied, "Hell, yeah." Just then, a big guy dropped his large hand on the hood of the BMW. It was a giant cholo-looking guy who had cornrows in his hair and gold teeth. He said, "Hey, get ready!"

Garrett snapped out of it, focusing back on the task at hand. The crossing lamp light went to yellow. Garrett took a deep breath squeezing the steering wheel with both hands. Then, the crossing street's lamp went red and a second later, the green lamp ignited. Some guys jumped the light and left the line before the lamp went green. Garrett stomped on the gas. There were a lot of cars squealing their tires, but the BMW, as expected, gripped and launched itself forward, pressing Garrett into the seat. Everything was working as planned. The RPMs quickly approached 6000. Garrett flickered the transmission shifter keeping them there for as long as he could, gaining ground before the street narrowed. The car was quickly doing 85MPH. It ripped northbound underneath I-55. The noise from the cars collectively sounded like a swarm of bees with as many decibels as if they were standing next to an aircraft. The group flew past a series of streetlights skidding erratically, avoiding accidents. Some oncoming cars stopped mid intersection and were crashed into by racecar drivers. It was very dangerous. Garret himself hit a pothole early that might have done him in for the remainder of the course, but it didn't. He worried about it and performed a series of S curves to see if the wheel bearings were still good. They were. As they maneuvered through the narrow neighborhood streets, the cars began to resemble an F1 segment, trailing the lead car in a straight line, avoiding bumps in the road, and avoiding oncoming traffic. From his rear-view mirror, Garrett could see a line of lights following each other, then the gaps where they all attempted to pass the driver in front of him. Some of the more aggressive drivers crashed into parked cars along the street. Garrett had no time to be fearful. He had to carry on forward and peered out to see in front of him. He was in 4th place.

The SUV carrying Sgt. Vega was speeding on Milwaukee Avenue. They were going to a Mercedes dealership when another call came on over the radio from dispatch. She said, "Multiple Five One Zero street racers northbound on Ashland. Be advised. Traffic is heavy."

Julissa muscled up a deep voice then she said, "What are we doing? That's us. Let's go!"

Sgt. Vega said, "This is closer. Let's see if we can help."

He took the radio speaking device into his hand and said, "Fred, you copy?"

Fred said, "Copy that."

The cars kept roaring up Ashland Avenue. As they approached the westside, the streets got worse and worse. All drivers began watching out for the smoother surfaces on the road to avoid breaking suspension components but still at high speeds. There was a car that might have been sixth that slammed into an oncoming car for not slowing down when they crossed the intersection at Roosevelt Rd. The Eisenhower Expressway also complicated things. There was heavy traffic and the bridge bulges high almost as steep as a ramp. Many cars got airborne, coming down hard, breaking suspension components, and crashing into other cars violently. Garrett did the best he could. He came away unscathed but lost a spot falling to fifth. The loudmouth guy from the parking lot driving the RX7 was who had just taken Garrett. He hit his horn as he passed him just to mess with him. Ahead of them still was a newer Camaro and a pair of GT500s.

The street widened again. The cars all picked up speed, becoming more daring, cutting around one another, attempting to make ground. The city streets had a lot of cars and people on them as well as distractions everywhere. Garrett was well-focused. From the corner of his eye, he caught a glimpse of a series of squad cars parked near a corner off of Division.

Inside the squad car, the officer was counting all the speeding cars as they went by, "Five. Six. Seven." After concluding most of the speeding cars, he said, "26. There are 26 suspects. Let's get them."

The other officer in the car reported it over the radio and said, "We have 26 vehicles involved in that Five One Zero northbound Ashland approaching 90-94 let's go! Let's go! Let's go!"

All of the squad cars made their presence felt. They exited the side streets and were on the closed routes off of Ashland, intimidating the young racers flying down the street. Fear sunk into their hearts. Others who had been arrested before were consumed with a high-level frustration, and just a few of them didn't care about what happened next. Garrett was in fourth place. He knew every action of his was being recorded. This was what he wanted to do with his life, drive fast. He would not be taken to jail or have his license taken. He would have to perform another great driving act to get out of this one and he was up to it because he loved it.

As Garrett approached North Ave., the police threw a set of spikes out onto the middle of the road. The drivers saw a gap on the opposite side of the road. They swerved to take it. Again, in a straight line driving over the opening, when the officers saw they missed the lead cars, they retracted the spikes then threw them onto the road again. This time, they caught several cars. The following ones had no choice but to hit the brakes and stop. A bus blocked the cars from turning the north in either direction. Several squad cars pulled onto the street acting like obstacles blocking the lead cars from passing. The cars scrambled in every direction to avoid hitting or stopping in front of the obstacles. Garrett himself climbed the sidewalk. Officers on the sidewalk had to dive out of the way to avoid being run over. The group of lead racers made their way to the 90-94 on ramp toward the loop. If they slowed down, they could have been slow enough to get caught by the police. They were driving out of control accelerating excessively. Garrett and a group of cars managed to control the oversteer and come up the expressway cleanly. A few other following cars had to drift around the police vehicles impeding entrance to the ramp. Only about seven cars were still in the race. The cars created a solid barricade, and they had several streets closed off. They caught everyone else.

Of the cars still in the race, the RX7 was now in the lead, followed by the GT500 in second, then the Camaro, and Garrett was neck and neck with a 350z with another 2 cars behind them. Garrett pushed the coupe hard on the expressway's straightaways. He looked down at his speedometer. It read 150MPH. It felt dangerous, but he lowered his brow and kept pace. They saw sets of flashing lights but most of them didn't stand a chance until one car began making serious ground on them. It was Officer Fred driving the Viper Interceptor. When the viper reached to top the six racers, Garrett's speedometer read 140MPH. The Viper seemed to hover behind them. None of the drivers were willing to leave the race. All of them pushed the speed limit even higher. The GT500 behind Garrett lost control and skidded into the dividing barrier, catapulting it straight into the air before coming back down into oncoming traffic. Then 350z spun out sideways and went off the road taking out a sign with him. There were 5 cars left. They approached a busier part of the roadway. More patrolmen joined in. The racers maneuvered past the heavy traffic southbound now nearing the Eisenhower expressway. A state trooper who was in the traffic ahead of them joined in and took a position to block the Camaro off to a shoulder that fed into a tunnel. He was in 2nd and now had nowhere to go. The RX7 seemed to still be in the lead despite the traffic. Garrett was weaving in between cars, avoiding accidents, and trying to keep up with the RX7 and the GT500. One of the other racers got bunched up behind regular citizens where he was pinned until a squad car caught up to him. It was now down to 3 racers and 2 police cars. The road began clearing. The speeds quickly climbed. The racers separated themselves from the pack. The RX7 remained in the lead, but the Interceptor Viper had chosen to pursue the leader. He was right on his tail. In second place was Garrett in the BMW and third the GT500 along with another state police cruiser behind him.

The racers continued south. They neared the exit for Cermak Rd. The driver of the RX7 grew impatient. He suspected he could lose the Interceptor or at least attempt to get him off of his tail. He decided to take an alternative route hoping the Interceptor would stay with Garrett or take his chances, losing him in the Southside. Garrett saw the driver of the GT500 swerve to the left, pulling the patrolmen with him, then when he was next to the quarter panel of a sedan, he cut his steering wheel to the right harshly into it making the sedan spin around and strike the patrolmen taking him out of the chase. The driver of the RX7 took advantage of the events to take the off-ramp suddenly hoping to catch the Interceptor off guard. Fred caught on to the move. He showed off the superior braking ability of the Viper. He would chase his prey, the RX7. The GT500 and the BMW flew on by him. The exhaust of the Interceptor roared as the throttle was cut wide open. He turned controllably down the ramp where the RX7 was nearing the end, but seeing the Viper still in his pursuit caused him to lose control of the RX7. He oversteered to the right. The car ended up spinning the rear end around in a 180-degree turn which then slammed the driver side hard into parked cars on Cermak Ave. The driver of the RX7 tried to move the car backward, but it was stuck. Then, when he tried forward, the Viper came around the corner and drove all the way up to the RX7 touching front bumpers. The driver of the RX7, the same loudmouth guy that had made the side bet with Garrett, scrambled to unbuckled himself from the racing seat then dove over his center console. He opened the passenger side door and dropped onto the asphalt. Fred exited his car and held him down with his foot against the ground, then he said, "Gotcha!"

The people who were at the parking lot when the race started were watching everything as it unfolded on their phones but when they heard the sirens approaching, they quickly left the parking lot. Some 75s had to be there to record everything. They had pre-made scenarios with the help of a few homeless people to be able to stay there and look normal. For the 75s, every one of them would be compensated for their role in the race whether anyone won or not, but they had to be there no matter what happened. That was the job. Some of them knew the kind of tricks El Diablo plays on people but that's the thing. They can't be helped by anyone. They need to arrive at the conclusion to do good on their own—a hard lesson for those amateur racers to learn, but it would need to be so. Those that continued seeking selfishness would find themselves chasing higher and more dangerous ways of sinful pleasures until one day, they run out and commit one from which even they cannot forgive themselves over. Agusto acted without concern and let the universe take its course. From what he saw, the righteous always found a way to prosper.

This was a proving ground to El Diablo. Let's see what you're made of. This was exciting for him. There were still two racers left. It looked like they would complete the race. They exited the expressway on Pershing then headed west to Ashland. The yellow line painted on the street also served as the finish line. Agusto looked on from the comfort of his warehouse in Aurora. Not one squad car was still in pursuit and neither driver showed any sign of giving up. The BMW and the GT500 were neck and neck as they took the ramp to get off the expressway then made the turn on Pershing. Garrett was downshifting and making wide, controlled turns. The GT500 had more low-end torque. It came out fast, maybe a little too fast. The rear end kicked out. He had to lay off the gas giving the German coupe sole possession of the lead. Garrett sped even faster, shifting quickly, but he knew the GT500 was completely capable of gaining on him. Garrett could hear it getting close. Ashland Avenue was coming up. They had to downshift and make one last turn before the finish line. If the GT500 gets it right, he could leave Garrett in the dust. They could see members of the 75s at the corner recording the action. Garrett was very excited to beat the RX7. He was about to come in 1st place. He would get to kiss Dayana. He was going to be $50,000 richer! The two cars again came close to being. Even the turn was again wide. It seems like both drivers coasted in the same spot to avoid crashing into one another, then took one final straightaway. They put it all on the line. Both cars had their RPMs peaked. They were producing the maximum amount of horsepower the powertrains allowed them to produce. There were members of the 75s standing on the sidewalk jumping up and down in excitement. Garrett and the GT500 roared to the finish line and crossed it. Throughout Chicago, people were cheering at the outcome. The BMW crossed first by a foot or two. Garrett beat the GT500 and shouted, "Yeah!"

Dayana was watching and let out a loud cheer, "Oh my God. Garrett won!"

The 2 cars crossed the intersection flaring loose the accelerator in relief as they cruised forward crossing the intersection. The Mustang driver was on the right side of Garrett. He looked over to him who looked back at him and gave him a nod and a wave of approval. Then, shortly after that, the guy slowed down and made a U-turn onto I-55 southbound. Garrett checked his phone. It was 10:40 PM. He pulled off to the side of the road. He called his mom and asked her, "Hey, has anyone gone looking for me?"

She said, "No, why? What did you do?"

He said, "Nothing, hey, I'm not going to be out late. If anyone goes looking for me, just tell them the truth, I'm not home."

His mother answered back, "Ok, goodnight."

Garrett answered, "Goodnight."

Dayana texted Garrett, "Dude, you are awesome. Great skills. I'd ride with you anytime."

Then he called her and said, "How about that kiss?"

Dayana answered, "Come on in. First beer's on me."

He sped up and began heading to Black Door. It was a feast from the moment he parked his car out in front. Dayana greeted him with a tall Lager then gave him the kiss he had so righteously earned. Everyone saluted him and praised him the rest of the night. His boss played replays over and over on the big screen and for that night, Garrett was a celebrity. He loved it. Garrett left before closing time. Dayana begged him to stay but he had already committed himself to go and visit his dad again bright and early. Agusto texted Garrett a simple "Congratulations." When Garrett replied asking about the money or any instructions for the car, Agusto never answered him back. Instead, some members of the 75s who were present told him, "Don't worry about it. You made every cent."

Music to the young man's ears, Garrett felt more confident in himself after having won the race. He found a profession he belonged in and people appreciated him for what he does. His voice was deeper. He could easily look at people in the eye and be proud of himself. There was no denying himself to anyone ever again.

CHAPTER 5

"I just wanna fly."

The following day, Garrett woke up around 7 AM. He walked over to his personal bathroom and threw some water on his face, brushed his teeth, and got ready to head down south. When he went outside to his car, he couldn't help but stop and admire it. *Wow!* he thought. *That is a beaut.* He reached Springfield by 10 AM where he stopped for a late breakfast. A steamy egg muffin sandwich along with a slushy, then he kept on driving, reaching Menard still at a good time for visitation. Garrett penned his sign at the bottom of a sheet to request to see Warren Lee. The wait was the longest he had ever waited for and finally, after nearly an hour and a half, his name was called. The guards brought his father around, but he looked distraught, almost as if he were ill, wasn't eating, or wasn't sleeping. It bothered Garrett. But even more shocking was the first thing Warren said as soon as he sat down. He said, "Are you hanging out with those 75s?"

Garrett said, "Excuse me? What? Dad, you look terrible. What's going on?" After a brief glance to make sure the guards weren't paying attention, he smiled and said, "Word gets around. Maybe a little high-speed driving? If you know what I mean."

Warren said, "So, it's true! Dammit, Gare!"

Warren looked around. El Bambino was sitting near Warren and could hear him, then he said, "Dammit, Garrett, stay away from those damn punks. They're trouble."

Warren kept turning to look at El Bambino then they happened to make an eye. Warren quickly turned away.

Garrett said, "Pops, I'm a little too old for you to be telling me what I can and can't do. Besides, I'm the best driver in town. There's no way I'm getting busted."

Warren lowered his head holding it with one hand, then he said, "Turn around and walk away. Just stop everything. It's made out of pixie dust."

Garrett said, "Hey, if they lock me up, Pops, so be it. I love driving and the way I see it, I don't drive for them or the money. I drive for myself."

Warren again repeated, "It's all a part of their game. You'll never win."

Garrett said, "Is that all you wanted to tell me? It's not about winning, Pops. It's not about a side or work. It's about doing what you love for all the right reasons. Even if you do cross the line, I love driving, Pops, and I ain't stopping."

Warren said, "I'll do what I can to protect you."

Garrett said, "You too, Pops. You gotta take care of yourself, man. Why aren't you eating?"

Warren said, "I've been a lil detached lately overthinking. But you confirmed my worst nightmare to be true. I'm sorry, Gare. I hate the idea of you becoming like them."

Garrett said, "I'll be fine, Pops. I own my world now. I heard you were out?"

Warren said, "Yeah, with the parole coming up, I told them I'm out. Start fresh, like I said, remember."

Garrett said, "You can do that?"

Warren said, "You always have a choice, son, even if all the cards are stacked against you. You can always walk away."

Garrett sat there taking in the words his father said, then Warren continued, "The only family I have now is you, son. Once I get out, if you want, we'll leave town."

Garrett said, "Sure, sounds good. I saw there's like a whole racing league down there. It'd be nice to let her loose there on a track."

Warren smiled and said, "Yup, let her loose." They both grinned. The mood had lightened.

After a while, Garrett's cell phone rang. The caller ID said it was 'no caller.' Warren said, "Don't answer that."

A pair of visitors behind Garrett later walked behind him and whispered, "Answer it."

The cell phone rang again but again, Garrett didn't answer. He and his dad kept talking. Later, an inmate near Warren who was walking by tugged on his shirt and said to him, "Your son works for El Diablo."

El Bambino looked toward Warren flared with a slight amount of anger, hearing something damning for the first time. El Bambino chose to investigate the matter. He was talking with his wife and his daughter. A display of violence did not favor him especially not after having obtained a stature of a peaceful person. Warren still had 12 more days at Menard. He wasn't going anywhere. The Outfit would surely get to the bottom on this. On Garrett's side, members who followed El Diablo hovered behind him as if they were protecting him until one of the guards yelled at the men saying, "Hey! That's good enough. Back to your seats, gentlemen!"

The phone rang again, and this time, Garrett answered it, then he said, "Yeah."

Agusto Reyes was on the other end and said, "Congratulations on your win last night. I knew you could do it."

Garrett said, "Thanks, hey, I'm kind of busy right now an—"

Agusto said, "I'll let you finish with your father but before you leave, give the man 4 spots to your left the middle finger on your way out. He operates the Outfit and is displeased with your father no longer wanting to be a part of his organization. What a loser. Next, I want you to come to Aurora when you're done. I have another race to talk about. You do want to race again, don't you?"

Garrett said, "Yeah."

Agusto only said, "Excellent," then quickly hung up the phone.

Agusto had invited his niece to a Sunday morning meeting at her favorite coffee shop. After he hung up, he looked at the screen. The name of "Garrett" still illuminated. Agusto smiled then said, "I'll get you, demon. Leave that boy at once!" In a few moments, Julissa arrived. She drove and parked exactly in the front where Agusto was in a fire torch her red Supra that her uncle himself bought her as a gift. She walked inside still with her sunglasses on then waved at him as he stood up. As they greeted each other, she was a bit pissed and exclaimed, "What the hell is going on! Tio, have you seen the news? My goodness."

Agusto said, "That bad, huh? Have you eaten breakfast? I can order us something."

Julissa said, "That'd be great, thank you."

Agusto signaled the waiter to come by, then he asked her, "So, how was your shift?"

Julissa said, "We were staking out that big race, the one everyone was talking about, but then, all these calls began pouring in, and dammit, Sergeant Vega second-guessed me. We go to this burglary and of course, it's too late. The whole thing last night was a disaster. Just a huge shit-show!"

Agusto said, "You'll get them. What about Sgt. Vega? What does he think of everything?"

Julissa said, "He wishes he was 20 again to pull 18-hour shifts. Oh, and, for some reason, still has that vendetta against you."

Agusto said, "Did he say something? Do you think the guys who tip you off are talking to him?"

Julissa attacked him saying, "That's private stuff, Tio, he wouldn't tell me."

Agusto said, "What do you believe?"

She sat back and let out a deep breath, "I know nobody talks to him. They usually end up arrested. But sometimes, I do wonder if he's right."

Agusto let out a light laugh, "Mijita, c'mon now, you're going to start thinking I run organized crimes? Is that cherry-colored car a bribe? How about my love, there's nothing there, c'mon? I wish I could fix everything, but I can't. I am only a man, no more than a messenger."

Julissa said, "What does that mean? I'm just a messenger? A messenger for the devil?"

He said, "The world has a message, a pace. It always looks for ways to correct itself. We are just here as passengers. Anyone can take your place."

Julissa answered, "Are you still dating that yoga chick? The one who plays the bells. Damn, how did you become so deep?"

Agusto began, "I'm just older than you, little girl, you'll get there."

She took a deep breath then said, "This is mixing family with my job, but I know how connected you are. Do you think you can look into this sudden crime wave and tell me what you come up with? I'm gone, Tio, I can't even think straight."

Agusto said, "I don't think that would be a good thing for you. You know, breaking one small thing usually snowballs into breaking something bigger. Take my advice, forget about it. Go out with your friends and have some fun. Who cares about some insured items getting stolen?"

Julissa said, "It makes me feel useless. Ashamed. Embarrassed. Failure. I'm desperate. Tio, help me out."

Agusto said, "Fine, I'll see what I can do."

Julissa said, "Could you find out about the race too? I heard from some cops that 2 cars actually finished it. You think It's true?"

Agusto said, "If they did, they must really be blessed."

They would enjoy a light Sunday afternoon lunch then go their separate ways. Agusto was a guy who was always thinking ahead. It bothered him that his niece would be timid over the events of last night. He cursed Sgt. Vega for leaving the big collar in order to assist a robbery he had no chance of stopping. "What a damn fool!" he said. As far as Garret, there were still many options ahead of him to make him fail. He could also see the 75s landing a big blow to the Chicago Outfit, cutting the head off the snake Joeblas Juerta. Warren was gettable. Garrett has a lot of worth as his personally sponsored driver. He just needed to get him out on the main stage and that's what El Diablo planned to do—milk him while he was warm. Garrett would fail sooner or later, he thought, and if he could make some money while doing so, well, that was just a bonus.

At the same time, Garrett was still visiting with his father. Garrett was the last person to be granted time so it would go all the way to the hour. Warren came back to the conversation about the 75s. He said, "Son, you're right. I can't tell you what to do. You're a grown man and have done fine for yourself without your old man. I'm sorry."

Garrett said, "Stop, Pops, the reason you did this was to provide for us."

Warren stopped him, ". . . and you? Who do you provide for?"

Garrett said, "Myself, and well, I met a girl."

Warren said, "Hmm, great, hopefully, you don't sell your soul, like I did."

Garrett answered, "Pops, it's different out there, being a good guy doesn't stand a chance. More money doesn't mean a lot either. Mostly, people just try to be as real as they can, I guess. Survival of the fittest, meaning the ones who aren't afraid to go for it, you know."

Warren asked, "Afraid? Afraid of what?"

Garrett said, "I don't know, rejection, embarrassment, getting used to losing. A lot of people carry things inside. I don't know, Pops. We're all just trying to make it. Then there's the devil."

Warren said, "Are you afraid of the devil?"

Garrett said, "Well, yeah, I guess."

Warren paused then said, "Hmm, you know it's close to like when I met your mother. I walked a thin line with the Outfit. There was always the fear of messing up. Maybe we all need to walk next to that line to grow a pair. Just don't make the same mistake I did."

Garrett said, "Which one?"

Warren said, "I got in too deep, stayed in for too long, riding that cash cow. Handle yourself, be conservative, trust yourself, remember what I've told you your whole life 'Don't give these bums leverage over you!'"

Garrett said, "About that . . ."

Warren said, "I figured." He pounded his fist to the counter in slow motion. "If you do the crime, Gare, you got to be willing to do the time. Build in the right direction. No one can blackmail you for a hundred dollars if you have two hundred. Be the hawk, not the worm."

Garrett said, "Thanks, Pops."

The guard yelled out behind Warren, "Ok, convicts, times up!"

On the other side, a person said, "Ok, let's get ready for the group of people."

Garret said goodbye to his father, "I'll see you later, Pops."

Warren answered, "12 more days, don't forget, see ya."

Garret got up and noticed the guys who were outside the visitor's area waiting on him. He caught a good look at El Bambino and out of foolishness gave him the middle finger. The act cemented Garrett as taking Agusto's side and inflicting further separation between the Outfit and his father. Warren had already turned his back on the organization, refused to further help them in any capacity, and now, Motors' son was disrespecting him? When Warren walked by, he didn't even look toward El Bambino. He just put his head down and kept walking. El Bambino was above loud actions, but rest assured, he would look into it. He had been offended his whole life, so what? When Cruz Santiago found out it was music to his ears, he said, "Good. I want all of ours helping Motors from now on. It has to look like he's the boss. Like he's deep in it. I want the Outfit to know. I want COs to know. I want the warden and the parole committee to know, even those phone snatchers on Halsted. I want them all to know that Motors call the shots from Menard. Then we tell Warren the Chicago Outfit is targeting his son for the disrespectful act today."

The member of the 75s who were with Santiago all nodded in agreement. The best way to beat fake news is not to pay attention to it, but what do you do when there is no way to avoid it? They were betting everything on Warren falling in. Most of us would do the same thing as Motors--think about it, letting our minds run wild with our worst fears.

Garrett left the correction facility. He stopped at a gas station and got himself a giant cherry-flavored slushy. He drove back to Aurora without a care in the world. Garrett had the windows open, letting the cool afternoon airflow through the inside of the car as he blasted down the highway at 85mph. Garrett enjoyed seeing the vast flat cornfields in the countryside of Illinois. He took a shortcut driving north on route 47 cutting through some old sleepy towns. When he arrived at Agusto's warehouse, Agusto had changed out of his street clothes and wore a dark blue onesie like the kind the mechanics wore in pit crews of racing teams. His name was on a patch on the left side of his chest. It read "Agusto." The warehouse's door was wide open. Garrett drove the coupe inside then Agusto signaled him to turn off the engine and to come over. Garrett shut off the engine then stepped out. Agusto said, "Took you long enough to get here. How do you think you did last night?"

Garrett was all smiles and said, "What do you mean I aced it? First place, baby!"

Agusto smiled, "No fooling you, huh. That's right. You came in the first place and made yourself some money. Let me ask you a question. You like that car?"

Garrett shook his head rapidly up and down then said, "Yeah!"

Agusto continued, "If I asked you to give me a percentage of your winnings for ownership of that car, how much would you give me?"

Garrett said, "I don't know. All of it? It's probably worth more than my cut."

Agusto said firmly, "Assuming the car is worth $1. How much money would you openly give me?"

Garrett said, "Half . . . half would be fair. I think."

Agusto said, "You are a good friend, Garrett. And I bet you do it naturally despite all the loss and anger inside you. You would still remain fair, huh."

They both stared at one another briefly, then Agusto walked over to a desk and pulled out a yellow envelope with a lot of money inside. Agusto dropped the bunches of bills over his desk and began separating them. He said, "I will provide you the same 50% friendship you would give to me. Let's start. The buy-in was $1000 which I paid so you owe me $500. The purse grew to $40,000. I said I would double it which made it $80,000. You won first place which was $50,000, second got 30,000, there was no third. Now, due to our 50% deal, $25,000 of it is yours minus the entry. It means you're at $24,500. Then, that little side bet and yes, I cashed it in already. I made $10,000 which you were generous enough to give me 50% so you add $5000 which puts you at $29,500. Not bad. Especially as you have also managed to avoid getting arrested. You're alright, kid. Now I tell you what else you get for being generous to me, the car, that coupe you modified, it's yours. Plus, I'll pay you for the upgrades, an additional $5000 topping. You at $34,500, you good?"

Garrett looked at the pile of bills Agusto pushed toward him. He was speechless but managed to say, "Ugh, yeah!"

Agusto said, "Garrett, the reason that you should keep the car is I'm not a bad guy unless you think I am. Am I a bad guy, Garrett?"

Garrett said, "No, of course not."

Agusto said, "Garrett, I'm not giving you this stuff. You earned it. Take it, enjoy it. Now, there's a racing event this weekend, in Houston. TX2K at Royal Purple raceway. Are you up for it?"

Garrett's eyes lit up. Everything he was hearing was like a dream come true. He said, "Yeah! Ugh, I'm ready."

Agusto said, "Alright, look, I know a guy who owns a high-performance shop in town. He regularly goes to these events. I can get you on his team. I'll get a car for you to drive. Just rest up and get ready to focus on your driving."

Garrett said, "I'm going to TX2K?"

Agusto said, "Yup, get ready."

Garrett said, "Sweet."

Agusto said, "Now, kid, this isn't easy. It's a quarter-mile. You put this car in the wall, and you're done, and this car is not $1."

Garrett then asked, "What about Pablo? Can he come?"

Agusto said, "We'll see. I'm expecting him later. I don't know if he will join you. Is there a girlfriend or a wife you might want to take with you?"

Garrett said, "No, I just met this girl, but I don't know. I'd be happy if I could just get a date with her."

Agusto jumped at the opportunity, saying, "Well, what's her name? Maybe I can help you."

As if he didn't know.

Garrett said, "Her name is Dayana Cuevas. She works with me over at Black Door in Addison."

Agusto said, "Well, dammit, Garrett, ask her out already. What are you waiting for? I'm sure she won't say no."

Agusto knew the biggest weakness to any guy since the beginning of time has always been a woman or their attractive counterpart. Garrett needed to lift heavy weights to build his mind, secure himself amid difficult times and build upon that, take life at its hardest, and have the confidence to know he can come out on the other side or fail miserably. Agusto wanted a front-row seat.

Garrett secured his cut inside the yellow envelope then pointed outward signaling he was leaving. Agusto stopped him then said, "I know this car is yours now and all, but there might be a lot of heat on this thing. Too many people looking for it. Tell you what, I have a pickup over against the wall. Why don't you take that instead?"

Garrett said, "Sure?"

Agusto continued, "Keys are inside. Come by on Wednesday so you can meet the team."

Garrett exited his office and saw the truck. He laid his eyes on the beautiful gem sitting alone in the warehouse. It was a 1992 454SS in mint condition with a set of aftermarket wheels and solid black window tint. Garrett stood there to take in the sight. He loved it. The keys were sitting on the sun visor. He dropped the sun visor, caught it before hitting his lap, then stared at the truck in awe the whole time. The keys alone were vintage Chevrolet style. He grinned at the nice rumbling sound it made once he started it up, then he began to maneuver it out of the shop. He waved at Agusto as he drove past him. Agusto approached the coupe. He was cautious in case he needed to use the car against Garrett. He moved it into a secluded part of the shop.

Garrett drove off toward the city. The truck just felt like a 1/4 mile drag car. It wasn't great stopping or cornering, but hey, "it's a truck." What it was good at was laying patches of tires on the ground using all throttle. He was all smiles. Shortly thereafter, Agusto received his next visitor, a customer who wanted him to work on a 4x4 plow truck that needed some welding work to get done. Agusto would spend the rest of the afternoon measuring, cutting, and welding steel to replace the decaying and broken pieces on it. He fabricated sheet metal and welded them together. Agusto enjoyed working. He would do it for free but needed to keep his customers honest as well. Agusto was deep in thought blasting heavy metal music when his next visitor arrived, Pablo. His security system let him know as soon as Pablo passed his front gate, but he also knew the guy was cocky and believed he was meant for something bigger. Agusto would give it to him, but he feared Pablo would find a way to use it against him. He had yet to break him. It made him weary that he was involved so closely with Garrett. Agusto wanted to know if he could give him a job and if he would do it without screwing him. To test Pablo, he trusted him to collect money from the criminals who had paid for the crime wave that happened the night before. El

Diablo knew Pablo should have collected thus far $125,000 dollars. They had a 40/60 split which meant Pablo would keep $50,000 if he played straight.

Agusto knew before Pablo entered his shop but he kept on working on his project as if he wasn't there. Pablo saw an aluminum pipe on the floor and had thoughts of cracking Agusto over his head. He looked around to see if he could spot any cameras, and sure enough, he saw one. Agusto still hadn't acknowledged Pablo being there and did not show fear toward Pablo. The loud music alone could have been intimidating, blasting throughout the shop area. Pablo yelled out, "Agusto."

Agusto failed to do anything new. He just kept on welding with his back still turned to Pablo. There was a mural on the wall behind the workbench where Agusto had been welding on. It was a beautiful female angel with her wings spread wide open, one going up and one going down. Pablo had seen the mural before several times in various places, but today, Pablo noticed something different about the drawing. The angel was crying while gazing upward. The drawing looked like the shape of the halo was a shroud around her head, not a halo. Pablo noticed the mural had squiggly lines he took for beams of light, but on Agusto's wall, the faint outlines looked like horns coming out of the angel's head. Once he saw them, he couldn't un-see them. This time, Pablo's voice was weak. He yelled, "Ugh, hey, Agusto."

Still no answer. The heavy metal music pierced Pablo as if it was growing in intensity. A series of goosebumps rapidly shot down his backside. He was fearful to actually be in the presence of the biblical satan. Pablo had been told the drawing was meant to be a reminder that your guardian angel was nearby, but he feared his new understanding of the drawing. Pablo was scared he thought about leaving. "Fuck this!" He thought he'll steal the money then let Agusto go look for him. Pablo was about to leave but he built enough nerve inside him to call one more time at Agusto. He raised his voice and yelled, "Yo! Diablo!"

Agusto turned around in a sharp, quick manner with his welding mask on. It had a scary, red Japanese demon face drawn on the front of it. He yelled from behind the mask with a muffled and eerie yell. He said, "What!"

Pablo was wide-eyed and scared out of his mind, yet he stood his ground standing firmly holding a bookbag in his arms unable to speak for a second. Pablo was sweating trying to regroup himself. Agusto took off his mask and asked Pablo to follow him to his office. They both entered the room. Agusto took a seat behind his desk. Pablo preferred to remain standing. Agusto said, "Relax. You're not in trouble."

Pablo looked afraid. He swallowed in his throat loudly.

Agusto then continued saying, "By my account, you should have $125,000 in that backpack."

Pablo said, "Sorry, but some of the guys got arrested and some of the others died last night. It's $90k."

Agusto said, "That usually happens when they go out looking for blood. They usually find it. Ok, you do know I'm going to check on that number. You know what happens if you're robbing me."

Pablo said, "C'mon, man, I deserve more of this. I could've gotten whacked. I got a crew to feed. I earned this."

Agusto said, "Don't be angry now. You're the one who set the break. Let's see. 40/60 $90k, that's 36k. You want more? Bring in more. Until then, pay up!"

Pablo was disgruntled. He started unpacking the bag and placing stacks of money on top of the office desk. 20 stacks with $4,500 each, then he pushed 12 stacks toward Agusto and began rolling up the remaining 8 stacks into his duffle bag.

Agusto said, "You know your math. I'm going to give you a way to bring in more cash. I want you to take my $54,000 dollars to Royal Purple raceway this weekend and run bets with my money on my behalf. I don't have to explain the booking to you. I know you've been doing it on a small scale. Well, this is your chance and if I like what I see, we can renegotiate your cut. Garrett will be there to race.

I need him to focus on his driving. Don't get him involved and try to stay out of trouble. Can you handle that?"

Pablo agreed, "Yeah sure, Diablo."

Pablo grinned as he put all of the money back into the duffle bag, then Agusto added, "Something else, I have a task for you in Houston."

Pablo began to leave the room, but he stopped, turned around, and gazed back at Agusto saying, "What's that?"

Agusto said, "Show Garrett a good time. You know women down there, introduce him to a few. Let's see how pure his love for his little girlfriend really is. Praise him every time he wins and encourage him to keep at it on his losses, make him arrogant, full of himself. Let's see how hard his backbone really is. See what he does?"

Pablo agreed and finally walked away, then Agusto yelled from inside his office saying, "And don't forget to tell your boys who they really work for!"

Pablo said to himself in a low whisper, "Fuck off!" Pablo felt as if he was being promoted but got shit on at the same time. *Who does this guy think he is?* he thought. Pablo understood the meaning of "Show Garrett a good time" to mess him up with his girlfriend. It was El Diablo's cold-hearted scheme to break people up. As much as he hated it, it was a job and he would always put himself first. He had to. Even if it meant hurting his friend Garrett. "Oh, he'll find another girl," he said to himself as he boarded his car. "So what!" As Pablo began driving away, it was still on his mind. He was debating whether he should pull Garrett his way, make him part of his crew, so he could keep Dayana. But then, Pablo shrugged his shoulders thinking, *He's young! It's not like they would end up together. Psh,* he thought, *Maybe I'm doing Garrett a favor. Maybe Garrett is destined for greater things.* Pablo wondered if these actions would come back and hurt him in some way. He wondered if he should turn back and shot Agusto. He reached under his seat and verified he still had the 1911 pistol he stashed, and he did, but he said, "Naw! Things will be just fine. It's all just money."

CHAPTER 6

"Many men wish death upon me."

At Menard Correctional Facility, Warren was living in an abyss. He feared for the path his son had chosen. Even worse, Warren was being isolated completely out of the know. Now, none of his old friends talked to him. The only guy that would get near him was that outcast Loro. The other inmates were hearing all about Motors and his kid. They wouldn't mess with him nor talk to him because he was becoming more dangerous and he had the appearance to match. They all assumed it to be true. The Outfit held back from confronting him because of the rumor that he was now calling shots for the 75s. It could trigger a war and El Bambino didn't want to risk that kind of exposure, not yet at least. Warren didn't mind. He knew none of it was true, so he passed the time just keeping to himself. Prison gives you the skill of appreciating your solitude. Sometimes, you can go days without saying a single word to anyone else nor wanting to. The Chicago Outfit was convinced Warren and his son were betraying them. Several guys wanted to kill him wherever they found him. They should have known this as soon as he denounced the Outfit. El Bambino remained stubbornly loyal to his teachings. Of a man being able to control himself, he told them, "Until he looks for blood, we cannot give it to him."

Cruz did a good job making it look like Warren was now against them, but Warren kept his discipline even if his son was involved. He wanted no part of the 75s. Warren was thinking of finding a way to talk with Cruz and ask him to name his price in order to leave Garrett alone, but he was not close to any of the 75s. The only friend he had was Loro. Warren hated the fact that his son was hanging out with them. Jake failed him. The Outfit failed him. His mother failed him. And finally, he had failed him. Motors understood the game from early on. Why had it become so difficult for Garrett to see? Warren further beat himself up. It was by his hand that he asked his son to be isolated from this life, and this is what happened.

Over the next few days, Cruz was a bit disappointed Motors wasn't feeding out his hand. He devised a lie to see if he could get Warren to play into their game. He had his guys speaking multiple times right in front of Warren to spread a rumor that the Chicago Outfit was on the hunt for a getaway driver, claiming, "He had stolen money from an Outfit stash house!"

Another person talked about the events near Warren saying, "There were several hired guns out looking for a Gare who was driving."

Then, Cruz told Loro to mention another part of the lie to Warren to remind him, "The driver of the getaway car was in fact Garrett his son!"

Warren reached his breaking point. Even with the pressure of his upcoming parole, Warren felt like he had to act. He couldn't wait until being released. He realized it might not even happen. He asked Loro for a meeting with Cruz. Initially, he refused but that didn't stop Warren from trying. More and more guys in his cell block believed Warren was losing his edge. At times, he even looked clingy with Loro. It was an embarrassment to the Outfit he had ever been associated with him for so long. El Bambino was wondering if attacking him would be a good time now, "Besides, he's not even a man anymore. Hahaha."

Garrett knew nothing of all the drama his father was going through. He went back to work that week and continued having productive days. Things were moving along with Dayana and it showed in his behavior. He was courteous and friendly to every customer he came across. He was a different man, full of confidence. That night, he would see her again. Garrett would find himself daydreaming of being with her instead of eating his lunch. He was falling in love. As soon as 5 PM came around, he quickly left to go to work at Black Door. It was drizzling. He paused to admire the beads of wax floating atop the top jet-black finish on the truck, a thing of beauty. He unlocked the driver's door, stepped inside, and got into the perfect spot of those custom bucket seats. Garrett placed his left hand around the steering wheel then took the single ignition key from the key chain in his right hand and slid it perfectly into the ignition cylinder. He flicked his wrist away from his body. Once he turned the radio on, for a second time, he ignited the dashboard, but the third time, it awoke the fire-breathing dragon. The loud steady hum of the 400+ horses galloping throughout the exhaust pipes took over. Even starting up the engine was very exhilarating to him. He leaned back in the driver's chair and took it all in for a few seconds before he pulled away. He cruised over to Addison feeling the raw power of the pick-up truck. It turned a few heads as he roared around town. His mind wandered. He wondered if the money was what had changed him. It surely didn't hurt. Maybe having the girl of his dreams was all a byproduct of it. He wondered if maybe there really was a greater power looking out for him. If Satan was pushing on him, testing his faith, someone else might also be guiding him. Garrett was overthinking. None of that mattered, only the road in front of him and the powerful pickup truck beneath him.

A light rain was beginning to fall as Garrett flew down the street. The beads of water floated off the windshield. He pressed the accelerator raising the speed. He unlocked the driver's door, stepped inside, closed the door, and got in just the right spot of those custom bucket seats. When he reached his job, he found a perfect spot to show off the truck, the first spot from the street. He took it. He walked in and immediately caught sight of Dayana behind the bar. His heart was infused with joy. He walked right up to her and gave her a kiss. He never bothered to ask about her descent, but he was now noticing her long, sleek, gypsy eyes that made his knees weak when they stared back at him. Garrett, still holding her, said, "Hi, am I dreaming?"

She looked excited to see him and replied, "I hope not."

Garrett said, "Hey, I want to tell you something. I'm leaving town on Wednesday."

Dayana brushed his arms, then she said, "What? You're leaving town? Like for good? No, Garrett, please don't go."

Garrett said, "Huh. No, just for the weekend. What's all this cuddling stuff?"

Dayana smiled then explained, "Oh, sorry, it's an old waitress scheme. See, when guys say they're going home or leaving town, I'm supposed to suck up to them, pleading them not to go." She smiled then said, "It works, huh, I've heard that back in the Capone days, like when Gangsters pick up prostitutes, they're supposed to say, 'I'm leaving town.'"

Garrett said, "So, are you saying I'm picking up a gal at a brothel?"

Dayana immediately frowned and said, "Oh, wait. You're not a gangster, are you?"

Dayana walked away then Garrett followed her and said, "I'm sorry, I know it's way too soon, but I wanted to ask you if you wanted to come to Texas with me?"

Dayana said, "You're right. It's too soon."

Garrett was confused as to how he got to have this conversation. He looked like he had seen the president participating in the macarena. His eyes were open lopsided trying to make sense of everything she had just said. His chin pulled back into his neck and his eyebrows pointed straight up wrinkling his forehead. Garrett said, "Hey, I really am leaving town and yes, I'll be back next week. I'm going racing in Houston. And how do you know all that Capone crap?"

Dayana said to him, "Sorry, but I find the 1920s very interesting. There's something off about you and I don't like it. Maybe this winning is going to your head."

Garrett said, "Let me make it up to you. Let's get lunch tomorrow."

Dayana said, "I can't. I'm busy, but if you really want to spend time with me after we close, we could hang out. I know of this diner we can go and just chill if you want."

Garrett said, "Yeah, that's great, that's fine." He kept nodding and trying his best not to crack a huge smile on his face.

Dayana said, "Cool after work tonight?"

Garrett said, "Sure."

Garrett walked back to the storage area. He needed a moment just to take in everything that had just happened. He had finally bridged the gap between him and the girl of his dreams. Things could have gone south really quick, but he recovered and even built on it. He liked her so much. He did believe she was the woman for him. He liked her more now than before and he couldn't hide it. Everyone could tell how happy he was. He tried to relax and maintain calm for the rest of his shift. The night went by easily, with no hits, no runs, and no errors. There were not a lot of customers. The cleaning began early and at about 11:15, Edgar decided he could let them go. He said he would cover the bar if anyone happened to walk in. Dayana changed from her skimpy skirt and loose blouse into jeans and a jacket, her hair grabbed into a single tail looped through a Cubs hat that she wore. She met Garrett at his truck and when he stared at her due to how awesome she looked, she blushed a little and said, "What? Got to throw off the creepers."

Garrett said, "Well, that's what I'm here for. I can defend you."

Dayana said, "Garrett, don't be stupid."

Garrett said, "Where are we going?"

She said, "It's called Maya's diner. They're known for breakfast, but they're always open."

He said, "Ok, yeah. I know where it is."

It did not take long for them to reach the diner. They walked inside and found a nice table toward the middle of the room. There was only another single guest seated near the kitchen watching a small television hanging from the ceiling. The waitress quickly came over to take their order. Dayana ordered 2 scrambled eggs and 2 strips of bacon. He ordered a roast beef sub. They mostly stared at each other and asked silly, useless questions to one another all night. Once their orders came, Garrett was thrilled by how big his roast beef sandwich was, but he dug in with no remorse. Then, Dayana asked Garrett, "How come it took you so long to talk to me before? Were you married or something?"

Garrett said, "Things just weren't right."

Dayana said, "Oh, and now they are?"

Garrett answered, "More than before, yes."

A couple walked up to the door. They made eye contact with Dayana, then they paused. The girl began snapping at the guy as if he and Dayana had something to do with one another, then they decided to leave and walk away.

Garrett said, "Do you know them?"

Dayana said, "That's my ex-boyfriend and that was my former best friend. I guess they were meant to be and found each other. No Biggie. Are you offended?"

Garrett said, "Who? Me? Naw. You really are strong."

Dayana said, "Sometimes. I've known them both for years and well, as you saw, it doesn't matter anymore. Tell me about you . . . so, racing?"

Garrett said, "Well, I'm on a racing team now and I'm their driver."

Dayana said, "So, how deep are you?"

Garrett said, "What?"

Dayana said, "Racing, how long have you been doing it?"

Garrett said, "Well, it's been my life-long dream as far back as I can remember, but last week was my first race, ever, and I love it."

Dayana said, "You know, most guys only have room in their hearts to chase one thing at a time. It's said that most guys can't love two things at the same time. Do you believe that?"

Garrett said, "Um, I don't know. Maybe?"

Dayana said, "Would you ever cheat on me?"

Garrett said, "Never."

Dayana said, "You see, it's a woman's world. We earned it. You guys just live here. We hear everything!"

Garrett said, "Wow, I never thought of it like that. Cool."

Dayana said, "I've heard that guys who accept that it's a woman's world have bigger dicks. Do you think it's true?"

Garrett said, "Well, uh, I've never seen the studies, but I would say sure, it might be true."

She acted as if a cold chill had gone up to her spine, then she curled her index finger and lightly bit down on it. Dayana said, "Are you for real, Garrett? Or are you lying to me?"

Garrett said, "I don't know how to lie."

Dayana said, "Well then, let me warn you about something. Success is a dangerous thing. No one has that much luck. There's always someone pulling strings and when you stop winning, they throw you away."

Garrett said, "Good thing I'm winning."

Garrett swooped in and kissed her on the lips, then she said, "Good thing you are."

Garrett said, "When I come back as 'a winner,' I want to see more of you."

She answered, "We'll find out."

They shared a final long stare in the center of the table which led to both of them smiling at one another before she pulled away and said, "I got to get home. It's late. I'll see you tomorrow?"

He said, "Sure, I'll pick up the bill."

She smiled and said, "I didn't ask, big winner."

After Garrett paid, he walked back to the table and had her accompany him to his truck. He opened the door for her then walked over to the driver's side and got in. He started thinking about what she said, about his success being manufactured, and to some point, he could see it being true. Agusto might be taking advantage of him, but why him? He dropped her off in front of her car near Black Door then took a long way home. He just wanted to bury himself in his thoughts a little bit longer. His thought was interrupted by a text message from Dayana who texted him, "Made it home safe. Tnx. Good night." He texted her back, "Good night." He erased all the false realities in his mind and went home. It was nearly 1 AM.

The next day was much like the day before. Garrett was a little bit tired but at that age, he managed nicely. He found out that Pablo would be accompanying him to Houston. It was great news, but Pablo wasn't on the racing team. It raised suspicions in Garrett which Pablo put to ease later when he told him, "Someone's got to take all the bets." Agusto sent Garrett a text message asking him to go to the performance shop that afternoon. They had received the car he would be driving and wanted to take some measurements to know how much room they had to play with. Garrett would meet the guys on the racing team for the first time. Garrett texted Edger asking for the night off. The worse part was he wasn't going to be able to see Dayana, but he figured he might stop by as a customer and flirt with her. He left NTB a bit later than usual then headed over to BMS Performance to meet Gene the owner and the race team, along with his new car.

Elsewhere, Sergeant Vega was attending a follow-up council meeting where his services were being evaluated for the events of that weekend. Sgt. Vega found himself being scolded. His command would be placed under review, an embarrassment for him for the events of Saturday night, yet not once did he mention the information that came into Detective Reyes, nor did he blame her for anything. Sgt. Vega claimed he acted and gave orders based on the intel that he himself had put together and although he left the car race scene early, he claimed it to be entirely his work. Sgt. Vega claimed he left to avoid further crime throughout the city, which he failed to do.

Julissa could not attend the council meeting. She suspected what was going on and felt a lot of pressure to call her uncle, which she did, but the call went straight to his voicemail. Little did she know he was right outside of City Hall hearing every word being said at Sgt. Vega's review hoping they would throw him in jail or at the very least, fire him. But it would not happen today. Julissa would be forced to do some old-fashioned police work. She worked until late with the IT department to backtrack city view cameras trying to determine where some of the stolen property had gone, but after nightfall, she had no new leads. She changed tactics and decided to backtrack people who were recognized in the area, backtracking their known locations hoping to get lucky and spot missing merchandise or any sales of property associated with these individuals. She couldn't make any matches. When she heard how bad Sgt. Vega had it at the meeting, it deflated her. It was after dinner time so she left home and decided to study and prepare to change her strategy again. She looked inside textbooks and journals from other detectives hoping to pick up on something that could help her, anything.

Garrett arrived at the performance shop and meet with the owner of BMS performance, Gene Paterson. The guys had picked up the car from a dealership which Agusto had paid. Then they drove it home and had it sitting in the center of the shop waiting for him. It was a brand-new Supercharged Demon. Garrett stood in awe. It was a car meant to be in some rich guys' collection and Gene and his team were about to heavily modify it to make it go faster, and hopefully, not put him into a wall. Gene helped Garrett breathe normally again. He was a car enthusiast himself and knew what a precious work of art they had before them. He offered to give him a briefing of his shop and introduced his technicians as he walked by them. Gene would also be driving at TX2K and knew how important this was to Agusto, a longtime friend of his. He asked Garrett what his strengths were and how he planned on staying alive going down a quarter-mile at 100 miles per hour. Garrett answered he had no idea. It would just come as he went, he answered, to which Gene said, "You're already a better driver than I was the first time I went down the track."

Gene said, "We've all seen what you did last weekend."

Gene and Garrett walked over to where two guys were browsing parts on a computer next to the Demon. Garrett admired a pair of aluminum cylinder heads sitting on a cart. Gene said, "This is Hector and Paul. They are going to perform the mods and travel with us down to Houston. Guys, here's our driver, Mr. No Fear himself, Garrett Lee."

Hector turned around and said, "What's cracka-lacking?"

Paul nodded then shook his hand saying, "How do you do it?"

Garrett said, "I-I don't know, man, it's like me and the car become one. Then, I'm just in the playground running around. I don't know."

Gene bumped Garrett in the stomach then said, "Paul was among the drivers last Saturday. I had to bail him out. We still haven't gotten his car back though."

Paul gave him a smirk then he began to talk with Garrett about their plans for the Demon. Garrett loved everything they were planning on doing. He approved everything, then Gene said, "How about we test Agusto's pockets and go with a larger Whipple Supercharger?" Paul and Hector smiled. They had one in the shop that could get modified to fit the Demon's intake. All of them were aboard. Garrett was asked to sit inside, then they used laser tracking to figure the roll cage configuration. They were also removing the passenger seats and adding a console capable of holding a laptop. There were different steering wheels they also talked about, just to make getting in and out of the car easier. They came to a configuration they all agreed upon. After that, they hung out, joked around, and laughed about finishing touches they could install. Not related to racing, their spirits were high. They all got along nicely. Garrett was easily one of theirs.

The following morning, Sergeant Vega called Julissa into an early morning meeting in his office. Once she arrived, she marched on inside, closed the door, and waited for further instruction. Juan got up from his chair, walked over to a window peered outward for a second or two still not saying anything, then he turned to face her. Both of his palms were firmly placed on his desk, then he said, "It's your uncle. I don't know how but I know it's your uncle."

Julissa said, "That's bullshit! I would know."

Sergeant Vega said, "That's how good he is. I need you to help me bring him down. He's the one pulling all the strings. Be very careful about your next words because I'm going after him whether you're on board or not. I can have you transferred. It's on you."

Julissa said, "I can't because there's nothing there."

Sergeant Vega stood in silence for a while then Julissa continued, "I met with him on Sunday. I asked him to find out who was involved in all the heists last week. I'm sure he will give us something, and he was going to handle it."

Sergeant Vega said, "That's not good enough for me. I'm taking you off this investigation for obvious reasons. Tell your uncle his luck is about to run out."

Julissa looked angry and said, "Tell him yourself."

She stormed out of Sergeant Vega's office. He suspected she had told him the truth. She wasn't the type to lie, but this behavior toward her partner was also new. There was something changing within her. He could tell even if she couldn't. Other officers standing outside Sgt. Vega's office quickly relayed the news, making its way to Agusto himself within a few minutes. What Sgt. Vega was doing going after El Diablo could be looked at as condemning himself. Agusto wielded a lot of power in Chicago. If he wanted to, he could be untouchable.

By late Wednesday, Garrett would have to get his things in order for traveling to Houston. He had another good day at work. Things between him and Dayana were still on the up and up. The worst thing was that it would be the last day he would be driving the 454SS. *There's no such thing as a perfect day,* he thought. As he packed and just moments before leaving to meet up the guys at Gene's shop,

Dayana texted him saying, "Good luck and call me when you get there."

Garrett made the last drive in the truck a good one speeding out of Chicago toward Aurora, making the exhaust scream just behind him. At every green light, he would stomp his right foot on the accelerator squealing the tires. When he got there, Pablo was already there waiting for him. He would ride with Pablo in his car the entire way there. Hector and Paul were also waiting for him. Both cars were loaded up inside 18-foot trailers. They were going over some final thoughts making sure they had everything they would need before heading out. Gene said, "Well, our driver finally got here. Anything else?"

Paul said, "No, we got everything. We should be good now."

Garrett took a peek at the Demon before they closed the liftgate. They added the roll cage and a set of competition tires all around that were much better than the factory ones. The paint was a deep Burgundy color. They fit it with a clear plexiglass replacement hood and removed the headlamps allowing for direct turbo induction. Garrett walked over to where the guys were and said, "Hey, guys, now the Demon truly is wicked." They all threw their hand waving him off and laughing at him. Gene replied, "You're like the fifth person to say the exact same thing!" Gene was driving a lifted dually pulling his racing trailer with his R35 inside. Paul was riding with him. Then, Hector was volunteering his own pickup truck to pull the shorter trailer with the Demon inside. Garrett would ride with Pablo. Gene shouted, "Ok, ladies, it's go time. Maybe we can make St. Louis by midnight."

Before the convoy left the gated area of Gene's shop, an Imported SUV arrived. It was Agusto stopping by to see why they hadn't left yet. Agusto saw they were leaving and stuck to small questions. He walked over to Garrett to have a quick chat with him. Agusto told him, "You know your job once you're on the track is to beat everybody. Don't get soft on me, alright. You gotta rip that Demon of yours a new one, kick the ass of every Lamborghini, every Ferrari, every German car, every Jap car, everybody and anybody even Gene. Take his lunch money! Make him your bitch! Got it?"

Gene was listening from behind the steering wheel of his truck. He rolled his eyes as if Garrett had a chance. Garrett believed every word Agusto was saying. He was dancing to the tune El Diablo was playing. He was pumped! Agusto further told him, "This is where you belong. Soak it in. This is your coming out party. Be free to meet some new big-breasted woman out there. Have fun." Garrett agreed and said, "Sure, that's what I'll do." Then Agusto padded him on his arm and said, "Good boy. I know you will." Agusto walked over and gave quick praise to the other guys on the team, everyone but Pablo. As Garrett was leaving, he rolled down the window and said, "Thank you, Mister Reyes. I won't let you down."

Agusto waved as he walked away. He didn't care about what happened, but he knew Garrett would soon be under his thumb. After Agusto left, Gene gave the signal. The convoy soon left the parking lot making a single stop to fill up on fuel before going south on I-55. They bought enough junk food to keep them awake throughout the night. They were not expected in Houston until Friday morning. Their goal was to sleep somewhere before Memphis, possibly off to the side of the road or in their vehicles at a rest area. The convoy made it to St. Louis by 11:15. Making good time, they rested near Memphis but still in Missouri around 2:30 AM. They awoke and recharged their batteries enjoying a good breakfast in Memphis before continuing to drive all day. Thursday, they crossed Tennessee and passed some beautiful country in Mississippi. It would be after 5 PM when they crossed into Louisiana. While they were driving, Pablo decided to get the truth from Garrett. He asked, "Hey, man, so are you always a tool, or do you just seem like it?"

Garrett said, "Who cares, man? I'm going to TX2K!"

Pablo asked, "Well, based on last week, and you firing on all cylinders at work, maybe I should always bet you. Bro, how do you do it?"

Garrett said, "I have no idea. A lot of things have been going well for me, bro. God is good."

Pablo said, "C'mon, man, not the boy scout answer. How do you do it? Are you paying someone? Greasing some palms or just too foolish to know about it?"

Garrett said, "You just don't think about that, you just do. And whatever happens, happens. Live like you're always going to be broke. Don't ask for more money and all the right things just happen. Well, I'm still trying to figure it out. Maybe my luck runs out this weekend. Maybe this is the last few days for me on this planet. If so, I'm alright with that."

Pablo said, "What happens if you ask for things? Or go on strike?"

Garrett said, "Well, I have never gotten what I asked for. Ironically, I focused on something totally different and things just happen."

Pablo said, "That might work for you but for me, I've had to take everything I've ever gotten and watch my back every day because somebody is going to creep up on me and take what I've gotten."

Garrett said, "Sounds like a prison. It also sounds like a bunch of theft; nothing is earned."

Pablo said, "There are no rules when you want to come up. As long as you do. Ever heard 'all's fair in love and war?'"

Garrett said, "Ever heard of the Geneva Convention?"

Pablo laughed then said, "Funny. We can regulate warfare but not hurting someone's heart."

Garrett said, "Love is forever. You're not supposed to hurt anybody. It should be pure and honest, bro, one for one. How many women have hurt you?"

Pablo got frustrated and said, "Alright, man, you keep your ways, and I'll keep mine. Maybe we can both go out in Houston and meet some new girls down here?"

Garrett said, "I don't know, bro. I think my heart is spoken for."

Pablo laughed and said, "We'll see. I got some friends down here that will have you looking for them in the daytime with a flashlight. Just be cool, Gare. I won't steer you wrong."

They both grinned at each other. Garrett was slightly open to the idea. Maybe his ego had been inflated higher than it should have been. He felt like he couldn't lose. Pablo asked another question, "So how much money are 2 Vatos from the westside of town making this weekend?"

Garrett answered, "A whole lotty dooty! Bro, we're in TX2K!"

The two guys were pumped. Pablo was convinced he was going to hustle from the moment he arrived until somebody stops him. Pablo did not understand what made Garrett happy, but he sure understood what made him happy and that was taking other people's money. *There was one woman who could possibly make Pablo happy, and God willing,* he thought, *he would get a chance to see her in Houston.* It was a very big coincidence. Pablo was an attractive guy. He could have any woman he wanted. He could turn on and off his feelings at will, except to one. There was Karina. He had been friends with her since the time he dated her friend Patricia. They still worked together. Pablo had not been involved with Patricia in years, but recently, he had begun talking with Karina. He even flew her out to Chicago to spend time with him and since then, she had become the one. Pablo was a guy who could make money doing anything he wanted. He chose to be an auto repair technician because it was something that interested him. In a lot of ways, he's a lot like Agusto, arrogant and with boss-like figures who enjoyed commanding from the front, attempting to exercise his will to the fullest. Garrett was oblivious to all of this. To him, willpower didn't matter. Men could not be manipulated. Nobody lied and every thief no matter big or small always went to jail. Garrett was a nice guy. He still didn't even believe he was a member of the 75s, but oh, yes, he was. They were exploiting his talents as we speak.

At Menard, Warren was getting worse. All the overthinking cornered his mind into a spot where that was all he thought about.

Warren was starting to get that crazy guy look on his face, the one where they always seem to be soaked in anger, squinting their eyes and looking hard at everybody. He was losing himself. The guards noticed and sent him to the med bay. They administered pills to help him and they did their job to balance his mind just for a while. Once he was fine again and in population, Warren did something really foolish. He asked Loro to help him get a stabbing device. He set his mind to threaten El Bambino into leaving his son alone or he would kill him. Warren would not let his son die at the hands of the very group he served for so many years. He was out and willing to kill to prove it. Loro answered, "I got you."

Loro wrote a message on a note and passed it along to a guy who was the right-hand man to Cruz Santiago. The note said Warren had approached him on his own and asked him for a stabbing device. He said he believed he would threaten El Bambino. Cruz smiled then he said to his follower, "Get Loro a shank."

The follower neared Cruz's ear, then he said, "Who's the target?"

Cruz said, "Don't worry about it, get it! I will cover the cost."

The follower said, "I know just where to get one."

Cruz nodded in approval, which was seen by Loro. He was told he would be found a shank to give to Motors. He just needed a day or two. Once Loro left, Cruz said to a second follower, "Pass this news to the Outfit. Tell them Motors wants blood for the Outfit playing him, going to prison, and being away from his son. Tell them he can't let it go and tell them he's got a shank."

The follower nodded then said, "I'll get on it."

Things were moving along for Cruz. He was happy to see his plan in fruition. Elsewhere, a guy walked into Black Door, a handsome, confident guy. He walked up to Dayana and flirted with her the entire time he was there, then he made his will known and asked her out. She was tempted to agree and leave with him that very night, but she thought of Garrett and declined barely. She kept a respectable distance from customers the rest of the night, but it wouldn't take long for him to leave. She later resented her choice. She didn't text Garrett to check up on him that night, but she noticed she wasn't fully with him. It bothered her.

Elsewhere, the convoy Garrett was riding with reached their destination. It was late when they reached Houston. Gene checked them in their room. Garrett texted Dayana, but she didn't reply. He peered out of his window facing north. An odd feeling came over him as if he needed to be somewhere else but couldn't put his finger on it. Garrett rubbed it out of his mind and tried to concentrate on the racing tomorrow. He laid down on a couch, soon got drowsy, and fell asleep. He awoke again. He checked his phone. The clock said 3:15 AM and Dayana still hadn't answered him. He paid no mind to it. Instead, he transferred himself in his bed under the sheets and soon fell asleep.

CHAPTER 7

"It ain't safe."

Garrett awoke to a bright and sunny Friday morning. Gene texted everyone to meet up in the hotel's cafeteria for breakfast. Pablo could not wait to begin placing bets. He circled around the tables picking out the high rollers, immediately making conversation with them. Pablo was also gathering information, studying the field, and assessing who the better racers were. He put together a lot of names on a notebook, people, and videos he would have to look up and study, trying to gain an advantage and create spreads. He didn't even have time to sit down with the guys. That morning, he ate wherever, left, and talked to guys outside in the parking lot, inspected a lot of cars, and took in money from guys who also wanted in on the shares. Pablo didn't care if the police were nearby. He openly did what it was that he wanted to do. Pablo had connections in town. It was a powerful street gang that he had already paid to supply him with muscle and although they hadn't arrived, everybody somehow knew they would protect him. When Garrett was going to back him up in case things got ugly, all he said was, "All you need to know is they're kind of like a local affiliate of the 75s." Agusto had made connections with different entrepreneurs in Texas. He offered his services and helped a lot of them strengthen their positions and they were appreciative of the friendship they had made. Pablo was in the know of who those people were. He looked for a way to gain leverage and build up his own anyway and anywhere he could. Pablo understood the power of deception. A simple introduction can go a long way he thought. He just needed to ride Agusto's train long enough to build one himself then jump off onto it. Pablo was rediscovering all his traits. Agusto said, "I would never teach him."

Pablo was made to be booky. He quickly devised a ranking system and scouted all newcomers to understand who would fall where. Friday would be head-to-head qualifying and as soon as the first two cars line up, he would be ready. Gene was well known among the veteran and returning drivers. Pablo dropped his name here and there to get himself into exclusive areas with known car builders. Pablo could get into a few garages and tents just by mentioning his name. Podcasters and promotors loved Gene. Illinois was being well represented in the TX2K. His mechanics Randy and Hector were also popular themselves. Pablo had no trouble getting personal with the other racers.

Once they entered, Gene introduced Garrett to several drivers also participating. Some of them had heard of the legendary street racer who won a race on the mean streets of Chicago a week ago. They were excited to meet Garrett but none of them thought he would do well at his first big event. They thought Garrett was too young. He got lucky, others thought. Gene had brought him to groom a new mechanic due to his knowledge of engine building but when asked where he learned it, Garrett replied, "I read it online." That comment would lessen Garrett's reputation. Some thought he was not even worthy of being in the event, to begin with. If it wasn't for Gene's trusted racing pedigree and him vouching for him, they probably would have kicked him out. What Garrett learned was that among deep pockets was a sense of entitlement. Gene noticed the aggressiveness of a few drivers then whispered to Garrett, "Don't worry. They probably never turned a wrench for a living in their life." A policeman walked up to Garrett and shook his hand. He said, "Gene must really trust you. That car over there, I bet it belongs to Satan! Be careful."

Garret answered, "Thanks."

Pablo finally came over to meet with Gene's racing team. However, the only thing on his mind was increasing his winnings. He was asking Paul, Hector, and Gene about different setups and tires to finetune his own understanding. Their cars were unloaded and the inspection team had already admitted them. Some were hanging around checking out the Demon and the mods. Gene had a blacked-out turbo R35 and Garrett was standing next to the Demon. The inspectors lingered around it, admiring it. Before they left, one of them got close to him and said, "Don't forget to give them hell!" Another said, "I'll keep the first-place trophy warm for you!" Garrett said, "Yeah, right. I'll be happy making it through today." The speakers were calling all drivers for a meeting near the launching area. At the same time, Pablo's entourage showed up. They set up a perimeter and made their presence felt. The racers all cheered after the introduction meeting. An email had gone out to everyone with class brackets and heat times, meaning the schedule for Friday's qualifying races. The Demon was one of the first cars to go in the first heat. Garrett was eager to start up the car and go to the staging area. Gene peeked his face near the passenger side window and said, "So, just checking. You're good right?"

Garrett said, "Yeah, I'm good."

Gene said, "Do you know what you're doing?"

Garrett said, "Ugh, stomping on the gas."

Gene reached for the tablet then turned it on and initiated a software program. He plugged in a thick cable with the other end disappearing under the passenger side dash. Gene said, "Turn the car off. Now set it to key on engine off. We're going to change the engine mapping and place the car into BMS's modified track mode."

He navigated the software and scrolled to a setting that read "TX2KDemon." Gene selected it. A whining noise was heard coming from under the hood. Gene locked the tablet on the custom-made console then spun it to face Garrett. He said, "Turn it on." Garrett fired it up. There were several additional gauges on its screen all referring to fuel trim and the stoichiometric ration. Garrett punched the throttle. The Demon roared loudly. Garrett then told Gene, "This program allows for an easier launch of the line. Leave it in gear and pull both paddle shifters, then once you release them, even one of them, the car will shoot out. Got it?"

Garrett said, "Got it."

Hector came over and checked his belts, making sure they were secure, then he handed Garrett a brand-new racing helmet. Then he said, "Don't forget to pray. This car scared the Jesus out of me just idling in the shop."

Garrett smiled eagerly to get the first one out of the way. He wanted to fly down the racetrack. Garrett believed in himself. He believed this was where he wanted to be. Garrett drove into the staging area. He turned and looked over at the guy to the left of him. He was driving a Challenger. It sounded mean, a slightly older SRT modified. Pablo showed his faith in Garrett. He placed a $1000 bet against the owner of the Challenger on Garrett. It was just qualifying but the heat was on. Garrett put on his racing helmet. He could see the team lining up along the fence ready to watch their car go down the strip. Garrett was signaled by the officials to advance. The lane was his. Garrett did a major burnout to warm the tires. He passed the starting line by about 5 feet, put the car in reverse, then drive again moving forward slowly to meet the starting line. Once both drivers were lined up, all the yellow bulbs were illuminated. He pulled back both paddle shifters. A buzzard could be heard coming from the tablet. Garrett pressed hard on the accelerator. The car revved up fiercely, staying perfectly on the line. Then the yellow bulbs began to turn off followed by the green bulbs going off. Time to go. Garrett let go of the paddle shifters. The car squealed lightly then gripped, launching the Demon forward at full speed. The front end lifted slightly but the car pounded the pavement with an excessively high number of decibels behind it. Garrett kept upshifting, hitting the paddle shifters just by listening to the sound of the engine. Gene was proud of his car as he watched it go down the track. Garrett looked into the mirror and saw the Challenger behind him, then just like that, it was over. The Demon ran a very quick quarter-mile, 9.903 seconds at 140MPH; the Challenger 10.3 seconds and 132MPH. Garrett was very excited. Garrett thanked the car by rubbing the dashboard. He said, "That win was all you, buddy, all you! Yeah!"

The guys were cracking jokes near the fence. Gene looked at Paul then Hector and said, "Guess he can tame his demons."

The guys lightly laughed. Paul said, "He's a speed demon!"

Garrett idled back to the trailer area. The guys slowly met up with him. Gene would race his car in the next heat. He needed to get his car ready. The heavily modified R35 sounded more like an Indy car with a very high rev and massive turbos on either side. Once Gene got to the staging area, he looked over and nodded at his competing driver, a friend of his from Michigan who would be driving a bright copper-colored Aventador, then when the green light went on, both cars fired past the starting quarter pole. They both sounded very impressive gripping the ground as well as anybody. When they reached the finish, Gene came in 10.232 seconds and the Aventador in 10.581. Pablo's scouting skills had paid off. He made himself a nice amount of money. Pablo bet on every race that happened that Friday, all 120 of them. Garrett raced 3 times staying consistent, earning a high-ranking position for his class for Saturday's events. By the end of the last race, the Demon was well known around the racetrack. Gene only raced twice and fell somewhere in the middle of the heavily modified class with a lot of competition. Gene wondered if the car was not running as well as it should. Hector and Randy were all over the GTR trying to figure it out.

Pablo convinced Garrett to join him and some of the other racers in a late-night cruise through Houston in search of illegal street racing. Garrett didn't know if he would street race. Besides, taking the Demon onto the streets was a very dangerous thing to do. Gene also had been instructed by Agusto to help "loosen him up." Gene encouraged the guy to go along with Pablo. Him and the two mechanics were going to be busy working on the R35 all night. He said, "I'm not your chaperone if you want to go go."

Garrett installed a set of street wheels on the Demon, then he followed Pablo who was being accompanied by some of the local 75 troops. Other racers grouped up. A small convoy of sports cars left the facility. Amongst them were high-end imports, exotics, domestics, and old-school muscle. The convoy went to various places along the loop which were known meet-up spots. They added more drivers then proceeded to drive downtown turning heads everywhere they went. They stopped across a gourmet tacos place and parked near a nightclub district. The flashy cars filled the parking lot. The expressway was not far and anyone who challenged another racer would go and race on the feeder road. Garrett had gotten his fill of racing for the day. He just stood next to the Demon as if he was guarding it the entire night. Pablo right away met some girls and brought them over where Garrett was. He acted friendly but entirely uninterested. Pablo's entourage didn't mind acquainting themselves with them. For Garrett, there was only one woman on his mind, Dayana. He looked for her name on his phone then pressed "call." She didn't answer. Garrett tried again but nothing. Dayana was busy working. It was a full house. Not only that but a guest DJ was performing. The same guy from the night before was again seated at the bar trying to entice her. She avoided him at all cost. She didn't trust herself. She wondered how Garrett was doing but not enough to call him. Doubt was creeping in. She just thought he was busy racing. He was her one and only true love. *He'll be back,* she thought, then she decided to concentrate on work.

Garrett shortly thereafter told Pablo he was leaving, heading back to the hotel. Pablo was too busy having fun, just enjoying the moment and planning to see the woman which he felt his heart belonged, Karina. Pablo would stay out until after her shift then hang out with her until 5 in the morning. Everything always turned out good for the guy. Garrett would awake the following day feeling quite well. He was wondering if he awoke to a dream. He said, "Am

I really at TX2K?" He smiled and got excited because he knew it wasn't a dream. He jumped out of bed and hit the shower. It was still before 7. Garrett decided he would go to the gym located inside the hotel. It turned out to be a very busy Saturday morning. There were a lot of people working out. Midway through his workout, Garrett caught sight of a stunningly beautiful woman. She drew his gaze toward her so much he couldn't help himself. It took so much of his willpower to look the other way. Garrett went to the far side of the gym as far as he could from her but then something funny happened. She completed her upper body workout where she was then walked over to a treadmill close to where Garrett had moved to. He smiled just because of the connection he felt with her. It was so strong it seemed to him as if they already knew each other but they had never met before. Every so often, he would glance toward her to see if he would catch her looking at him. He was so gritty that he wanted approval from her before he approached her. Some kind of a glance, smile, or a nod but he got none of those. If Garrett wanted to talk to her, he was just going to have to man up and walk off the edge of the cliff. Garrett could feel that connection between them, then he said, "Whatever happens, happens." He walked all the way up to her. She was cooling down from a quick jog. Once next to her, he put his hand on her shoulder. She faced him and all he did was stand there smiling at her. She looked at him uninterested, then Garrett began talking. He said, "Hi, how are you?" She did not reply, then she pulled out her small earphones from her ear and said, "What?" Garrett had a redo but went a bit further this time. He said, "You look amazing."

She blushed then said, "Oh, thank you."

Garrett now spoke up a bit. He said, "How, uh, how is your workout going?"

She smiled and said, "It's good. How about yours?"

Garrett said, "Wow, that's awesome. My name is Garrett. Pretty crowded in here, huh. Where are you from?"

She said, "Dallas. I'm here for TX2K."

Garrett said, "What? Me too."

She said, "What kind of car do you drive?"

Garrett said, "I'm with BMS. I drive a thousand-horsepower Demon!"

She said, "Wow. A thousand horsepower, huh, just had to bring that up?"

They both laughed for a quick moment. Her name is Liz, but she withheld that information from him for the time being. Liz said to him, "Mine is a Huracan, and the horsepower, well, you're just going to have to wait and find out."

Garrett said, "Yeah, I don't know if we're even in the same bracket. Like we might not even race against each other. There's like hundreds of people here."

Liz said, "Then, we'll street race."

Garrett said, "Uh, the car's not even mine. Can I invite you out sometime?"

Liz smiled then said, "I only date real racers."

Liz got off the treadmill and began to clean the machine. Garrett asked her, "Can I at least get your name?"

Liz said, "If you beat me, I'll give it to you."

She just made Garrett want her even more. She walked away flaring her hips from side to side. She had so much swag about herself she was on another level. Dayana seemed like a distant memory to him watching Liz walk away. The fact she was a racer too was a bonus. He couldn't wait to race against her or see her in any way at the racetrack. Garrett flipped through blogs and posts of people in attendance of TX2K online until he spotted her. Her name was Liz Michaels, a second-year participant. Liz owned a high-performance shop in Frisco specializing in Italian cars. Garrett looked up the shop and looked at her website, a picture of her bright neon green Lamborghini Huracan was boldly displayed. He was infatuated by her and all her accomplishments. She was true to herself and enjoyed racing cars just like him. Then Garrett's own perspective of himself demoted him. He thought she could never be interested in a ghetto guy from Chicago like him. He logged off and used his will once again to keep on working out. Dayana entered his mind. He called her, but she was still fast asleep, unable to answer his call. Garrett would finish then go back to his room. He ordered breakfast, watched some TV, and got ready for racing. The hotel was close to the racetrack. The parking lot was littered with trailers, race cars, and pickup trucks. Garrett drove the Demon to the racetrack and before reaching Gene and the others, he came across Pablo who called to him saying, "Hey, Garrett, come here a sec."

Pablo was working the field making conversations with older gentlemen who were looking to bet on Garrett but after meeting him, they were inclined to bet against him. They looked like they took cheap shots at him. He was still very unknown as a driver. People wanted so much to bury him for the success he had on the streets of Chicago and on qualifying. Several racers dismissed him as an amateur claiming it was only a fluke performance. A lot of people were eager to drive against Garrett and his Demon. Pablo closed the deal. He knew Garrett would win. The pick favored him. Garrett stood there for a few seconds taking it all in. He stood there in disbelief. It took the good words of Pablo to tell him, "Garrett, do what you do best til the cows come home! Fuck 'em!"

Garrett couldn't believe it. He woke up so good this morning "ready to take on the world and everybody wanted to piss in his cornflakes all day." *Well, that's it*, he thought. He was pissed. He returned to Gene a changed man on a mission. Garrett mounted the drag wheels and got his car ready. His first race would come at a heat starting at 2 PM. Gene told him, "Hey, Hector brought subs if you want one." Garrett had a look that was all business, and his response was as fierce as if it could bite his head off. Garrett said, "I'm at TX2K and I'm going to kill it."

Gene answered, "Well, that's the spirit, so do you want a sub?"

Garrett answered, "Yeah, man, you got meatball?"

Gene said, "I don't know. Go check."

As Garrett neared the track, he thought about Liz, the girl he had met that morning. He couldn't stop thinking about how beautiful she was, and he wondered if he would like to see her again, then he felt guilt due to not having talked to Dayana lately. Ugh! It turned his stomach over. Why was this happening to him? His heart in the discussion of a potential mate was tearing itself apart in indecision. The only thing keeping him together now was the love he had for racing. When he was behind the wheel, he was one, and that was what he chose to concentrate on, then the pain went away. Garrett saw Gene and the guys walk over to the Demon while he was in the staging area. Gene said, "Just don't put her in the wall."

Garrett pulled his helmet near his mouth and yelled, "I'll try not to."

Gene said, "I have a feeling this Demon is going to win it all."

Garrett said, "No! the R35 is going to win it all."

Gene answered, "Oh, no, no, no, no, you, my friend, are one bad hombre. I got a feeling about you and that Demon."

It may have just been the way Gene got Garrett pumped up before his first race. Garrett idled the Demon over to the starting pole he was next to race. Across from it was a Z06 Corvette. Pablo was speaking to Garrett very loudly. He turned to look at him and said, "There's a punk 16-year-old kid in that Z06. His dad just bet me $10,000. His kid will win. Smoke him!"

Garrett tried not to think of the money. He probably wasn't going to see any of it anyway. He had to concentrate on the race and get as much experience as he could. He was ready. It was hard to believe that 2 weeks ago he was at home playing video games without a clue that he would be at TX2K today! Especially, he didn't expect driving a 1000 horsepower Demon. Garrett blanked out his mind, closed his eyes, gripped the steering wheel, and tried to feel the car, the steering wheel, his hands, then all the way up to his mind, and there it was, he had become one with the car. With his eyes closed, he could see the components inside the steering column all the way to the steering rack and the bolts going into the chassis. He could see the suspension sitting with potential energy, waiting to push the weight of the car into the tires all the way down to the pavement. He could envision the crankshaft rotating, the 8 pistons alternating among them, the valve train working letting cooled boosted air from an intercooler in, then being exposed out through the exhaust. Garrett could also see the firing order of the engine blasting. In his mind, he slowed it down. It all made sense to him. It said, "1-8-4-3-6-5-7-2." He tightened both hands around the steering wheel and tapped his right thumb to every odd number and the even numbers with his left thumb. He matched his thumbs with the firing order and whispered, "1-8-4-3-6-5-7-2. 1-8-4-3-6-5-7-2."

The track official signaled him to pull forward. It was now the turn for the Demon and the Z06 to warm up their tires. They passed the starting line then reversed to stage their cars behind it. The father of the Z06 driver took off his sunglasses then walked over to cheer his kid, then he gave Garrett a middle finger. The smoke was still clearing when they approached the starting line. They locked eyes for a split second then immediately focused on their goals. Garrett pumped on the accelerator pedal slowly until he was ready. He didn't know if he was going to win or lose but he was going to give it his best and focus. He said to himself, "Whatever happens, happens."

The Corvette finally lined up all the yellows. Garrett had the left lane. A staff member was signaling the drivers. They were both ready, then as soon as he ducked away, the tree began coming down. Garrett had little time to get the brake torque launch set up. He would end up launching without it. The green lights turned on. He pressed the accelerator as hard as he could. Both cars expelled from the starting line with so much force it seemed as if one of them would break, but neither did. They both roared loudly down the track in apparent unison. The Z06 driver had a better reaction time coming out the gate than the Demon. Garrett held the accelerator down and shifted the car very aggressively. It helped him to hold the lower top-end gear longer. He held it nearing the redline, then quickly flicked the next gear. The mighty Demon was screaming loudly. He caught the Z06 and shot past it beating him as they passed the second pole. For their times, Garrett got 9.878 seconds at 147 MPH; the Corvette time 9.999 at 144. Garrett let out the throttle and gave off a cowboy yell, "Yee-haa . . . Yes."

Pablo was ecstatic. He took a picture of the board with the time on it then ran up to the Demon. Gene, Hector, and Paul also stormed the Demon. They tapped the body of the car whirling and making noise and gave Garrett a high five. Garrett was to remain in the staging area. He would soon race a mean-looking ZL1 Camaro. The driver already had his helmet on. Soon after, it would be time for the two cars to line up then race time. When they warmed up their tires, the two cars spun their rear tires hard against the pavement unleashing a huge cloud of smoke. They lined up, then when the green light flashed on, the two beasts rumbled out of the gate, shooting down the track. Garrett won the race. The Camaro did a flat 10.00 seconds at 136 MPH. Garrett ran the 1/4 mile in 9.82 seconds at 139 MPH. Garrett had advanced to the next bracket of the tournament. Pablo had found a driver who wanted to race against Garrett really badly. They made the request with the officials and they allowed it in between heats. Garrett lined up again for his third race. The team performed a quick inspection of the car then Paul dropped the hood and gave Gene a thumbs up. The race was on. The team got up and began to walk away from the Demon as he needed to get ready to race down the track again.

There was a beautiful 01 NSX lined up next to him. The driver was sitting on the passenger side of the car. The car sounded heavily modified. The driver was definitely a Pro. Pablo went up to Garrett and said, "Hey, how do you feel about taking one for the team?"

Garrett said, "Fuck, no!"

Pablo said, "Good, good. A lot of people are betting against you. That's money in the bank! The guy says it could run low nines. Yeah, right."

The secret was out. Garrett's Demon was consistently breaking under 10 seconds, not an easy task to do, but guys who also could break 10 seconds wanted to beat him. It put some stress on Pablo. The guys who could possibly beat Garrett all had deep pockets. The stakes were high, but he had to be smart about it and know which of these guys were worth betting on. The NSX revved its engine really high on burnout. It did not make as much smoke as the other cars nor was it louder than the Demon but what mattered was how fast it went down the quarter-mile. Garrett was a bit from his edge. He was first to line up but had enough time to prepare his launch and do everything right. The NSX was also giving enough time to be fully prepared, then a few seconds later, the yellow lamps began to ignite going down toward the green ones. The NSX leaped forward before the Green had gone off. A red flashed on his side of the track highlighting his mistake, but the two cars completed their race flying down to the finish line. First, the screen signaled 9.983 seconds at 150 MPH for the NSX. Garrett's time was 9.90 seconds at 144 MPH but the NSX had been disqualified for jumping the start of the race. Garrett had won. There was an argument with the driver of the NSX and his friends against Pablo in the parking lot. He had a bunch of his friends from Austin with him, but once Pablo got the 75s involved, he eventually paid up. Garrett went back to his trailer to get some much-needed rest and refuel the Demon.

Gene hitched a ride. Hector and Paul soon followed. They invited Garrett to walk over to the viewing area with them, but he declined, then he caught sight of Liz's Lamborghini Huracan. Garrett quickly made his way to the track then hung his bare arms over the fence exposed to that hot Texas afternoon sun as he watched the Huracan line up against Gene. The Huracan was missing the rear bumper cover. A single large turbo could be seen behind the passenger rear tire with a large intercooler behind the left one. The plumbing wrapped around the rear of the vehicle. All of it looked custom-made. Clearly, the girl had skill. The neon-green Lambo bulled up to the starting pole. Both cars were all-wheel drive. They warmed up then lined up before the yellow lights came down followed by the green lights. Garrett watched both cars fly down the track. The race looked neck and neck, but the scoreboard displayed the victor. Gene won the race by the smallest of margins. His car did 10.3 seconds at 135 MPH and the green Huracan did 10.34 at 134 MPH. Garrett respected her a lot more after seeing her go down the track and nearly beating Gene. He yearned to get a chance to meet with her again. Right away, she was hassled by the 75s to pay up on a losing bet. Garrett saw the whole thing but before he went over to intervene, she called over a mechanic from her team who paid the guy. Garrett thought about walking over to her. She wasn't more than 30 yards away from him, but he thought she might be in a bad mood. He decided not to. Garrett stood there and saw Gene race again. He would advance, then he saw Liz race again in an elimination race that she managed to win and stay alive. She would race for a third time cementing herself into the next bracket of the tournament. As Garrett was leaving to meet up with Gene and the race team, Pablo sent Garrett a text message he said, "Where r u. Get the Demon n come 2 staging. NOW."

Pablo had a major bet going on. Garrett did just that. He fired up the car and went over to the staging area where he found Pablo holding a spot for him in line for the Demon to squeeze into. Pablo was talking to a guy inside an MK5. The guy looked like a supermodel. He was a professional soccer player from Spain who had a thing for races. Garrett was all business. He flipped down the visor on his helmet and got ready to race. He couldn't wait. Pablo came over to the Demon and said, "Hey, this guy ran a 9.750 earlier so I need you to really be on your Ps and Qs. No fucking around, alright?"

Garrett nodded then said, "Let's go!"

When their time came to race, Garrett noticed Liz was standing against the fence much in the same spot he had been standing in earlier. He grinned. The cars warmed up their tires, then they lined up until all the yellows came on. The yellows came down the tree a bit slower than Garrett. He did a near-perfect launch off the starting line. Garrett could see everything in slow motion. The car felt great.

He turned his head and looked over to where the MK5 was relative to his own car. It was right beside him. Garrett could hear the MK5's exhaust through the sound of his own. He could hear the engine revving and the harsh metallic cling as the guy shifted through a manual transmission. Garrett neared the last stretch just slightly ahead. He held 6th gear just a bit longer. The engine was well at 6500 where the powerband was at its highest. Before the Demon crossed the finish line, it looked like the MK5 had tied the Demon but when the times flashed out, the Demon had crossed the second pole before the soccer player's car. Garrett crossed the finish line at 9.736 at 151 MPH and the MK5 had a time of 9.750 at 150 MPH. Pablo was jumping for joy over by the grandstand. There were several people that made bets for the MK5. Pablo had made a big payday for himself. Pablo netted $76,425 from that one run alone. There were several people who were upset thinking the game was rigged in favor of Garrett, but no noise was heard from the soccer player at all. The driver of the MK5 took the biggest loss of all. He bet Pablo $50,000 which he calmly paid from his cell phone via an electronic transfer. The guy shook Garrett's hand and remarked, "Oh, well. That's racing. Hey, buddy, good race."

The team went back to the trailer area. None of them were involved in this heat. Garrett noticed a missed phone call from Dayana while he was racing. He tried to reach out to her but she didn't answer. Garrett walked over to Pablo and was in awe of all the money Pablo was making. He had guys quickly count and sort out cash in plastic bags and after every race, large amounts of money were being distributed. Just as fast as he collected money, he had to count it and organize it to be passed out. Pablo caught Garrett staring at him. He took a few hundred-dollar bills, raised them, and yelled at Garrett, "Here, go get dinner. A bunch of pizzas. It's on me."

Garrett didn't mind. It gave him something to do. He strolled over and Pablo handed Garrett 8 $100. As he walked away, Pablo said, "Hurry back."

Bets had slowly died down. Most of the people in the stands had already lost a lot of their money. There were no more secrets as to who the fastest cars were. There were other Dodge Demons racing that crossed the finish in the lower 10s. There was a Ferrari doing 11 seconds and an EVO that broke 10 seconds. There were some pickup trucks running 12 seconds and one that broke 11 seconds. It was an exciting day of racing. Occasionally, people put $100 on themselves with Pablo. A teenager bet him $20 bucks and made $40. "Good for you," Pablo told him. "Wanna make it $80?" The guy wised up and just kept his $40. He said, "No thanks." Garrett was near the pizza trailer when he spotted Liz again. He walked on over to her and said, "You are easily the prettiest gal in all Texas."

She turned and smiled at him, then she said, "Thanks, you are one heck of a racer after all!"

Garrett answered, "Mostly, it's the car. I'm currently in seventh place. I think there's one more run for me tonight. Let's see if I can improve on it. And you? How are you doing?"

Liz said, "I'm currently in the twelfth spot. Tough heat."

Garrett said, "Well, technically, I beat you racing, so how about your name, Liz?"

Liz said, "You cheated!"

Garrett said, "Well, maybe I could get a phone number this time?"

Just then, his phone got a text message. Garrett thought it was Pablo, so he reached into his pocket and slowly pulled out his phone. Liz looked at his screen. Garrett did too. It said, "Dayana 7:45 PM—I miss you, baby. Good luck."

Liz looked back at Garrett with disgust then said, "I don't think so."

Garrett was not a player. He had never been smooth with the ladies, and right now, he had just bombed out like one. He was in shock. He didn't have a clue what his heart wanted but the fact that he did not chase Liz meant he still gave preference to Dayana. He was closer to being an idiot than anything else when it came down to handling a woman. The only thing he knew how to do was drive. Only then can he follow his heart without scrutiny of the outcome. Garrett and Dayana were still just friends, he thought. Yes, things had happened, but he believed he was still single, and all these recent events had boosted his confidence allowing him to express his desires more freely. It was just a coincidence Dayana texted at that very time, he said to himself. Liz liked Garrett. Seeing him winning and accomplishing things made her want him. However, she naturally held up her defenses. She more than likely had met guys who had previously vanished out of her life too soon, guys who preferred their own success to being held down. But wasn't that what drew her to them in the first place? People really are crazy. Over time, Liz had adopted a strategy most women resort to, making a guy work for it. In these specific situations, everything had to take a little bit longer, everybody had to be more patient with one another, and both parties had to seem "not" interested but yet very interested at the same time. "Crazy, I know." All of this as a precaution of not being hurt again. People can destroy themselves when they give more than they receive. The scales are not equal, so people usually give the bare minimum and hope the other person to do the same, playing the long game to accomplish anything, something Garrett knew nothing about. He believed to act out on his desires. If it hurt, he cried. If it was funny, he laughed. If he wanted to drive, he raced. Why hide what you want? Liz was the same way, too, hiding to be a hardened self. She was upset, even more when she noticed she was weakened by Garrett because although she had moved away back to her trailer, she still thought about him. A friend of Liz, one of her mechanics, knew exactly what troubled her. He said, "Hey, don't worry about things. You can't force anything. Let's race. If it's meant to be, it will be."

Liz was naturally a nice person, a rare trait nowadays. Everyone could read her like a book and she hated it. Due to her interest in cars, most of her friends were guys. She sometimes thought like a guy, bold and commanding. Liz built up a shell in which she could live in, a confident steamrolling gearhead who could lift weights and do everything a guy could do and even better! Liz was 26 years old. She had a degree in forensic science, but she never used it. Her dad had been a long-time Italian dealership mechanic who fixed a lot of older cars. She had 5 sisters and no brothers yet her love for her father strengthened when he taught her everything he knew about fixing cars. Then, she opened her own shop paying homage to him and learned a lot more. Liz took pride in racing. She kept her feminine attributes while competing against apple-knockers and the high-collared pricks of the world, all the while wearing the shortest pair of Daisy Dukes she wore beneath her racing suit. She loved every minute of it.

Pablo was already making plans to meet up with Karina that night. Everything had been going great for the guy and he planned on ending the night with a bang. Garrett was confused and had mixed feelings about women so when he heard Pablo was going out afterward, he volunteered to go with him. Pablo figured it would add to what Agusto wanted, for him to meet a new woman. Who knows Garrett might see something he liked and make things happen on his own? Maybe El Diablo would recognize Pablo's talent, his creativity. Garrett completed his last race and won it. He was done for the night. Gene was scheduled to race again. When he was in the staging area, Pablo got a bet going with the guy that was racing against him. It was a guy driving a 72 Chevelle with a huge 671 supercharger sticking out of a hole cut into the engine hood.

Pablo looked over to Gene then asked, "How about you? You wanna put some money on this R35?"

Gene said, "Alright, I'll put $20 grand on me finishing before his Chevelle."

Pablo looked at him as if he wasn't sane, then answered, "You're on."

Gene lined up next to the Chevelle in the right lane. The Chevelle did a massive burnout heating up the rear tires not going past the starting line then easing into his starting position. Like a seasoned veteran, the guy knew what he was doing. Gene's car could run mid 9s or even quicker. They began working their way until all the yellow lights were on. The tree ignited downward then the green lights turned on. They both roared past the starting line. The Chevelle was so loud you could almost see its exhaust gases shooting out of the tailpipes in wavelengths as it zoomed by. Gene was pulling on the paddle shifters very quickly. His eyes danced all around as he looked on from his instrument cluster to the front of the car. A sinking feeling took over his stomach as he caught a glimpse of the Chevelle that was next to him but now slowly creaking ahead of him. When they crossed the finish line, the Chevelle's time was 9.90 at 157 mph. Gene crossed at 10.225 at 151 mph. Gene had lost. He pounded on the steering wheel after he caught himself being out twenty thousand dollars, but worst of all was costing himself positioning in the tournament on the following day. Gene idled all the way back to his trailer. It was late. He wanted to help Hector and Paul load the cars onto the trailers. It was awfully quiet as they helped him out. Gene was pissed. It wasn't long after that Pablo caught up with Gene at his trailer, asking about his payment. He said, "Tough loss, Gene, time to pay up!"

Gene replied without turning to face Pablo in a "fuck off" manner. He said, "Tell Agusto to take it from my cut!"

Pablo snared a bit and said, "You don't owe Diablo. You owe me!"

Gene turned to Pablo. They really didn't know each other very well. Gene in his younger day was quite a brawler. He attended Northern Illinois as a wrestler. He still had those huge shoulders and bear-like fists. He had that crazy stare from his younger days on his face. He took off his prescription glasses and set them down on a tool cart next to him. The tension was escalating. Gene walked toward Pablo. He reached for a floor jack pipe. He twisted it off at the handle. There were four guys with Pablo who caught on and stood tall, ready to back him up. One of them lifted his shirt showing a polished pistol handle that he had tucked in the front of his pants. Gene saw the gun then just squeezed his lips together, deciding he was not going to go out by these guys. He shook his head no then said, "Let me get my checkbook."

Pablo stood there feeling a bit bigger than he was. His entourage paid off. Too bad it was against his own team. Gene paid him then they nodded at one another like nothing happened. Pablo's entourage slowly crept away watching their backs following him. All these guys who were with Pablo had been promised a measly $100 by El Diablo while Pablo had already told them he would give them $500 each and promised another $500 for their loyalty. Loyalty to him, not El Diablo nor anybody else in Texas who wasn't putting it all on the line for them as he was, and they loved Pablo for it. Pablo had a hunch. He would need them if things between him and El Diablo get ugly. Either way, in the long run, Pablo was determined to find his own way in life. At the end of Saturday, the amount of money he had gathered was nearly 1.5 million dollars. He witnessed firsthand the kind of person he could become, the kind of power he can have, and he loved every second of it. Making a solid person like Gene bend his knees was so delicious to him, more than an orange-flavored slushy with vanilla ice cream in it. "Wow," he said.

Gene told Garrett, "Hey, we're going up to The Woodlands for a barbecue. You want to come with us?"

Garrett said, "Naw, I'm going out with Pablo."

Gene said, "Just be careful. Be ready for the finals tomorrow."

Garrett said, "I'll be alright."

Paul and Hector went with Gene in Hector's pickup truck. The cars were staying on the lot inside the compound for the night. Garrett left with Pablo in his STI along with 3 other guys from his crew who he gave a ride to their houses. Before soon, it was just Pablo and Garrett riding in the car.

Garrett asked, "Man, it was a whole other experience out here."

Pablo said, "You loved it today, didn't you?"

Garrett said, "It was epic."

Pablo said, "You deserve this and much more. You're actually talented."

After a pause, Pablo said, "You know I've met some guys here that are connected to professional racing teams. I could get you in, Gare. Just don't fuck it up."

Garrett said, "Bro, I'm trying to concentrate on my driving. TX2K."

Pablo said, "You sure you're not concentrating on that bartender chick at Black Door?"

Garrett looked away briefly, then Pablo continued, "C'mon, bro, Dayana is not even your girl. Yeah, you smashed, so what? Hey, you're single and there is so much more just waiting for you. Don't give 'em anything they can use against you."

Garrett said, "Don't give who?"

Pablo said, "Nobody. Fuhgeddaboudit." He turned and smiled at Garrett.

Garrett looked a bit worried. Pablo went on saying, "Look. If you guys can withstand this, then you're probably meant to be, but please, don't ever sell yourself short, alright? That's it. Don't think about it. Think of it this way. What would have happened if you had brought that piece of crap BMW to TX2K, huh? Go with the flow. You're an ace. Live like one."

Garrett looked like he wanted to laugh. In better spirits, Pablo said, "See, there it is! Exactly! You got wings, brother. Use them. She's got wings too. If she wants to be with you, it'll happen, bruh. Until then, fly, young demon. Fly."

The guys entered the parking lot of a large nightclub on the outskirts of town. It was named Chulas. Pablo drove up to the front. He had his car valet parked then the two men strolled into the place like they owned it. Most of the women working there were wearing lingerie. Garrett was in heaven. Pablo spotted Karina as soon as he walked in. He went over to a spot near the bar where she was bartending. As soon as she saw Pablo, Karina walked around the counter and laid a really big kiss on him. Garrett just watched in awe, amazed at how everything the guy did always favored him. She was introduced to Garrett as Pablo's "girlfriend." Garrett chuckled because he didn't believe the guy knew how to be a one-woman man. Karina walked them over to a table, then she asked them what she could get them for starters.

Both men decided on tall lagers. Garrett just wanted to unwind and relax. Karina asked him if he liked anyone there, but he replied, "I'm ok," to which Pablo ignored. He knew more than anyone you can't force a guy to do anything. They would have to do it on their own. Pablo wondered, "What's wrong with this guy anyway?" So he asked him, "What's wrong?" Garrett said, "Nothing." Sure, all of the women there were attractive and inviting, but Garrett didn't see himself adding another relationship with anyone, especially not on long distances. Pablo on the other hand was a natural. Two girls came up to him and he openly flirted with both of them. He squeezed in between them standing in front of their table there, rubbing on the guy. "How does he do it?" Garrett asked himself. Garrett finished his glass then broke loose slightly. He attempted to talk to the taller-looking gal who Pablo had his hand around her waist. Much to his surprise, she flirted back. The guy was in. Pablo let her go and she drove herself deeper into Garrett's arms. *Wow,* he thought. *This is fun.* Garrett found himself talking about Bugs Bunny and Bad Bunny for some oddball reason. The girl was laughing at every word he said, then Pablo got up to go to the bathroom and the second girl came over and wanted to know what was so funny, but just at that precise moment, her phone received a text message. The message upset her, the mood changed, and the woman quickly moved away from Garrett. They stood up ready to leave when Pablo got back. He looked straight at Garrett and said, "What did you do?"

Garrett said, "I didn't do anything, bro."

The taller girl said, "It's her ex. He's over there with his friends always trying to start shit."

The shorter girl near Garrett said, "He's so stupid, won't leave and won't man up to keep me! Hey, do you want to piss him off?"

She leaned in really close to Garrett as if she was going to kiss him, then she said, "I'm not even going to look. I bet he's with another girl right now. Let's mess with him. Kiss me."

Garrett looked around the room to see if anyone was looking and said, "I don't know."

Then she said to Garrett, "What do you want? You seem like the kind of guy who always goes for it. So, go for it!"

The tall girl sitting next to Garrett pulled his chin and kissed him, then the shorter girl climbed on Garrett's lap and Garrett kissed her. Pablo smiled greatly because he had done it. He had broken Garrett's will. Garrett caught himself and said, "I was thinking of sleeping. What do you want to do?"

The two women turned to look at one another then giggled, "I told you, you're hilarious."

Garrett had no idea of the small war which almost broke out as he was making out with these two beautiful women in the back of this nightclub. The shorter one's boyfriend was heated after seeing his ex-girlfriend making out with Garrett. He walked aggressively in their direction. All it took was a nod from Pablo and the three guys stood up and blocked him from taking another step further. Pablo could see the guy was arguing with them. Three of his own friends got up to confront Pablo's guys, then an additional five guys stood up to make the barricade with a total of eight guys. Security came and asked the guy to leave. He was furious. That was when Pablo stood up, walked up to the guy, and shook his hand. He waved off the security guy then he told them to walk with him, which they did. Pablo said, "Life is about what you don't do. The guy in there making out with your girl, he's my boy, but he's going to get his. Alright. If you want blood, I'll give it to you, but right now, I need you on my side so I'm going to help you. He's not going to fuck her. You have my word and if you want her, you know, as your bride or whatever, it's simple. Ok, pay attention cause this part is very important. Just don't fuck it up!"

The guy was older than Pablo and had intentions of turning around and unleashing hell, but Pablo patted him on the back, shook his hand, and left him confused. "What the fuck is going on?" he said. Pablo said, "You're on my side now. If you want her, just behave. The whiteboy, don't worry about him, he'll get his. Go home, compa."

When Pablo came back, he pulled the shorter girl from Garrett then said, "Time to go, girls."

They had to regroup themselves. Karina was standing there watching what was happening. She admired Pablo just a little bit more. There was no doubt to her that he was a real boss. Karina asked a girl that worked alongside her, Patricia, to go over and flirt with Garrett to get those two skanks away from him. She did. Patricia was Pablo's ex. However, she had since moved on and continued enjoying herself. The DJ was playing Tejano music. Patricia swooped in and pulled Garrett to his feet liberating him from the grips of the taller female. Garrett showed no type of willpower. He was as flimsy as an old kitchen counter rag. Patricia was a great dancer. She led and fancied most of the crowd with her work, even made Garrett look like he knew what he was doing. At the pinnacle of the song, the two women knew they had been beaten and slowly faded away into the crowd. Once the song finished, Patricia walked Garrett back to his table and said to him, "What can I get you, babe?"

Garrett was in awe. He felt as attractive as a member of the Backstreet Boys at the height of their success. He tried to kiss Patricia but she caught on and quickly looked the other way. She said, "Whoops, maybe you've had too much?" Garrett touched her hand. He then raised his right index finger signaling one then he said, "One beer, please."

Patricia did not have an attitude as perky as Karina nor did she have as thick a Southern accent as Karina either. She had a classier look but was still very attractive. Garrett was in awe. When she returned, she said, "Are you alright?"

Garrett said, "You are very pretty."

Patricia said, "Thank you. Are you here racing? You don't seem like you belong here tonight."

Garrett said, "Yeah, I'm a race car driver. I'm here with Pablo."

Patricia looked at Pablo then said, "Figures."

Garrett said, "Hey, let me introduce myself. My name is Garrett. Garrett Lee and you?"

Patricia extended her hand to shake his and said, "Patricia, but everyone calls me P. Nice to meet you. I gotta go but just let me know if you want anything, alright?"

Garrett said, "Anything?"

He smiled at her. She took it nicely and she grinned at him as she walked away, saying, "Sure."

Just then, Karina walked up to Pablo and pressed her chest into him then said, "Hey, Pablo, you should stay until we close. Maybe we could get some drinks later on?"

Pablo played it cool and said, "I don't know. This guy is my golden goose. Looks like we're going to have to leave soon."

Garrett sat there sipping on his beer not saying anything, barely awake. A single thought entered his mind. He couldn't help but think about Dayana. Garrett reached for his phone and began to text her. Pablo said, "Bro, don't do that."

Of course, he did. He pleaded with Dayana and told her that he loved her and always wanted to be with her. What a sap! When Garrett didn't get a reply, just sitting there for a few minutes, he started noticing Patricia more and more. He liked her. Pablo told him, "If you want to go up to the bar, say goodbye. I think we're leaving soon." Garrett did as he was told. Shortly thereafter, some guys joined Pablo at the same table where Garrett had been. They were bosses of local gangs and farther ones, aligning themselves with Pablo. Pablo appreciated their comfort, but he crossed the line when he asked them, "If I told you I'm going against El Diablo, would we still be friends?"

Pablo smirked. He got up from the table and said, "Go to Dallas and ask them the same question, and don't worry, I'll hear the answer." As big a boss move as any he had just done, Pablo walked near the door and greeted local 75s. They all reaffirmed to be strictly under Pablo; "no one else." Pablo took some wads of cash that he held in his pocket, nearly 4 grand, and distributed it amongst them. The guys who were at his table from earlier met Pablo then agreed saying, "We're with you, Pablo! Fuck Diablo!"

Pablo smiled. He might be over his head just a little, but he started this. This weekend, there was no going back. He asked the guys to follow him outside. He got his keys from the valet then walked to the trunk of his car where he told them, "Here, take this." "What is it?" they asked. Pablo answered, "There's $50 Gs in there. One bag is for you and another is for my peeps in Dallas. They need to say they are with me and denounce El Diablo. I will need all of you shortly." The guys agreed. Pablo followed it with, "I'd tell you to keep it quiet, but word is going to get around. I'm counting on it. Now get out of here." The guys did just that. Pablo walked back inside. Garrett was falling asleep where he sat at the bar. Pablo went up to him and hovered behind him. He looked on at Karina. Patricia came up to Garrett and said, "Are you good?"

Garrett asked Patricia, "Hey, can I get your number? I'm leaving town tomorrow. Maybe we can hang out or something?"

Patricia said, "Um, no, you can't get my number."

Garrett said, "I said, I'm leaving town."

Patricia said, "Um, maybe you're thinking of someone else."

Garrett thought, *Wow, maybe that whole asking for sex by saying I'm leaving town doesn't apply to Texas.* He told her, "Never mind. So how do I get to see you again?"

Patricia said, "You keep coming in. Maybe over time, yeah, we could hang out or something."

Garrett said, "I think you want to make me an alcoholic?"

Patricia said, "Take it or leave it."

Garrett smiled. Pablo reached over him, dropped a $20, and said, "We're leaving. C'mon, Gare, look at you. You're falling asleep." The two men began to leave. Pablo kissed Karina and said something to her, then he returned to meet Garrett. Garrett was so infatuated with Patricia. He took a pen and wrote his phone number on the back of a receipt saying, "In case you change your mind."

She looked at him like he was dumb but said, "Thank you. Drive safe. Good luck tomorrow."

Garrett met Pablo outside, then the two men began walking to his sporty sedan. Pablo said, "Struck out, huh?"

Garrett replied, "Yeah 'n you?"

They mounted the car then Pablo began driving away. He said, "You know what happened in there, don't you?"

Garret said, "What?"

Pablo told him, "You can't decide who you're going to love and they all took advantage of you. You were closer to a puppet than a man."

Garrett said, "Screw you."

Pablo said, "Hmm, puppet, that's a good name for you."

The guys went straight to the hotel. Garrett dosed off a bit but managed to walk himself fine to his room and shut the door. Pablo turned on the TV, laid in his bed, and second-guessed what he was doing. Could he challenge El Diablo? He had garbage bags in his room with over a million dollars in all kinds of currencies. A text message came in. It was Karina. She was asking whether he was still awake. Pablo answered that he was. He invited her over to which she agreed. Pablo told her to text him when she arrived so he may go downstairs and get the door for her, and that's what she did. When Karina got there, Pablo walked outside and greeted her. In her Mustang outside, he whispered to her, "There is not a man alive that can break me, but you make me feel weak all over. I want you to be with me always. Let's go inside."

Katrina said, "Sure, let's go."

They both enjoyed each other's company the rest of the night. When the sun came up, Pablo had no doubt about what he was doing. He was meant to destroy El Diablo and begin a new reign. He slept on and off wondering if he should just take Karina back to Chicago with him or not. When she awoke, he asked her to come with him Sunday night. But she turned him down saying she wasn't ready. He pleaded with her but again, she said "no." Pablo was hurt. He offered her money, $100,000, then Pablo said, "I'll come back for you."

Karina said, "Keep the money. Just come back."

He said to her, "Dammit, Karina! It just makes me want you even more."

They both smiled, then she leaped onto him, kissing him repeatedly.

CHAPTER 8

"Sicko Mode."

Sunday was the third and final day of TX2K racing. There were other events scheduled for the morning and early afternoon, including a car show and a burnout competition. Garrett got his good rest in then made his way to the events. Several guests recognized him and finally gave him props over his driving at TX2K. A few bloggers and writers interviewed the rising star. He blushed once they began recording, flattered. Gene pulled Garrett by the back of the neck then told him, "A bit of advice. Don't mess with stuff you don't understand before the fight's over."

Garrett answered, "Are you superstitious, Gene? I looked pretty good on camera."

Gene said, "Everybody gets burned sometime."

Garrett said, "Did you forget to have breakfast? Bad barbecue or something?"

Gene laughed and said, "Saying that kind of stuff in Texas is a sin. Naw, just don't jinx yourself. You see any other racers giving interviews who still have a chance to win it? It's bad voodoo."

Garrett smiled, "I have a chance to win it?"

Gene said, "You do some good driving today. You just might. That Demon is quicker than hell and you aren't afraid of her so, we'll see. C'mon, let's go."

Hector and Paul were already unloading the cars. They pointed to a pot of coffee inside the trailer if they needed some "pick-me-up" juice. Gene pointed to Garrett so he could join him near the trailer. Gene looked at Garrett as if he was a child, then he said, "Son, I don't know how you got involved with Agusto or Pablo, but they're both bad news. Stay away from them. You've proved yourself to be a good racer. The doors will open for you on their own."

Garrett said, "Agusto is a good guy. He's the first adult who ever trusted me."

Gene said, "Kid, the money's dirty! You don't want his help and trust me, as soon as he figures a way to keep you without paying you, that's it! You're his! You don't want that."

Garrett thought about his father telling him, "I got in too deep then stayed longer than I should've." Garrett said, "Does he own you? How'd you meet Agusto?"

Gene said, "Much the same way you and that guy Pablo met. We went to school together, but he was already tainted after that. Well, we both make moves in the community. I was talking to the publisher of SCCA weekly last night. They want you to be in Kansas City next month so bad but take my advice, kid, please. You can do great things behind a steering wheel but staying loyal to these guys is going to get you hurt."

Garrett didn't know what to make of this new knowledge. He had also just met Gene. Why was this happening to him? He began to wonder who really was his friend. Was Gene trying to distract him so "he" could win the whole thing? Pablo had been working with him at NTB for some time, but they were never this close before. How deep was Pablo in the underworld and did it matter? As far as Garrett knew, most things were lies and playful teases. For all he knew, it probably wasn't even true. Besides, the guy always lands on his feet. Nothing could stop him. If anything, he might want to hang out with Pablo more often. Maybe he could pick up. How he does it and act a little bit more like him, he admired the guy. Pablo was a popular guy who knew how to talk to women and usually got them.

Money was easy for him. Life was easy for him. Garrett nodded up and down in front of Gene, then he said, "I understand. I'll stay away from those guys."

Garrett spent the rest of the morning rather quiet keeping to himself. He went about his business trying to hide inside a hardcore emotionless shell as he had trained himself to do since his youth. No one likes to be told their wrong ways or pointed out things they were doing wrong. Mentally, Garrett was still young, so he sucked it up and did as he was told. Gene noticed and wondered if he was hurting the kid but then he thought to himself, *If I lose friends because of what I said to him, I'd accept it. If I gain good friends, so be it.*

Around 3 PM, they called for a private meeting in the main building behind the racetrack. Garrett was treated like an all-American star. Everybody wanted a piece of him. When asked what his expectations for the day were, Garrett simply said, "I don't know what's going to happen, just go out there and drive the Demon the best I can." Gene was nearby watching and noticed that those words were forced and manufactured. He grinned because he knew he had changed the guy. Sounded good, but at 9 AM, there was no way he would have said that.

Agusto was also watching the racing events and noticed certain cruelty to Garrett as he spoke. He called Pablo, but he didn't answer. Agusto was forced to go to his inside man, Cuervo, who had been among Pablo's elite circle. The downside is he specialized in not knowing things, so he usually didn't. Cuervo had gotten news on everything Pablo did, minus the more important inner circle stuff. His inside guy assumed Pablo was going to Chulas to see Patricia. He knew nothing about Karina, and as far as Garrett, he suspected he would turn his back on El Diablo. He was too good to stay anchored to Agusto. If he couldn't give him the racing world, he was begging to be a part of it. Cuervo told El Diablo, "Secret's out. If you don't keep him driving, someone else will."

This angered El Diablo. How was this kid beating him? And what was Pablo up to? His inside guy didn't know Pablo nor the exact number of money Pablo was making. He assumed the payments were all on behalf of El Diablo even though Pablo made them denounce him. His informant didn't mention any of that so he would not be disciplined. He hid information from him. Agusto seemed to benefit greatly from his broken background. His rags to riches story gave him an extra sense. He could detach himself from all the luxuries because he didn't start with them. He could peek inside the eyes of people and decipher them because he shared the best of himself with everybody who came across him. Agusto learned how to speak by trial and error working out the kinks, and now even if the slightest gap was an abyss, a mile wide to him, he knew something was wrong. But he also knew that if he dwelled on this single thought, it could consume him. He buried it and decided the truth would show itself. This way of thinking made him rare at such a young age. Agusto believed he was meant for bigger things and he had risked everything to get to be where he was, much the same as Pablo was currently doing. Maybe Agusto could feel a shift in his allegiance. There were things he just felt as if the air around him was speaking to him, but he needed to remain strong. He repeated to himself, "You are alive! The world is out there waiting for you. Go get it."

As Agusto sat there in his office, he took his mind off of the race by remembering where he came from, how he had pivotal moments in his life, and how people always let him down. He remembered how he lent a friend $10,000 to start up his own business. He held his hand and gave him step-by-step instructions on how to succeed and yet the guy still failed. Yet, El Diablo didn't give up. He overcame by crossing the line. He tricked the guy into becoming a viable citizen by whatever means necessary. He knew that he smoked marijuana, so he arranged for the "citizen" to buy some marijuana from a second guy who he was also trying to help. The "seller" had just met a girl he liked so Agusto took it upon himself to help the guy better his relationship. Both guys completed the transaction, then he held it over their head to get them to do what he wanted them to do, for their own good, things that they had asked for, and it worked! Agusto pressured the seller into getting married because the girl knew he was a seller and the only way to have her testimony thrown out was to get married to her, which he did. The buyer, Agusto, constantly raised the prices of his weed, and every time the guy needed money, Agusto put him to work, slowly decreasing his weed and increasing his pay. Of course, after a year of doing this, the guy finally stopped smoking. Agusto was so thrilled. The guy had no idea that within that year, he had paid Agusto back on the $10,000 loan he lent him a year earlier, then Agusto sponsored his business but told him he needed to keep coming in or he would "break his legs." The guy was accustomed to working nearly every day in the following 5 years. He never missed a day. Agusto enjoyed pressing people into doing good things, but he couldn't figure out what Pablo was up to. But he knew it was nothing good. He knew he would be forced to upkeep his image and if Pablo looked for blood, he would be forced to give it to him. Those were the rules. He didn't set them, but he understood them.

The overhead speaker at Royal Purple Racetrack buzzed, signaling someone was about to talk, then it said, "To all the drivers competing in heat Alpha, please take your positions in the staging area. Again, to all the drivers racing in heat Alpha, please take your positions in the staging area. Thank you."

Gene said to the guys, "That'd be me. Wish me luck, fellas."

Hector, Garrett, and Paul said, "Good luck, Gene. See you on the podium."

Gene flipped the toggle switches that feed the fuel cell holding 105 octane racing fuel inside, then he pressed the red ignition switch that ignited the engine. The car idled very good. It sounded exhilarating if you are the kind of person who enjoys loud cars at the racetrack. He made his way to the staging area and noticed Pablo had appeared and looked a bit disappointed. There were bets going on but not as much as the days before. When he saw Gene, he walked up to him and said, "Bygones are bygones, right?"

Gene answered, "Yeah, whatever!"

Pablo said, "Do you think you can beat him?"

Gene answered back, "You've taken too much money of mine already. I'm going to pass."

Pablo looked over at his competitor, an S2000 that sounded like it had a 50 grand under the hood, then Pablo said to Gene, "Too bad, you might've won this time."

Pablo felt uninterested in playing bookie this morning. It was the main day of the competition. There were a lot of top racing officials and professional teams everywhere, a lot of heat and not in a good way. Gene warmed up his tires as did his competition, then they lined up on the starting line. They waited for all the yellows to turn on then flashed down to the lucky green ones. Both cars flew out of the gate on the command. The S2000 proved to be a worthy adversary. It stayed neck and neck most of the 1/4 mile with the throaty sounding R35. But once they crossed the finish line, the results showed that Gene had beaten the S2000. The positioning of the remaining drivers would mix racers several times that afternoon. No one remained perfect out of the 16 cars in Gene's class. They continued raising winners until they came to the final 4 of which Gene found himself in the 3rd place. Gene would have another run to attempt to go for the first or second place. His opponent was a guy they called Thunder Dan from a town just southwest of Tulsa. Thunder Dan had a 72 Nova with a huge supercharger sticking out through the hood, massive slick tires on the rear axle, and trailing arms that extended way past the rear bumper. Thunder Dan was a fan favorite who often came to race at Baytown's racetrack. The fans cheered loudly for him. The R35 and the Nova were signaled to advance to the starting pole. They violently heated up their tires then took their places at their respective starting points. Gene was confident he could beat Thunder Dan's Nova. He beat him on Friday during the first day by a very slim margin. Gene would have to be completely focused. The green lights ignited; Gene's car exploded forward. The Nova lifted the front tires off the ground. As the car roared so loudly, the exhaust was like a series of cannon fire shots going off on the dragstrip. Gene never had the Nova behind him.

At the start of about 200 feet, the Nova just pulled away ever so slightly. By the time the Nova crossed the finish line, it was traveling 150 MPH crossing at 10.090 seconds. Gene crossed at 10.385 at 148 MPH. Gene was eliminated from further competition. He could place no higher than 3rd. His weekend was over. Thunder Dan went head-to-head one more time for first place this time against a 1963 Falcon with a huge blower and a set of massive slick tires to boot. The cars lined up, the yellow lights ignited at the top, then hurried downward before the green lights turned on. Both cars shot out, lifting the front end and getting a little squiggly. The smell of burned rubber along with high octane fuel flooded the grandstand area. The two cars looked like rocket ships blasting off into orbit. When they crossed the finish line, Thunder Dan had the advantage. He won first place in a very tough modified class.

Gene was excited and thrilled just to have participated in the weekend. He had witnessed another great weekend of racing. Even if he didn't come out on top, he felt rewarded for having brought his A game. From here on out, he was a spectator. He parked his car near his trailer, locked the doors, and partially took off his racing suit. Gene walked over to a nearby stand and bought a bowlful of steamed corn with mayonnaise and parmesan cheese topped off with a bit of chili powder. *Why not?* he thought. Once he finished, since he was in Shiner country, he bought 3 cold 16 oz Shiner Bock beers, walked over to Hector and Paul, then handed them one and said, "Thanks for coming out here, fellas. I appreciate it."

Paul said, "No problem."

Hector said, "Thanks for bringing us."

They raised their bottles in the air to acknowledge the hard work and dedication that led up to this weekend. Gene smiled with great acceptance. Garrett was hanging out with the Demon going over tire pressures and installing a fresh amount of racing fuel into the fuel cell. He would have to wait until his class would be called, the last one for the day. He was a bit nervous, at ease only when he thought how good the car had been to him this weekend. Garrett decided to give the car a light wash since he was waiting. He scrambled around the trailer looking for anything carwash-related items. He found some dish soap, a bucket, and he purchased a shammy towel from a nearby seller. Garrett was used to doing things by himself. He didn't mind people walking by him and not interacting. He wrapped it up then heard his heat being called to the staging area. It was "go time." Garrett turned on the Demon and idled his way to the staging area. Garrett looked over at who his opponent was. It was Liz in her neon green Lamborghini Huracan. Liz had her helmet on, but the visor was lifted. He knew it was her. They locked eyes for a second. Garrett waved then she threw up a peace sign with her right hand. Her Huracan looked magnificent. The pearly neon green really shimmered in the afternoon sun. Garrett admired her even more but now, it was strictly business. Garrett hung a camera from his windshield. He pressed the record button then approached to do a massive burnout getting the tires ready for the race. He pressed a record button that engaged a camera mounted on the rear windshield facing forward. Garrett lined up ready for the green light to turn on. The Demon was shaking and rattling beneath him furiously ready to go. Once the green lights turned on, he launched the car out of the gate. He immediately left Liz's car behind him but then Liz began making a quick ascend. She nearly caught Garrett especially because he missed a shift as he couldn't believe what he was seeing. The Demon revved in high gear for just a second, more than it should've. He regained focus and, in a panic, completed the shift then rushed across the second pole nearly giving Liz a chance to catch up. It was a lot closer than Garrett would have wanted, but it was too late. They had already crossed the finish line and Garrett had won. The Demon crossed the finish at 133 MPH in 9.9 seconds; Liz 10.215 at 128 MPH.

Garrett turned and headed back to the staging area. He would advance to race on. Garrett wanted to exit his car and go and talk to Liz, but the staff advised against it. He would quickly be entered in another race. Liz was signaled to remain in a staging area for an elimination match. Garrett waved at her, but this time, she gave him the middle finger. Garrett would retain his focus and beat a pair of competitors: first, an R8 then he beat an RX7. To become a champion, he would need to beat a brand-new NSX. All cameras were watching the last two performers in the last class in a mano-to-mano final showdown. Liz would be eliminated. She had some very good races although the best she placed was 6th. She was now spectating and enjoying watching Garrett and his Demon. Liz walked up to him before his final race and said, "Hey!"

Garrett opened his visor and said, "Hey! What's up?"

Liz said, "You know what? When you focus on only one thing at a time, you're pretty good. Maybe you can be taught."

Garrett said, "Well, I love this."

She said, "Exactly."

Garrett said, "What? I didn't get that part. It's kind of loud!"

Garrett turned off his car, then she leaned in to talk to him, "I race to feel free because the world at times can enslave you."

Garrett said, "Wow, that's awesome. Some of us, all we need is that one shot."

Liz said, "Hey, good luck. If you want to hang out, I'll be around."

Garrett said, "Sure, I'd like that."

Gene, Hector, Paul, and Pablo were on the dragstrip close by the officials and began telling Garrett they were ready for the championship race. Garrett nodded up and down quickly. Liz stood there for a second and watched as Garrett fired up the Demon then pulled forward to get his tires ready. The announcer called over the speaker and said, "Ladies and gentlemen, please put your hands together to welcome our finalists Maro Steinberger in the 2022 Acura NSX type R, and Garrett Lee in the 2022 Dodge Demon SRT."

Garrett was a little bit nervous. He loved the way the NSX sounded. He had spectated the car a few times and knew how good it was. He knew it was a hybrid with twin-turbo V6 and electric motors in the front. Garrett did his usual burnout then looked over to see Maro perform an all-wheel-drive burnout—very impressive. Garrett took a deep breath then gripped the steering wheel firmly. He lined up then set his launch. Maro did the same. Garrett used his launch control. He revved up the engine then attempted to predict the speed of the bulbs as they descended to the green light. The green lights came on. Garrett's launch time was minimal. He had predicted the launch perfectly and did nearly half the time of what the NSX's launch time was. Garrett was in the lead most of the time. Garrett's eye flared wide open. It seemed like he stopped breathing. He just pushed the car equally hard as he had all weekend. He took it all and held it. Both men were riding rocket ships. The 9 seconds seemed to last an entire hour then both men crossed the second pole. Garrett was now free to take in deep breaths. He was excited and thought he won. The NSX was slightly behind him. The ending barricade wall was coming up really fast. Garrett reached the end of the track, turned around, and verified he had won! Maro turned around in the opposite direction. He extended his left hand out the window waving at Garrett.

The Demon came in first: 135 MPH at 9.887 seconds, his best run of the afternoon, with Maro right there next to him, 134 MPH at 9.94 seconds. Once they made it back to the grandstands, people mauled both drivers. Gene sprayed Garrett with Michelob's. Garrett removed the steering wheel, opened the door, and took off his helmet. Liz was there celebrating with him. He hugged her then the officials would give them a few minutes before conducting a podium ceremony. Garrett was emotionally riding high. He was all smiles. Several people were recording it all as it unfolded before them. The officials handed Garrett the trophy. Everyone cheered. He raised it as high as he could then he said to Gene, "I'm going to do the podium thing, but I want you to have this. It's yours. I'll win the next one on my own soon enough."

Gene said, "Stop that. This is yours. You defied death today on a 9-second tight rope and won. It's yours!"

They hugged each other from pure joy. Garrett was a star a lot of editors and bloggers wanted to write about. It was a very good afternoon, one he won't likely forget. Eventually, he made his way back to the trailer area and caught Liz again. Before she was leaving, he went up to her and said, "Hey, are you all packed up?"

Liz said, "Yeah, hey, um, can we take a picture together, just you and me? Here? As friends?"

Garrett said, "Sure, as friends."

Garrett didn't have his phone on him. He was still in his racing suit. Liz pulled out her cell phone. She took the selfie with both of them in it. Then she said, "I'll tag you. Take it easy."

Garrett said, "You have to friend me first."

Liz said, "I just sent it, but here, put your number and I'll message it to you if you want."

Garrett said, "Sure."

Garrett returned to the trailers. The cars were nearly secured and ready to go home. Garrett got out of his racing suit and prepared to leave with Pablo. The convoy slowly left the racetrack and found their way home. Garrett was re-living every single detail of the weekend the entire way back. He soon dozed off and fell asleep. By the time they exited Houston, it was very late in the afternoon. They stopped and rested outside New Orleans before changing their route Northward along I-55. They drove the entire day Monday crossing into Illinois late in the afternoon. By midnight, they were back at Gene's garage in West Chicago. The Demon was just a loner. Garrett would never ask Agusto for a paycheck and was curious if he would get paid for the weekend at all. Pablo was cool and calm, joking and signing the entire way back. He still had several grocery bags full of money with him. Garrett wasn't the type of guy who liked to gossip, but before they parted ways that night, Garrett asked Pablo, "So, where's all the money?"

Pablo said, "What money?"

Pablo had this don't-ask-me-look about him. He didn't believe Garrett to be a soldier. He didn't think he had it in him to do what would need to be done if push came to shove, so he preferred not to get him involved. Pablo got along with Garrett, so he turned to see him then began saying, "Let me ask you something. If things begin to change with El Diablo, where would you stand?"

Garrett said, "What do you mean?"

Pablo said, "Remember when I told you you were a member of the 75s?"

After a pause, Garrett nodded yes as if he remembered. Then Pablo said, "Forget about it. See you tomorrow."

Garrett said, "Sure. See you."

Garrett didn't really know what Pablo was talking about despite being around Pablo this weekend, despite living in a city like Chicago and having a father who was in prison for his involvement in the Chicago Outfit. Garrett just didn't see the friends in his life as top mob figures or active participants in organized crime. Crime was foreign to him. Garrett was of good heart and thought the same of everyone he encountered that they too were good people, but it's not always the case. His isolation kept him in the dark. It was his way of naturally seeing the world, and the rest of it, well, he just couldn't see it. Maybe he refused to see it? Maybe there are a lot of people who try to convince themselves of that world not existing because it takes so much from them if they participate.

Garrett began getting a feeling in the front of his mind as if something bad was going to happen, possibly related to what Gene was mentioning to him. He couldn't tell what it was, but he would try to follow Gene's instructions. Pablo drove off knowing the end was near. He would have to make his move soon. He drove from Gene's shop to his home thinking about what he was going to do. Pablo knew Agusto was well connected. Maybe he had someone monitoring him the whole time he was in Texas. At the end of his thought, he didn't care. Pablo was offended. Some of his longtime allies would take money from Pablo and plan against him. He took in multiple situations and decided on possible solutions for each. *Nothing I can't handle,* he thought. Pablo said, "I will control my own fate!" Agusto would hold no quarrel. He would figure Pablo out and destroy him in the long run. Pablo had to quickly take advantage of his opportunity and point the spear in the direction of his master because he may never get another chance. Little did he know Agusto secretly admired his confidence. He thought Pablo should have served in a better place closer to him, strictly under his guidance, but Pablo was too much like Agusto. They were the type of guys who couldn't be tamed.

CHAPTER 9

*"I wish the wind was cold.
I want to hold you, baby, hold."*

At Menard Correction Facility, the word was out: Motors had a son who ran with the 75s. El Bambino did not judge his son's actions, but he was very carefully watching Motors' every move. The 75s had already told the Outfit that Warren was buying a shank and that he was targeting members of the Outfit. El Bambino replied, "Let him attack. It would be the last thing he ever does."

The guys were back in town. Warren had reached out to Jake and scolded him for allowing Garrett to get mixed up with the 75s. Jake pleaded it was out of his reach. "Garrett made his own moves!" Warren pleaded with Jake to look after him. He didn't care what it would take and to remember how he helped him get wise behind bars. "The only thing he was asking was for him to repay the gesture with his son." Jake said, "I'm on it." From there on out, Jake would try to instill himself in Garrett's life. He probably wouldn't be able to pull him out but maybe they both could figure something out and stay alive just a little bit longer. Warren was still wearing himself out. He wasn't eating and he wasn't sleeping. The outcome was beginning to take its toll on him. Again, Warren was made to sleep in the med bay for a few days as they watched him recuperate himself. He hated it. Motors had four days up to his parole hearing. The staff wanted to keep him away from pop to try and help the guy out, especially due to a rumor of Motors attempting to retaliate against the Outfit. They needed to do everything they could to avoid any trouble, but Warren didn't care. If his son's future was on the line, he was willing to do what he needed to do.

Agusto had called Pablo to his warehouse the following day. Pablo was nervous. It could be his last day alive. He loaded a shortened shotgun and worked on his 1911s making sure they would operate nicely and cleanly if he should need to use them. Before leaving his house, he asked Virgen Guadalupe for her blessings because he had a tough thing to do. When the STI made it to the warehouse, Pablo tucked left the shotgun in the driver's chair with the window down then tucked his pistol under his shirt before grabbing multiple garbage bags from the trunk and walking inside with them. He had done a lot of counting in his hotel room before he left. He was planning on giving Agusto only $178,500, which is good, but Pablo was funding a war against him with his own money. He was keeping over $125,000. As he walked inside, Pablo constantly looked around. There was no one else here. He could hear Agusto working near his workbench. Now, Pablo was checking for defensive positions where he could take cover from oncoming gunfire. He reached where Agusto was and said, "I'm here."

Agusto motioned for him to follow him into his office. As soon as Pablo entered, a faint chime was heard. He was looking at the doorway. It had a sensor embedded into the frame. Agusto probably knew he was carrying a firearm. Agusto took a seat behind his desk. Pablo placed the garbage bag on the floor next to it then Agusto said, "What is this?"

He tore open the bag allowing Agusto to see inside. He didn't bother counting it or going through it. He didn't want to get too close to Pablo. He didn't trust him. Agusto said, "Pablito, how much is this?"

Pablo said, "$178,500."

Agusto turned angry then said, "You imbecile, you disappoint me!"

Pablo said, "Hey, man, people weren't betting then I took a few hits, and it is what it is."

Pablo was still among the few guys to ever talk back to El Diablo. He knew Pablo was robbing him but wondered how he could turn it against him. He also knew things could get ugly. Agusto had reasons to go for his gun beneath his desk and kill him, right there, right now. Maybe Pablo would never learn. Then it sunk in that if he was wrong and Pablo could fall in line, it would be as if he was hurting himself. Agusto tried to concentrate on what the universe was telling him. He knew Pablo was stealing from him, but he preferred to have his service than to waste a single bullet on him. If he had squirmed like a coward, he would have definitely shot him, but he didn't. He kept his stare and defied him. Agusto said, "Don't worry about the money. We'll make it a 50/50 split. Go ahead and when you're done, take a seat."

Pablo was calmer than Agusto was now. It bothered Agusto. Pablo sorted out the cash equally then he took a seat on a recliner behind him. Agusto said, "Gene told me the kid did well. What do you think of him?"

Pablo said, "He's a good driver. I think his talents might be going to waste here in Illinois. Maybe Gene could get him on a professional team."

Agusto said, "I've been watching him online and it looks like he won't need Gene to get a job. Several car builders around the world have shared their interest in him. The only fucked up part is I won't be with him, have to let him grow on his own. What would you do to get me more money from him?"

Pablo said, "He loves racing. Let's give him another race."

Agusto thought of it as a perfect opportunity to get both of them pinched. He said, "Absolutely! And I want you to organize it! This week!"

Pablo said, "Man, it's too soon, we'll have to find a track, make reservations an—"

Agusto butted in, "A street race! I have people who love to race. Outside of the city, people with deep pockets who loved the action they saw going down make it happen."

Pablo said, "Who exactly are you talking about?"

Agusto said, "Bosses, and their best drivers. Now, you're going to represent me, so I expect the best of treatments. Go all out. Put $1 million on the line. Draw the course and I'll cover the cops."

Pablo thought about saying something smart like, "Oh, like last time?" But this was an entrance to Agusto. Not only that but he was literally handing him his contacts throughout the country. Pablo grew wise and went with it. He said, "Man, of course, you can count on me and if it's like that, I may just enter myself in the race."

Agusto felt like he would soon have Pablo pinched by his associates. He got excited. He could promise Pablo protection over a failed race. Agusto grinned and said, "Perfect."

Pablo began to get an uncomfortable feeling. He rose to his feet and began to make his way to the door. He would kill him once he had his operations. He could make his own connections on his own, but this would solidify himself as El Diablo's victor. Agusto didn't want the guy to hang around. He walked with him out but as they neared the doorway to his office, he held himself. He could feel Pablo's intention, but a slew of questions came up, doubting himself. Would Agusto slip up? Could Pablo handle the pressure of having the Chicago police department down his neck? Would Pablo crack and do something stupid? Could he hurt his niece? Maybe El Diablo should just end this right now!

Pablo reached his car, opened the door, turned toward Agusto to draw his gaze from the loaded shotgun on the seat, then said, "We'll be in touch."

Agusto said, "Sure."

Pablo got in his car and drove off. Agusto watched him leave the lot then turn down the road. Pablo noticed there were members of the 75 guys loyal to El Diablo standing nearby awaiting orders. Agusto knew all the people who lived in his neighborhood and he knew he could count on all of them on-demand, at any time. Agusto walked to the end of his lot. He crossed the street and walked right up to them. A big guy said, "Hey, Mr. Diablo, what's up?"

Agusto said, "Keep up the good work. There's a guy coming by in a few minutes you might scare. How about you guys go get some 40s at la Garita, take 5."

Agusto handed them a wad of rolled bills. The big guy nodded, "Sure thing."

The big guy turned and walked away waving. The other guys followed him.

Agusto was expecting Garrett in Aurora. He would arrive shortly after 6 PM. The first thing he did was congratulate him for his efforts in Houston. Agusto had hoped the environment would be too much for him to handle, but Garrett came out clean on the other side. Agusto was guilty of the man Garrett had become. Agusto had raised a lot of guys above their comfort zone too soon and most of them had failed miserably. They needed a few attempts to finally get it. Even Agusto needed to be broken a few times until he understood the pleasures the world had to offer and how to enjoy them. Agusto replied joking to Garrett, "I heard there was no police chase this time."

Garrett said, "Yeah, I'm disappointed about that too."

Agusto studied Garrett's body movements. He was a changed man. He grinned back at Garrett laughing slightly.

Garrett sprung a question at him, saying, "How's the BMer. Can I take it?"

Agusto said, "Sure, you can, it's yours. Let's go find it."

The two began to walk inside. Garrett said, "Cool. Hey, is there any pay for winning TX2K?"

Agusto said, "Only Satan pays demons. Do you think I'm Satan?"

Garrett said, "No?"

Agusto reached for a beer from a nearby fridge. It pleased him. Garrett still believed him not to be El Diablo. It also sucked because he couldn't break the kid, but he was doing good and making money, so, who cares, he thought. Then he said, "I netted $178,000 this weekend. You made me zilch! But you did win. Tell you what, I covered your tabs and bought the car. I already sold it to Gene, but I guess I could pay you $10 grand."

Garrett was all smiles and said, "Oh, man! Yes!"

Garrett found the German coupe tucked neatly inside. He climbed inside. The keys were on the driver-side sun visor. He turned it on and revved it a couple of times. Agusto had gone into his office, counted $10,000 and put it in an envelope, then gave it to Garrett as he drove the car through the shop outside. Agusto handed him the envelope. Garrett said, "Should I count it?"

Agusto said, "Only if you don't trust me."

Garrett nodded and said, "Cool."

Agusto said, "There's another race being scheduled this weekend. I want you to be in it."

Garrett smiled and nodded, "Yeah, I'm in."

Agusto said, "Well, I guess you'll be quitting that shop and bar now that you're a pro racer?"

Garrett said, "Not exactly. Until it happens, I gotta do what I gotta do."

Agusto agreed then said, "Soon. Hey, if Pablo tries to recruit you to be his driver, just say no, alright? You drive for me!"

Garrett said, "So, what kind of race is this?"

Agusto said, "It's a street race through Chicago and it won't be low budget. Some guys with some very deep pockets found out about the race last week and want in on the action. So, what kind of a supercar do you want?"

Garrett said, "An NSX type R."

Agusto said, "Gotcha, but hey, let's keep this close to the chest, alright? And get ready for this Saturday night."

Garrett said, "Sure."

Garrett sped away. Agusto stood there watching him drive away. He whispered to himself, "Damn! He even screwed me out of $10 grand. Well, ask and you shall receive." He then looked up to the sky and said, "What should I ask for?"

Agusto wondered where his friendship with Garrett was going. Maybe the guy really was unget-able and was worthy of his rewards. He wondered how Garrett could be living in such a toxic environment and still have enough will to not see it and resist all temptations. He must have a lot of willpower! Agusto had heard of the downfall of Warren at Menard but he had yet to eliminate El Bambino or himself. He wondered if it was possible. Had they changed their evil ways? Why hadn't the universe revealed its true nature?

Agusto decided he would not stay with his hands tied. He would add more pressure to both Garrett and Pablo. El Diablo would again have 75s attempt to pull Dayana away and to leave Garrett, to weaken his high spirits. Then, he sent a text message to his niece himself. Once she replied, he called her himself. He said, "Hey, I got a lead for you regarding the street race."

Julissa said, "Oh my God. Thanks, Tio. I needed this so bad."

Agusto said, "I heard there's a guy who organizes big illegal races. I have a name and a place where I believe he works. Now, be careful. I heard he's very dangerous."

Julissa said, "I'll be cautious. Who is he?"

Agusto said, "Pablo Gutierrez. He works at an NTB. And I heard he's planning something. You might want to just watch him for a while, and again, Angel, please be careful."

Julissa said, "Thank you, Tio. I will."

El Diablo hung up then smiled. He knew that Pablo had his days numbered. This was something he could no longer hide from. His niece was not the type of person who gives up and she is smart enough to get him. *A collar like this will do her well,* he thought.

Julissa went in to work bright and early to do research on Pablo Gutierrez and figure out who was this guy her uncle had been told had something to do with illegal street racing. She found he had done a very short stint in Juvenile, completed probation, and was not listed to be working with any street gang. Everything she found about the guy made her believe he had his life put together. He had a gym membership. Julissa thought for a 25-year-old guy, he had a hefty bank account, not Kingpin money but over $100,000. On a mechanic's salary, it seemed odd. Then, the home he lived in was in his mother's name, but he was the only person receiving mail at that location, then she noticed his mother owned 3 houses in Cook County and all of them were paid off. His mother also had over 10 cars. Something else was odd because, from all of the cameras at Archer and Ashland, none of them showed any images resembling Pablo or any vehicle associated with him. She found the picture from the EVO when it sped past a speed trap camera, but it did not look like Pablo was driving. There was someone else driving. She found out there had been an attempt to pull over the EVO, but the car left, then when she looked for the evidence or recording from the police car, she found that it had been made unwatchable. The recording was there but the image was just a dark screen. Nothing could be made out of it. It happened to all squad cars involved in a limited pursuit of a sedan that fits the description of Pablo's which was photographed. She began to think her investigation was being tampered with, but by who? And how was her uncle involved? She knew something was up. She decided to begin surveillance on him, herself. It was shortly after 11 AM when Julissa arrived at the NTB where Pablo worked. She watched from afar and looked around before stepping out of her car to approach the building. As soon as she stepped inside, a guy addressed her loudly, saying, "Can I help you, ma'am?"

Julissa replied, "Hmm, I'm just browsing."

The guy said, "Ok, well let me know when you're ready."

She walked around the customer's lounge until she spotted him and after that, she couldn't unsee him. The first thing she noticed was how attractive the guy. How he carried himself with so much confidence, he joked and smiled with everyone like he didn't have a care in the world. Then, he stopped in his tracks, as if he could feel Julissa's gaze upon him. He turned his head and clearly stared back at her, trying to remember if he knew her. They both held eye contact for a few seconds. She was overcome with confusion. Her brow curled upward near the center of her forehead, then she decided to turn away. She walked over to a coffee machine and poured herself a cup. The guy at the desk took a look at her. She would slowly glance toward the technicians making sure Pablo was no longer staring at her. He wasn't. Then, she noticed a guy who looked a lot like the driver of the speed trap picture, Garrett. He was a fellow employee. She took a picture of an ASE certification with Garrett's name and picture with her phone. She would conduct research on Garrett and find out how he was attached. Julissa decided to leave. As she walked by the guy, he greeted her and said, "Can I interest you in another cup of coffee?"

Julissa said, "I'll pre-order some Comp-Tas."

The guy waved as she pressed on the door to leave. He said, "Have a good day." Then once she was gone, he said to himself, "You, cheap bitch. Oh my God, she has an MK5 too? Total chick car."

She walked back to her car. She wasn't picking up anything offensive from Pablo. She would have to do more digging and see if she could come up with something more solid. She started up her car and drove away, peeling out a little bit of rubber on the asphalt as she left. Pablo had taken notice of Julissa. He was curious as to who she was. He casually walked upfront and asked the guy at the desk about her. Pablo said, "Hey, what's up with that chick that just left?"

The guy said, "I don't know. I think she was checking you out. Maybe one that you left hanging last night?"

Pablo knew he had never seen her before. Her eyes were as sharp as swords piercing through him it captivated him. He knew their paths would cross again, soon. Pablo returned to the shop and kept on working. Shortly, Garrett and he left for lunch together. While driving, Pablo mentioned he was going to host a race that weekend. Garrett said, "You're hosting a race and didn't tell me about it all weekend?"

Pablo said, "I just found out about it yesterday. How about you drive for me?"

Garrett said, "I would, bro, but I already got a car for the race."

Pablo said, "What? My race? Not that old German car. I'm planning on bringing big power cars."

Garrett said, "I'm getting a new car, an NSX."

Pablo said, "Wow. That's great. How are you and Dayana?"

Garrett said, "I haven't heard from her. I'm going in tonight to see her."

Pablo said, "I hope everything turns out good for you."

Julissa arrived at the precinct and got to work looking for anything she could find on Garrett. There wasn't much, 22 years old, clean record, but what did show up was he had several visits to Menard Correction Facility. She found out everything about Warren Lee. But once she began looking into the Chicago Outfit, she was asked for authorization. She walked to Sgt. Vega's office and knocked on the door. When she heard him asking her to enter, she went in. Julissa asked him, "Why are there files related to the Chicago Outfit that are off-limits?"

Sgt. Vega said, "That information is restricted to a very special task force. One that you are not a part of."

Julissa said, "Why not?"

Sgt. Vega, "Because sometimes I don't know if I can trust you. What are you working on?"

Julissa was furious. She said, "There's a guy Pablo Gutierrez. I believe he was responsible for the racing on Archer."

Sgt. Vega, "And how does the Outfit figure into this? They haven't had any operations in this city in years."

Julissa said, "There's a guy, Garrett Lee, son of Warren Lee who is a known Chicago Outfit member and I'm looking into all possible leads, sir."

Sgt. Vega, "Well I'll tell you right now. The Outfit only exists behind bars, and let's keep it that way. I wouldn't advise you to take to anyone about the Outfit."

Julissa rose her voice and pleaded, "But, sir, this can lead to getting El Diablo. I can—"

Sgt. Vega, "Those files are off-limits! You want something on Garrett, don't look at Warren. Get Garrett!"

Julissa stormed out of his room, frustrated. She returned to her office and looked for addresses related to Garrett. She was determined to catch him when he slipped. Maybe then she could get the information from the Outfit which she was looking for. Garrett would walk into Black Door that night, as a guest. He took a seat at the bar and watched on as Dayana ignored him most of the night. Garrett did not know how to act. He wanted her so much, but he couldn't figure out what it was he had done wrong or what he was supposed to do. It hurt him to be ignored by her. On top of that, he saw her being flirtatious with other guys who walked in, more attractive than him, better suited to be with her. Garrett took it as a loss. He loved her, but he couldn't be with her. He figured he might as well leave. Jake was inside the bar. He was witnessing what was happening. He purposely walked over to the guy who was flirting with Dayana and told him, "Take a hike. I don't ever want to see you here again."

The guy understood who Jake was and he wanted nothing to do with him. He stood up quickly then fumbled through his pants, but Jake said, "Don't worry about it. I'll cover your beer."

The guy hurried out of the bar, then Jake walked up to Garrett and said, "Hey, you're that race car driver guy, right?" Jake raised his voice and said, "Hey, everyone, we got a real champion up in here! Make some noise for Garrett, everybody." The few gathered on a Tuesday night, raised their glass, and cheered for him. Jake whispered to Garrett, "Don't be so gloom. Smile. And don't worry; you can't lose what wasn't yours. If you want her, go get her."

Garrett smiled. His reception by Dayana also improved. They looked at each other immensely once again. Garrett was in for a good night.

Wednesday morning at Menard came around. A guard and a nurse entered the med room where Warren was then a guard and said, "Stand up, please." Warren stood up wearing a thin white shirt with no pants. He was in his underwear with his socks on. The nurse handed him a cup of water and a small thimble with an assortment of different colored pills inside, then she said, "I need to see your mouth when you're done." Warren took the cup and ingested the pills, then he finished the cup of water. He leaned toward the nurse for her to see his open mouth. She had a small flashlight in her hand which she used to take a better look then said, "You seem to be doing much better. I'll be back to check on you after lunch." The guard handed Warren a tray of food. He said to him, "Here's breakfast." After Warren took the tray, he said, "Looking good, Motors, keep it up."

Warren gave the guard a thumbs up although he didn't know if the guard had seen the gesture or not. On the opposing side from him across the hallway, an inmate stood at his door. There staring back at him was a member of the Chicago Outfit. He had a smile on his face as if he knew something that Warren didn't. Warren turned over and attempted to block it all out of his mind. The meds were doing their job, slowing down his thoughts. Warren had forgotten what a cold beer tastes like. He ate his breakfast and imagined himself drinking a bottle of Old Style while flipping meat on an outdoor grill. He said, "Yup, those would-be good times."

Garrett was at work enjoying a good day. Things ended well for him on Tuesday. He just felt good inside and out. Dayana sent him a message that said, "I can't wait to see you tonight XOXOXO." Garrett got excited for the prospect of being with her but maintained it out of his thoughts. He still had a full day's worth of work ahead of himself. His confidence was enormous. He felt as if he could do no wrong. Agusto bought a brand-new NSX type R and drove it to Gene's shop where he instructed them to immediately create performance add-ons to increase the horsepower and torque. Along with a weight reduction and newly fabricated pieces for improved speed and handling control, he then asked for the car to be ready by Friday. A tough assignment on such a new product, Gene said, "I'll see what I can do."

Jake took the liberty of stopping by NTB and having a conversation with Garrett, which he felt he should have had a long time ago. He stayed in his car watching Garrett wondering what his reaction would be if he told him everything his father had asked him to do. Then how would he try to explain what his mother told him? And would Garrett believe him? He knew the 75s had gotten to him. He could see Pablo nearby. He thought Garrett would reject him. Jake exited his 71 Mach1 then walked toward the wide-open door of the shop to him. He would tell Garrett the truth as he knew it. He would say, "You're being played. Agusto is El Diablo and he's using you to destroy the Chicago Outfit."

Pablo knew who Jake was and as soon as he saw him walking toward the shop, he went into the parking lot to confront him. He said, "Can I help you?" Jake said, "I'm here to see Garrett."

Pablo said, "No, I don't think so."

Jake and Pablo stared at each other down for a second then Jake said, "Yeah, alright."

Pablo answered, "I'm hosting a race this weekend. Buy-in is $100,000. If you're up for it?"

Jake turned and said, "Yeah, sure, I'll be there." Then he began to walk away. It was slightly insulting to Jake, but he knew Garrett had value. Garrett wouldn't talk to him again if he knew he was violent. So, he decided to lay low. He would get more chances to see him, and Jake was into racing himself, he would enter the race. Jake started up his car and left. With Pablo around, the shop was not the best place to approach Garrett. He would go to Black Door and hope to see him there.

Jake sat at the bar at Black Door slowly sipping on a tall beer. Around 7 PM, Garrett showed up ready to begin his second job. Dayana greeted him with a kiss on his lips. Then Jake extended his hand. Garrett knew him from the night before, so he gave him one of those long hand tags and fist bump handshakes. Jake smiled. Garrett tied an apron behind his back and got to work. He also served as a bartender now which was ok because it gave him a chance to talk with Garrett. Jake said, "Hey, how's it going?"

Garrett said, "Good, thanks for yesterday, so, you're into racing?"

Jake said, "My guy Flash, remember? Guy with the RX7 from the first race. Remember?"

Garrett answered, "Oh, well, I'm not looking for a sponsor."

Jake said, "No, I'm not here for that."

Garrett said, "So, what are you here for?"

Jake said, "Just a beer."

Garrett said, "Alright, nothing wrong with that."

Dayana butted in and said, "Hey, Gare, who's your friend?"

Jake loudly answered, "Well, actually I just met the guy. My name is Jake. Jake diEscasio and Garrett is one lucky man. What's your name, beautiful lady?"

Dayana blushed a little and Garrett just sat there like a dummy green and jealous of how smooth this guy was. Dayana answered, "Dayana. Nice to meet you."

Jake said, "That is a gorgeous name. Are you seeing anyone?"

Dayana said, "Well, me and Garrett are kinda talking."

Jake said, "Oh, I'm sorry, I didn't know, but you might want to handcuff this guy because I think he's going places. Have you heard of his driving skills? The guy is blessed. What a madman behind the wheel."

She paused and squinted, looking hard at Garrett. Then Garrett said, "I wouldn't say all that."

Jake smiled as he and Garrett locked eyes. Jake told Garrett, "Could I get a Guinness?"

Dayana butted in confused a bit and said, "Sure, I'll get it."

Jake wanted to bump fist with Garrett, which he did, but then he leaned into Jake and said, "Dude, what the hell! Hey, man, if you want me to drive with you, I can't, ok?"

Jake shook his head no, then he began, "You are a blessed man. Think of me as a really good friend. I can hook you up in all types of ways."

Garrett was skeptic and said, "What do you mean?"

Jake's beer arrived. Dayana walked by, squeezed a smile, then walked away. Jake said, "Thank you."

Garrett stayed with Jake as he took the first sip, then Jake continued saying, "That guy, Agusto, wake up man, he's not a friend, is he?"

Garett looked down in a deep stare but before he could answer, Jake said, "You know he isn't, huh?"

Jake carried on saying, "Garrett, have you ever felt alone amongst people you know? I know why, alright. There has always been a place for you, where you would have been good, but you never received help before because . . . you didn't need any."

Garrett answered frustrated and said, "What! I don't need help. WTF are you talking about? I'm doing great."

Jake said, "When was the last time you talked to your dad?"

Garrett crossed the counter and shoved Jake. It's amazing what a beautiful girlfriend and some money do for a guy's self-esteem, probably equal to carrying a weapon. Garrett said, "Don't you ever bring up my dad. You don't know him! You don't know shit!"

Dayana was scared. Edgar came upfront from the back. He was taking Jake's side and said, "Hey, is everything alright?"

Jake raised his hands and tried to straighten things out with Garrett. He said, "I'm on your side, your father's side. I'm here to help!"

Garrett stormed out angrily. Dayana caught sight of what was happening and tried to hold him from leaving but it was too late. He pushed open the door and walked out. She followed. Garrett always felt passionate about his father and what he had heard about friendships and gang life in Chicago was basically the same his entire life—"stay away" and "just say no." His father wanted Garrett to be a strong person, a natural-born leader, but what he grew into was a life with a lot of isolation, poor social skills, and disappointment the few times he tried. How does one learn to be a leader with no clan to lead? Proving Agusto was in a way really liberating him. Garrett did like what was happening to him in the last 2 weeks and if Agusto was trying to screw him, he didn't care. Dayana calmed him down and asked him not to leave. He didn't, but shortly after she walked inside, Jake walked out and said, "Look, yeah, I know your dad. I did some time at Menard a while back and he told me to take care of you. Your dad needs your help."

Garrett didn't answer. He would be at the Parole hearing in Southern Illinois Friday morning and see his father. He wanted nothing to do with anyone in the Chicago Outfit. Garrett went up to Jake and said, "I know my dad is not in the Outfit and neither is Agusto." Jake nodded then left. Garrett tried to put the whole thing behind him, a skill his solitude had taught him well to put the little things behind him. Later that night, he sent his dad an email, but Warren was unable to read it that night. Garrett was going through a lot of turmoil in his own right. His mind kept thinking over and over as to who Jake was—some gangster or drug dealer? What could he teach him or do for him? Garrett tried to block it all out, but he remembered when he saw Jake at the race two weeks ago, he had pulled with the locals and his demeanor that night demanded respect. Who was he? His mother could tell something was wrong. He wasn't his usual cheerful self as he lately had been. She went to the door and asked him, "Honey, is everything ok? Do you want dinner?"

Garrett said, "No, just sleepy, I'll be fine."

His mother left him alone. He began thinking about what a great time awaits him this week. He was going to Southern Illinois for the last time on Friday for his fathers' parole. Then, the big race on Saturday. His dad might even be there to watch him come in the first place. Now, that would be a pleasant dream. He wanted to believe everything was coming together but a bad notion rested in the back of his mind telling him that, "He was wrong!" It frightened him. The more he thought about it, the more he realized something wasn't right. He felt as if he needed to see Agusto, right now! He checked the chat room for all the members of the 75s but it was silent, nothing, no chatter at all. It was 11:30 PM. Garrett texted Agusto and said, "Hey, what's up?"

Agusto was on the west side of Chicago helping a man who "didn't know his limits" drown himself to death on cheap alcohol. Agusto sat next to him in a dimly lit bar, surrounded by misery pushers and money extortionists. The man couldn't follow orders and had always pressed his own hand. He had lost himself too many times becoming a burden on everyone who attempted to help him. Now, it was time for Satan to help the guy awaken himself or die trying. Jazz music was being played in the background. Agusto knew all the muscles that hung out at that bar. The owner of the establishment, certain patrons, and El Diablo mutually agreed to be compensated $150 for every 12 ounces and $200 for every shot of liquor the man ingested. The house was now up to $3100 but the mark showed to still be in his elements. Having a good ol' time, everyone encouraged the guy to keep drinking. El Diablo bought him dinner and brought a woman to dance with the guy so he would stay on his feet and keep on drinking. Agusto saw the text message from Garrett but chose not to answer. Garrett slowly gave up and dozed off, alone that night just as he always had been. Maybe Jake was right. Agusto doesn't care about you.

Around 12:30, his phone began ringing. It was Dayana. He answered the call and slowly said, "Hello".

Dayana said, "Hey, babe, what are you doing?"

Garrett said, "I was sleeping."

Dayana said, "Hey, some friends came by the bar and we're going to go out to a club tonight. You want to come?"

Garrett said, "Naw, I'm good."

Dayana said, "Some of them are guys. You sure you don't want to come?"

Garrett was just tired, so he said, "Naw, go ahead."

She said, "I'm going to be dancing with them. You sure?"

Garrett said, "That's fine."

Dayana answered, "Ok, I'll talk to you later."

Garrett said, "Ok, bye."

He hung up and turned over burying the side of his head deep into his pillow. Then, like 30 seconds later, the phone rang again. It was Dayana again and she said, "I'm not going."

Garrett said, "Oh, and why not?"

She answered, "Because I'd rather be with you."

Garrett said, "Sure, me too. Can you come over?"

Dayana said, "Yeah, I'll be there in 20 minutes."

Garrett said, "Ok, but I'm going to need you to be quiet. My mom and ugh—everybody is here."

Dayana said, "Ok, I'll be there soon, bye."

Garrett hung up his phone then smiled. *That'll definitely take my mind off of the Outfit,* he thought. Garrett jumped out of his bed and noticed he had already pitched a tent with his shorts. Just thinking about her, he laughed. He went to his private bathroom in his room and brushed his teeth, splashed some water on his face, and put on some deodorant. Garrett checked his junk and noticed he hadn't groomed well lately, then he noticed he only had a few minutes to spare. He had that morning tight dehydrated bod thing going on so he could skip doing a few push-ups and sit-ups before Dayana arrived. He had a set of electric clippers in his bathroom he kept for grooming his private areas, but he did not like how it might make too much noise, so he took a simple approach using scissors. He pulled down his briefs, put one leg on the edge of his bathtub, pinched some pubes with his left hand, then squeezed the scissors with his right. When completed, he took a second to admire his work then he properly disposed of all traces and kept things looking clean. He had never had a girl in his room before. He didn't know what was going to happen if she would enter his bathroom or not. But he wanted it to be nice and not seem like he had to get ready for sex. Garrett did a nice job. His member looked gorgeous as always. He made a mental note to himself to invest in some Nair hair removal cream for men and groom more often. His phone gave off his text message alert. Garrett lost the briefs and scrambled a pair of baggy shorts, then he put on a graphic tee shirt from atop the dresser. He once had purchased a black light bulb just for this occasion and would finally get a chance to use it. He rushed through his drawers looking for it until he found it. Garrett unscrewed the overhead light bulb quickly fighting with burning his hand, then in pitch-black darkness, he screwed in the black light bulb until it was secure. Now, he figured he was ready for sex. His room had a nice purple glow about it. Garrett looked around admiring it, then he smiled. His toes also tightened with joy. He casually picked up his phone to see her text message. It said, "I'm outside."

He casually texted back, "I'll let you in."

Then she replied, "Ok."

He hurried down to the front door, slowly opened it, and greeted her. She was wearing blue jeans and a pink zip-up hoody. As soon as he opened the door, she sprang into his face and kissed him. Dayana had a bottle of Jameson whiskey with her tucked near her armpit. She showed it to him and said, "Get some glasses 'n maybe some water?"

He was excited. He had mistakenly made a lot of noise fumbling through the kitchen cabinets, but he got everything she asked including some ice. He signaled her with a flick of his head using his neck for her to follow him to his room. As soon as she entered, she said, "Somebody got the right idea."

Garrett said, "Yup, to chill."

Garrett set the glasses on a table, put ice inside of them, then began pouring shots in a hurry. She kissed him very passionately on his face. She groomed his head with both of her hands. He leaned in and squeezed her thigh and buttocks with his right hand. She enjoyed that. With his left hand, he was being subtle just holding her above her waist near her right-side kidney. She rolled her body tipping her breasts into his chest then withdrew from kissing him to admire his face. He wasn't the prettiest of Caucasian guys. His facial hair was getting out of control. It looked like a teenager's chin growing in his first beard but to her, he was hotter than Brad Pitt. She said, "Let's do a shot?"

He dropped his thought and nervously began waving his head up and down saying, "Sure."

Garrett had crept away from the glasses. He stretched reaching for her glass and handed it to her, then he picked up his and they downed the first shots of the night. They both made harsh blowing gestures due to how strong it was. Dayana suggested he pour another round which he did. They tipped back the second drink for each one. Garrett grabbed ice from a tray he brought and put it in his mouth. Dayana requested ice for herself. Garrett said, "I'll give you your ice if you take another shot."

Dayana said, "Deal."

Garrett poured the third round into the shot glasses. Dayana stole the ice from his glass and told Garrett to add a fresh piece of ice to her cup. He did. They drank the third round which now hit them both very nicely. They stared at one another for a pair of seconds, then she went for it groping him. Garrett laughed frantically, stood up, and hugged her throwing both of his hands around her waist. He smiled. He didn't have the abs of an MMA fighter, but she didn't mind. Dayana extended her arms over his shoulders, kissing him, his hands squeezing her slightly, his left hand tight around the small of her back, and his right hand up near her bra latch but he fumbled with it. He pulled off a great maneuver lightly clawing with his right hand. Using his fingers curled inward, he pressed against her back, lightly scratching her. Dayana laughed because he missed unbuckling the latch again, then she said, "Need some help?"

Garrett took it as a silly insult. He said, "Here, help me first." He turned around giving her his rear side. She was shorter than him. She had to really throw her arms over him as she pulled his shirt up over his head. He ducked a little. She took a step back and snapped the t-shirt at his butt as if they were locker room buddies playing with a towel. She reached around him pulling down his shorts, with both hands now on his hips, then she worked one after the other to the front just south of his belly button. It was obvious he was awake. Dayana bit her upper lip as she caressed the best part of the man. Dayana was caught behind him. She rotated him to face her then got down on her knees. The experience alone of undressing him had gotten her going. He stayed with his hands on his waist waiting to see what she would do. Of course, he would have no objection. She whispered to him, "Men don't have to prove themselves on the streets. It's at home where it counts."

He squinted saying, "I agree."

Dayana laid a hard open-handed slap on his left butt cheek. She said, "That is the most beautiful thing I've ever seen. Kudos on the lighting."

She caressed the extent of his manhood holding it upward, no help needed. She kissed the lower area where it began to protrude away from his body. She then began to give a series of small kisses to the sides of the shaft sinking a little bit of a pinching feeling with her teeth. The feeling of her teeth was weird for the guy. He felt like giggling. She maintained a firm grip caressing him with her index finger and thumb in a slow pumping motion. The guy was truly in heaven, but he was eager to return the favor. To him, she was the center of attention, so he stopped her then flipped her away from him as he began undressing her. All those years of being rejected by other women or thinking of all the time he had wasted not approaching her, it all disappeared. All it took was the following moments. Garrett undid her bra. She was not a very busty woman but had a nicely filled c-cup. He squeezed the sides of her breasts from behind her, pulling them forward then pressing them into her stomach while holding her areolas. Garrett kept thinking to himself, "Take it slow, this is going to happen, take it slow this is going to happen."

Garrett pulled back, lowered her bottom, then took a deep breath admiring her perfectly circular behind. He said, "Damn." She didn't approve of him staring, maybe a bit of uncertainty with her own body or maybe it was putting a pause on the show. She rotated to face him then began kissing him. For the record, there was no reason to disapprove. Garrett's muscles became more enhanced. All of his senses were being nurtured. His strength multiplied. The masculinity in him won out. Garrett lifted her off the ground with both arms and flung her onto his bed. As he did, she let out a brief cry, "Wow." Garrett reached for both of her ankles then pulled her body toward him. She flung her legs upward then Garrett put his nose between the area where they met. Dayana said, "Be gentle."

In Garrett's mind, he kept repeating to himself, "Take it slow, it's happening, it's happening, it's happening."

After a few hours went by, they continued to lay in his bed exhausted. The clock on his wall said 3:55 AM. I doubt anyone got much sleep that night at his house. Garrett laid there thinking, *Could this have been influenced by El Diablo? Or Jake? Was his whole life a set-up? But if it was getting you laid, who cares?*

Garrett's own mind had become his worst enemy. Time passed by until the alarm on Dayana's phone went off. It was now 6 AM. She awoke then gathered her stuff, claiming she had to leave. Garrett studied her every move feeding his own paranoia, and after she left, he was still undetermined. Everything she did was genuine. Why would she do anything other than that? He laid in bed a few moments trying to convince himself she really did love him. At work, somehow, everyone knew the guy had gotten lucky the night before but not once did he admit to it, not to anyone especially Pablo. This came from spurts of advice his father had managed to give him, to "respect what happens in private" and "no one likes a blabbermouth." Garrett concentrated on the tasks at work and he got stuff done. He almost set a personal best for hours booked in a single day. It's amazing what a guy can do when he feels complete.

CHAPTER 10

"A seven-nation army couldn't hold me back."

Warren had a visit with his psychiatrist on Thursday. He was cleared to rejoin gen-pop for what could be his last night at Menard. Warren was excited. He was eating and sleeping well. He felt healthy and fit. He did 100 pushups, 100 sit-ups, and 100 v-ups in his room. A few guards gave him high fives in the hallway as he walked to his old cell. He had energy in him that radiated and affected people around him. How was it possible? When Warren rejoined the group of his cell block, they were having free time watching television and mingling in the cell block before lunch. Loro walked up to Warren and said, "Hey, I got that thing you wanted."

Warren remembered he had asked Loro to buy a shank for him, and he had found a bargain for him. Warren had more than enough money to pay for it, but it was no longer on his mind. He had different thoughts now. He was thinking about leaving the whole prison life behind him. Warren said, "Naw, I don't need it anymore. I'll cover the cost, but you hang on to it just in case you need it one day."

Loro turned and looked at members of the 75s behind him frightened. They had gone through extreme lengths to acquire such an item. They had orders to report as to when Warren would use it. This was not what they wanted to hear. They immediately went to Cruz and reported what Motors had said. They added it to be an insult to their organization, wanting blood either from Warren or Loro. But Cruz knew it really was his plan and he wanted his adversaries to make that choice of taking somebody's life, not him. Cruz declined to show force. His followers were confused by this reaction, then Cruz said, "If you build it, they will come. Don't worry. I'll cover the cost."

A big bodybuilder guy who never really liked Cruz said, "What's that mean? Are you fuckin' with us?"

Cruz was an elder gentleman now, known back in the day for having been explosive and damn near psychopathic. He was still fit today, and one constant is that he never let anybody intimidate him. It didn't matter if you had more brains, money, or mass at any given time. He believed he could break you physically. Cruz stood there and squared up the guy, locking eyes with the giant. He broke eye contact and looked to the floor as if to say sorry. Then Cruz said, "The blade will be used, one way or another, capisce?"

The big man and the others nearby nodded up and down in agreement. Cruz walked away then snapped his fingers to a guy who handed him a smuggled phone. He dialed and called Pablo on the other end. Cruz said, "Does your papa know about your moves in Tejas?"

Pablo said, "I own Tejas and the 75s now. One way or another, you will beg me for my support."

Santiago laughed then said, "As long as El Diablo is around, you don't."

Pablo hung up on him. Pablo was furious on the other end. He slammed the phone on the exterior of a building he was standing near.

Cruz wondered if the young man could get the job done. He made another phone call this time to Agusto. A crisp hard voice quickly came over the line, "Yes!"

Cruz said, "Diablo, you might have a problem."

Agusto said, "Let those with blackness in their hearts exert their own force against themselves."

Cruz said, "This might be related to destiny. I think you've been fucking up. I've heard of what this Pablo guy is doing. He's smart and I think he has the balls to go through with it. Dallas is with him. Are my assets still safe with you?"

Agusto said, "With me? Always! His planning is a testament to the lack of faith in himself. I on the other hand am always prepared. Send him my way."

Cruz said, "Weird words. Sounds like witchcraft. Who knew Satan was so poetic?"

Agusto said, "Dallas will fold and take a lesser deal, punishment for taking swords."

Cruz said, "There are a lot of hungry dogs out there. Watch your back."

Agusto said, "I keep all of mine well fed. I advise you to do the same." He hung up.

Agusto broke the long silence on the 75's chat line. He announced the race on Saturday night but did not disclose the time or place. He signaled out to Pablo and mentioned he would greet him in his penthouse overlooking the finish line. The course had been set by Pablo. The buy-ins were coming in every day. El Diablo was giving him power on thoughts of it being used under him. But if Pablo wanted to go against his ruler, Agusto hoped it to be on his terms. Pablo knew about his top-floor penthouse near Greek Town on the corner of Van Buren and S Desplaines which he told the participants would be close to the finish line. Agusto got wind of it. Pablo understood the writing on the wall; Cruz and Agusto were not ready for Pablo to rule. The old-timers still wanted to have more time in the limelight. Pablo was planning for an ambush while Agusto was on his way to his Greektown penthouse. He began secretly recruiting his capos, but again, Agusto heard about his supposed attack. It forced Agusto to look into Pablo for a vulnerable spot and hit it. Pablo's most loyal soldiers were coming from out of state, and it would take nearly his entire fortune to bring them here, a decision he was willing to make.

Even though Pablo acted like no girl could come close to his heart, Agusto took a chance. The closest of any woman he knew him falling in love with was a woman who worked at a bar in Houston. That always tormented the guy. Agusto knew he had visited that same bar last weekend and he was sure he had gone there specifically to see her. Agusto would hurt Pablo by hurting his girl, Patricia. Agusto didn't have many loyal people in Texas at the bottom level anymore. For some time now, he gave them more liberties to grow on their own. Other bosses had come and gone but he always kept an eye on them from afar, which they hated. He contacted a single quiet agent of his which he knew had always been loyal to him. He always treated him right. He never made much noise and always went along with the flow, never saying much nor stepping on any toes. He was perfect for El Diablo. There were a few entrepreneurs who were also close friends to Agusto yet never publicly seen together. Besides, he felt like he couldn't trust most of them. The only way anyone was going to help him was at a price of course. Pablo had strategically disbursed his fortune in all the right places. If his bosses heard of what Agusto was up, he may lose these few loyal people as well; it was the perfect time to act.

Agusto searched through his contacts then pressed against the screen. He listened to the phone ring, then a guy known as Cuervo answered. He said, "Si, patron."

Agusto said, "I have a job I want you to watch over."

Cuervo said, "Sure, what's the job?"

Agusto said, "It's Pablito. I have to test the future ruler. There's a young girl over at that Chula's bar on the west end. A lady P. She needs to hurt Pablo in ways I never will, by never waking up again. I have a lone gunman. I need you to make sure the job gets done. Can you do that?"

Cuervo said, "Diablo, I got you, if you want, I can do the job myself right now!"

Diablo said, "No, not you. You are too valuable to be there. Besides, I wonder if you would get cold feet."

Cuervo said, "But I can do this—"

Diablo stopped him mid-speech and said, "Calm down. There is a paisa there who I'm sure has no ties to Pablo and to who I already gave the contract. I met him there once. I saved him from overdosing and took him to a shelter. I asked him what it was he wanted in life. He told me if he ever grew to have enough money to return to Venezuela, he would immediately leave and never come back. This may be his chance. Just follow the signs. They will put you in touch with him. Be ready."

Cuervo said, "Yes, Diablo, as you wish."

He hung up. Shortly thereafter, Cuervo received a text message, his first instruction. It was for him to go to the Azteca de Oro off of Westheimer and San Pedro Avenue. He will receive new instructions once he got there. When he arrived, he was told to leave his car in front of the building and walk toward the door but not to enter. Someone was going to hand him a red suitcase. The suitcase had clean clothes for them to wear after the hit. All of their current clothes had to go back inside the suitcase and be returned. Shortly after, he stood outside. A guy came outside of the building and placed a single red suitcase on the floor outside of the entranceway. Cuervo took it and returned toward his car. Then he received a text message to approach a blue sedan parked in the first spot to his left, leave all of his possessions including his phone inside his car, and leave it unlocked but to bring the red suitcase. Cuervo looked around the lot then he spotted a badly faded blue car that may have come from a junkyard sitting in the far-left corner of the parking lot. It was an old Caprice police interceptor. The windows were rolled down or missing. Some doors were missing the inner door trim panels, but he glared his eyes toward an anomaly on the back seat. There sat a solid, white, clean bed sheet, concealing objects beneath. He lifted the blanket and saw a box of nylon gloves along with 2 ski masks and 2 black handguns both automatics with extended clips protruding from the handles.

Cuervo reached into the box of gloves on the backseat and put on a pair, then he very cautiously entered the vehicle. As he pulled the driver's door open, it screeched and popped against the fender and caught on a dent in the center of the fender. Cuervo made a cross with his right hand over his head, looked upward to the sky, and said, "Forgive me, father, for doing the devil's work." Once inside. he noticed a note left on the dash. It read, "Wait for the homeless lady." Cuervo looked around the car. It had no key but a switch signaled "fuel," then a button that said "start" next to it. El Cuervo did as he was told. He sat inside until a woman exited the bar slowly and approached him. She seemed like a homeless drug addict. Cuervo waited for her to approach the car and say to him, "Hey, um, you're Cuervo, right?"

Cuervo was already very nervous and shaking. His forehead had sweat running down it. He looked around to see if he was being set up, then he slowly replied, "Yeah."

She said, "Hey, man, I just saw the sign, alright? Calm down. Here, this is for you."

She handed him a badly written note that had liquor stains on it. It read, "Take the blue car to the Sport smart on Kirby and pick up the guy. He's wearing a yellow Laker Jersey. Don't worry, Diablo will follow you." This creepy-looking goth woman walked away then someone else, seeing her job was done, slipped a rolled-up amount of money into her palm while she kept walking by him. Cuervo started the car, which sounded mean, tumbling and shaking like a top fuel dragster ready to go down the racetrack. Cuervo gave it some gas and did a burnout as he pulled off the lot where he picked it up. He grinned at the enjoyment of driving a "Sleeper." When Cuervo approached the Sport smart parking lot, he had a clear view of his accomplice, El Venezolano. Cuervo stopped to see what the guy was doing. He was hanging out with some other guys in the bed of a lifted pickup truck snorting cocaine. He could hear them partying and El Venezolano was saying, "2 years clean, but tonight's a special night."

Cuervo got a bad feeling about what was going on. This guy was going to get them busted by the cops. There's no way he could trust him. Cuervo wanted to call Agusto and call the whole thing off. His gut was telling him just to leave and claim he didn't find him. El Diablo was probably watching him right there where he was. There was no going back on this. Cuervo stayed for a few minutes just watching this poor guy demoralize himself with other losers who probably knew all about what was going down tonight. What a waste. What'd you expect from a person willing to commit murder? He would have to be this twisted to even want to pull off this job. After about 10 more minutes, the guys from the truck got another call to sell narcotics somewhere else. They shook hands with El Venezolano and parted ways. Finally, Cuervo went to pick the guy up so they could get it over with. Cuervo drove slowly through the parking lot approaching El Venezolano, but he may have forgotten his instructions because as soon as he noticed the slow-moving car, he took off running. Cuervo sped up to catch up with him. The guy fell and smacked his head against the floor. He was strong and attempted to get back up, but his head was bleeding. Cuervo got out of the car and walked toward him quickly, looking back quickly to make sure that no one was watching. El Venezolano kept saying, "Oh no, it was a test and I fucked up. I fucked, man, it was just a little bit of coke. Tell Diablo I'm sorry I fucked up. Please, man, don't kill me!"

Cuervo said, "Shut the fuck up! I'm with El Diablo! Get in the fucking car!"

The guy maintained his wide-eyed look. He was in his young twenties, a skinny small guy with scars on his arms of all different shapes. He had some discipline to himself demonstrated by a nicely built muscular long frame. His head was bald with no facial hair. His skin color was dark as they come. The front of his head was bleeding. Cuervo grabbed the guy and helped him to his feet then escorted him to get in the passenger side of the car. El Venezolano fell into the front seat then Cuervo walked around the front scanning the floor to see if either of them had dropped anything. Cuervo noticed a small bag with cocaine in it. Cuervo walked over and picked it up. He held it in his gloved hand before tucking it in his pocket. Cuervo got back inside the car then reached behind the steering column and pulled the shifter down to the letter "D" and accelerated forward. El Venezolano said, "So, the job is on? I was expecting you an hour ago, man!"

Then, El Venezolano said, "What? No music in this bitch?"

Cuervo said, "Shut the fuck up. You got your instructions, right?"

El Venezolano said, "Yeah, I'm supposed to—"

Cuervo said, "Wait, wait, I don't wanna know."

El Venezolano said, "Fuck you, I'm telling you anyway."

Cuervo said, "No! No!"

El Venezolano started telling him anyway. He said, "Her car alarm goes off and when she goes to the parking lot. Bam. The bartender dies."

Cuervo turned and looked at the guy like he had just condemned him for all of eternity. El Venezolano said, "I saw you pick up my coke. Give it to me, please?"

Cuervo said, "Man, fuck your coke. You're flying out of the country tonight not like that! Huh! No way."

Cuervo threw the small bag of cocaine out the window while they were driving onto the expressway. El Venezolano started yelling, "You, son of a bitch! You threw my coke out the window!"

He started punching Cuervo who began serving on the interstate. Cars next to them began honking their horns. Cuervo was about to have a heart attack. He was fully aware of what was at stake. Cuervo said, "Stop it! Stop it! You're going to get us both pinched before we even get to the job!"

El Venezolano yelled at the top of his lungs, "Fuck you!"

Eventually, they both cooled down a bit. They arrived at the bar shortly after 7 PM. It looked like a full house, happy hour. Cuervo parked the car a few buildings before the place to get a good look at it. Cuervo reached for the ski masks and placed one over his head like a wool cap. He handed El Venezolano a mask then said, "I'm going to stay away from all their cameras, right about here near the street. Let's wait for the car's alarm to go off, then you do your thing."

El Venezolano reached for the 2 handguns one at a time. He inspected them. He cocked a bullet into the chamber then waved one in the direction of Cuervo. Cuervo wondered if he were still upset from earlier. El Venezolano pulled down his ski mask and stepped out of the car without saying a word. He walked all the way to the entrance in a straight line. There were two guards at the door. One of them saw him coming. He withdrew his sidearm and fired toward El Venezolano who showed no sign of slowing down. El Venezolano had a firearm in each hand. He lifted his right arm and delivered a single burst that took out both guards along with a guy who was being carded when he arrived. He walked into the main corridor, made his way inside, then using his left hand, sprayed the entire bar area shattering several bottles and hitting several bystanders until it clicked. He looked at his left hand. He was all out of ammo. Several people had taken cover or attempted to make their way out from an exit behind the kitchen. Patricia was his target. However, he was told to make it look random. Only Pablo would know what happened. Patricia and Karina were huddled behind the bar along with a busboy who was caught there dropping off clean classes. El Venezolano couldn't find his mark around all of the scattering women, but when the busboy attempted to play hero by throwing a beer mug at El Venezolano that missed by about 2 feet, he gave themselves away. El Venezolano walked toward him, lifted his right arm, and pulled the trigger, then he caught sight of his mark, Patricia, who was huddled along with Karina. Both of them were shaking frantically. Karina would never know this was happening because of the love Pablo once felt for Patricia, when in fact, she was the true love of Pablo. El Venezolano lifted his right arm and unloaded a final burst that hit several objects behind the two women. 12 bullets may have been unloaded. It only took 2 to find their way, one hitting each of the two women in vital locations. Both were immediately silenced. El

Venezolano ran out of the building the same way he had entered. Sirens could be heard in the background. People were seen standing near their cars taking cover. Some even shot back at El Venezolano missing him badly. Groups of people were still hiding behind the building peering through to see if the coast was clear.

El Venezolano was suddenly completely sober. He spotted the Caprice rolling past the parking lot on the street to the following lot. Cuervo was watching the events unfold, all of it probably taking 20 seconds. El Venezolano ran as hard as he could. He came up to a short fence separating the lots to one side. He figured it could shield him from any attack, so he aimed to cross it. In one bound, he cleared the fence on his side, but unfortunately, there was a 5-foot drop with a small waterway in the brush on the other side. He landed harshly in some tall grass, his feet wet to his ankles. He dropped a gun from his left hand but even in the dark with all this towering grass, he was able to rapidly find it and keep going. He caught up to the Caprice which continued rolling slowly. He threw the guns in the backseat then jumped feet first in through the front passenger side window. Once he was in, Cuervo sped away. There were no police cars chasing them, nor people watching them. They drove aggressively but eventually, slowed down and blended in, leaving the chaos behind. Inside, both gunmen got a sense that "Yeah, we made it, we're going to be ok" mentality. Neither said a word. They just kept driving. While they were stopped at a flashing red light near the outskirts of town, a black Mercedes pulled up next to them. The window rolled down and a guy said, "Follow us."

Cuervo did as he was told, They turned to leave the city then continued for about an hour. The roads kept getting smaller and smaller. They then turned and passed a gate. They again continued for about 5 minutes until they reached a small home on somebody's property. All the lights were off. They followed the Mercedes behind the house then stopped before it turned around with the lights facing the Caprice. The guys in the Mercedes stepped out and signaled for Cuervo and Venezolano to exit their vehicles as well. They did. There were three guys inside the Mercedes. One of them was a young Hispanic guy in very suave business attire. The other two were wearing bulletproof vests and all-black gear. One of them was Hispanic and the other was a white guy who, as soon as he stepped out, went to the tailgate and opened it. El Venezolano and Cuervo got out, then the Hispanic guy in the tactical gear walked around the Caprice and inspected it with a flashlight. He checked the guns and verified they were empty. He retrieved the red suitcase then walked back near the Mercedes.

The business guy said, "There's a camera on the front windshield of this vehicle. Smile at your boss El Diablo."

They were both very frightened. Cuervo had trouble cracking a smile especially when the white guy stepped away from the rear of the vehicle with a huge, modified sniper rifle. Then, the business guy said, "Don't be shy, wave, say something?"

Cuervo waved then El Venezolano said, "Patron, it's done, I did—"

The business guy interrupted him saying, "It's not done yet. There's still one more test."

The white guy held up the rifle, then flicked a switch on the side which shot out a clear red laser onto the chest of El Venezolano. The two guys opposite this scope were afraid, then El Venezolano frowned deeply, put both hands in front of his stomach, nodded his head in acceptance, and said, "Fuck it. I deserve it. Go on."

The business guy got some chatter to an electronic earpiece, then he said, "Congratulations, you passed the test. I need you to change your clothes then get in the truck."

Then, the white guy aimed the laser at the center of Cuervo. He began saying, "C'mon, Diablo, Agusto, I'm your—"

The business guy yelled saying, "Not another fucking word. You'll get us all fucked. Shut up!"

Cuervo gasped and remained still. He understood loyalty can get you killed in this business or any business. You had to look out for yourself. Cuervo remained motionless, frantically staring toward his assailants who could easily set him apart from this world. He was perfectly still except for his left hand which began shaking. Then suddenly, the white guy took his aim away from Cuervo's chest and shot him in the center of his left hand. The recoil stopped it from shaking. Cuervo fell to his knees and pressed on his wound with his other hand. The bullet had gone straight through in the front and out the back. Cuervo was yelling in pain.

The white guy started going over his gun and disassembling it. The business guy walked up to Cuervo then reached into his bright blue sport blazer. Cuervo had a brief thought he was going to get shot again, but the business guy pulled out a hanker chief then said, "Relax. He knows you don't talk. No one trusts pussies. Be thankful it was just the hand. Now I need you to change and get inside. I got a place where they can stitch that up for you. C'mon."

All of them made their way to SUV. The white guy pulled a 3rd-row seat from the floor and sat in it. He apologized to both guys and said, "Nothing personal." He and El Venezolano became quite friendly, cracking jokes and singing songs as they rode away from the property. El Venezolano leaned into Cuervo and said, "Sure wish you had some coke right about now. It helps with the pain."

Once they reached the main road, there was a tow truck waiting for them. The driver of the Mercedes flashed his lights at him. Then the tow truck flashed its lights back before making its way toward the isolated property. Cuervo held his hand tightly. He could feel himself slowly growing weak throughout the drive back. Once they entered town, they stopped at a large well-lit gas station where a woman was ready to pick up the businessman and El Venezolano. He gave the two soldier guys a hand signal. The two soldier guys understood and carried on with Cuervo as their only tripulant. He laid down across the second row slowly dazing in and out of sleep, possibly losing consciousness. The driver said, "Sleeping? We're almost there."

The white guy noticed he didn't look so good. He jumped over the bench seat and sat up next to him in the second row. He had a small syringe of epinephrine which he tore the package open and injected Cuervo with a dosage, then Cuervo became more animated. He said a few words, but it all sounded like mumbling. To Cuervo, everything began getting blurry. He had trouble keeping his eyes open. The truck was driving into the downtown area and the driver was obeying the speed limit and stopping for all lights. The white guy slapped Cuervo on his face lightly. He saw the skin around his eyes began to get pale with dark rings around them. They were stopped in front of a Catholic church. Cuervo's eyes looked over to the entrance. To him, there was light coming from inside the doorway. In his mind, El Cuervo was saying, "No, stop. Let me out here. Let me in!"

The white guy said, "Dude, he's muttering some weird stuff. I think we're losing him."

The driver said, "What? I took eight rounds in Baku."

The white guy said, "I think it's his time."

The white guy looked up and saw the church dim and dark, barely visible, but to Cuervo, it looked totally different. To him, the doors opened, and the interior was full of shimmering gold and silver light. The driver disobeyed the red light and stepped on it. He sped for another 5 minutes until he gushed through an alley and stopped at the back entrance to a dry cleaner where immediately, a guy stepped forward waiting for them. The Hispanic guy opened the rear door. The guy who approached the truck was a Vietnamese man who may have been a medic before immigrating to Houston. He hurried over to the open door, took some basic vitals of Cuervo, then looked up at the gentlemen who brought him and said, "Can do nothing. This man has passed. I'm sorry."

CHAPTER 11

"I'm a straight ridah.
You don't wanna fuck with me."

Friday morning came in Chester Illinois. Inside the parking lot of Menard Correction Facility, a man stepped out of a Chevrolet station wagon. He took a few steps outside then felt a sudden sinking problem in his stomach. Last night's dinner was a microwave burrito that had been in the back of his refrigerator a bit longer than it should've been, but he ate it anyway. This morning, his own previous actions were testing him. He was running late because he overslept. He had trouble sleeping then decided to watch TV. To his delight, the late show had his favorite actress Scarlett Johansson on the set. He stayed up and watched the entire show. This morning, the parole council member thought he could live with the pain and make it through the day. Within 2 hours, he would be interviewing Warren Lee to see if he was fit to be released. He walked into the building through the front door. He showed all his proper credentials and was greeted along the way. The man was the first to arrive inside the reserved room where the parole council met. He found stacks of files with various inmates' names waiting to be reviewed. He could barely control the pain in his stomach. There were 6 people who served on the Southern Illinois Parole council. It was now nearly 9 AM and there was still one councilperson missing, a senior member. Then a call came in stating she was having car troubles and would be unable to make it to today's hearings. A rescheduling would need to take place. The guy with stomach problems breathed a sigh of relief. He could go home and tend to his symptoms. Too bad the convicts he was failing to review could not do the same. Warren was sitting in the hallway when the council members were dismissing the room. Warren was in shock and disbelief. How could this have happened? He overheard one of the guards being told, "All parolees would have to be rescheduled. A council member is having car trouble."

Motors was in shock. The staff had gotten his clothes from storage for him to put on for his hearing. He woke up extra early that morning. He had been waiting for that moment for a long time and now, he would have to wait a little bit longer. Frustration took over his fragile spirit. The guard who had been his longtime friend was tasked with returning Warren to his cell. Both of them said very little the entire way there. Warren hung his head as if a dagger had been placed right through his heart. He was first escorted back into the processing building to change back into his prison pullovers, then walked back to his cell block. The guard tried to give Warren positive thoughts. He said, "Don't worry, Warren, sooner or later, you'll be out. Just you see."

Warren tried to look at things on the bright side but walking in his state-issued clothing really demoralized him. It made him lose a lot of hope. None more than when he reached his room and the door locked behind him, reality set in, he was angered. He failed himself, he failed his son, Warren couldn't take it anymore. He kept thinking about the way it happened because a single council member had car trouble. Really? I could have fixed the car had I been outside, then he thought, *For sure it was the doing of the Outfit.* Laughing back at himself, he said, "Ruining my parole."

A few moments later, another guard went for Warren to his room so he could join the group from his cell block. They were enjoying rec time in the yard. By now, everyone knew Warren had a parole hearing. Seeing him back with a frown on his face only meant one thing: he wasn't getting out. It was a blow to other inmates who looked forward to one day having a parole hearing of their own, a wound to everyone's morale, a sense of rejection. Cruz took advantage of seeing him like that. He suggested to Loro to go up to him and offer him the shank again. Loro walked up to Warren and said, "So, no parole, huh?"

Warren angrily replied, "One damn councilwoman didn't show up."

Loro said, "Man, I'm sure the Outfit had something to do with it."

Warren said, "So, you have that blade?"

Loro looked over to Cruz. He nodded then Cruz smiled.

Pablo was emotionally destroyed after he heard about what happened in Houston Thursday night. He took it as a direct hit to hurt him specifically, which it did. He wanted to run the show and have Karina sit beside him as his queen. Now, that part of his dream was gone. He questioned whether he should go on with the whole thing. Pablo questioned whether he could ever get back at Agusto or if he was ever meant to. He kept thinking of how they both would still be alive if he had never dated them. There was also a heavy amount of guilt on his mind. He figured the monster was him and his punishment was to live with this. He wanted to be El Diablo. Through these obstacles, he would become him. The thought frightened him, but the gears were already set in motion. There was no turning back, but he didn't know if he could carry on. He didn't know if he wanted to. Some of Pablo's most loyal guys went to live in his house serving as protection. The 75s used other methods to further twist the knife in Pablo's side including taunting images on the chatline. One such image was a leaked forensic picture of both women deceased lying next to one another with a caption that read, "Hey, Pablo, isn't that your girl?" The horrific picture was deliberately placed there to break Pablo, and for everyone to see what happens when you challenge El Diablo; you lose. Pablo would lock himself in his room and cry all morning. He sat on the floor just staring at a picture of Karina which she had posted 2 hours before she died. Pablo deciphered and admired every single line, every single color. He lost himself in her gaze. He thought about her and remembered every single word he had ever said to her. His eyes and cheeks would turn red from losing all of his tears.

Pablo didn't go to work. He didn't want to see anyone and just drowned himself in his thoughts all day. At times, he wanted vengeance so badly, but then his heart ached, and he figured he couldn't do it. He didn't believe he could beat El Diablo. He had thoughts of giving it all up. He convinced himself he wasn't good enough alone. He wanted her. He needed her. He felt lower than dirt. His associates in Texas wanted retaliation. They had already begun the trip to Chicago. Pablo was not in any mood to lead a charge. The only reason he didn't give the command to have them turn back was that he lacked the mental strength to do so. Before the end of the day, Houston investigators who had looked into the victim's pasts immediately assumed the culprit to be a disgruntled lover. Pablo was atop the list of HPD's suspect list. They would make multiple attempts to speak with him. He refused all calls. Around noon, Pablo finally lost it. Pablo yelled at the top of his lungs and trashed his own room, topping over his dresser and punching the walls, creating multiple holes, then a lengthy quietness followed. His bodyguards left the living room and hurried upstairs to aid him, but the door was locked. They knocked and called for Pablo to open the door but heard nothing. Then, they heard a gagging sound from inside the room. The guards kicked in the door. They saw Pablo hanging from the ceiling by a noose. He was trying to kill himself. The guards lifted him up from his legs while another cut the noose. It was made using his blanket and leather waist belts. They lowered Pablo to the floor gently, his face already blue. One of them began pressing his chest to get air in him, then shortly thereafter, he began coughing frantically. The guard said, "Boss, you're better than this."

Another of the guards said to Pablo, "El Diablo did this because you can beat him."

Another guard said, "This is what he wants. Patron. don't do it."

The first guard who was overlooking operations that afternoon said, "C'mon, the reinforcements are going to arrive tonight. They need to see you strong and sturdy."

Pablo sat up a little from the floor. He slowly nodded up and down, then he said, "Alright, Let's get him."

Inside the precinct, Juan Vega dropped a file in front of Julissa's desk and said, "See. This is how teamwork works. This is your guy Pablo, right? Houston PD called my buddy Ron over on Monroe. He said a guy from Illinois named Pablo Gutierrez is a suspect in an 8-person homicide from a bar in West Houston that went down last night. Here, they sent over some pictures. Is this your guy?"

She opened the file. There was a copy of his driver's license along with those of the victims, then there were social media printed pictures that tied Pablo to both women that were murdered along with report copies, email addresses, and reference numbers from witnesses. She looked at it and said, "Yup, that's him, but I just saw him here on Wednesday, Houston? Last night, something's up."

Juan Vega said, "Congratulations, the file's yours, no take-backs. We know he was in Houston last weekend. He could have hired gunmen to do the hit."

Julissa said, "From these pictures, it looks like he loved her. Maybe it's from an opponent or a third disgruntled lover?"

Sgt. Vega said, "We know he's dangerous. We do this together, understood?"

Julissa said, "Will do."

Garrett did not go to work on Friday. He drove all the way to Southern Illinois just to hear his parole was postponed. Garrett couldn't even talk with his dad since it wasn't a visitation day. He drove all the way there and back for nothing. He was very frustrated. Garrett was asked if he wanted to go to work at Black Door early which he agreed. While he was there, Jake stopped by for a late lunch. After a while, Jake said to Garrett, "Did you hear about what happened at this bar in Houston last night?"

Garrett said, "Nope, what was the name of the place?"

Jake said, "Chula's, sound familiar? This is what happens when Agusto doesn't get his way. He's El Diablo, bro. Stay away from him."

Garrett said, "I don't need you telling me who I can and cannot hang out with. Get lost."

Jake finished his last French fry, stood up, and dropped a $50 dollar bill on the counter. He said, "Don't say I didn't warn you. The door is always open to you if you want to walk through it. See ya."

Garrett checked to confirm the news on the chatline. It was all everyone was talking about. It was stunning. He was just there. It saddened him to see those girls dead. He didn't want to accept it but maybe Jake was right. Garrett reached out to Pablo, but Pablo never answered. Garrett carried on working. Dayana was scheduled to clock in at 4 PM. Garrett was a bit serious. The news bothered him when Dayana out of the blue asked if he had seen his friend Jake again. Garrett replied, "Why would you think I would want to talk to him?"

Dayana said, "You seem lonely. You should have more friends."

Garrett said, "The only friend I want is you."

Dayana said, "Aww, that's sweet, but I'm serious. You're kind of too serious tonight. Make friends, get out there, do stuff."

Garrett said, "I'm going to visit my friend Agusto later. You want to come with me? He lives in this quiet little town named Aurora. It has this small-town charm about it. I'd love to take you there."

Dayana said, "I can't. I'm working til close, so when am I meeting this Pablo guy? Does he still work with you?"

Garrett said, "Why all the questions? Are you wearing a wire or something?"

Dayana said, "Dude! What's your problem? Why would you be worried about the cops? What aren't you telling me? You know my friend Kelly broke up with this guy who started stalking her then she got a new boyfriend and then her ex-boyfriend ended up fighting with her new boyfriend one night in the parking lot and one of them died. Don't hide things, Garrett."

Garrett said, "Is that what you think of me? I'm a brute?"

Dayana said, "I just really like you and want you to be happy."

Garrett said, "This is who I am. Sometimes, I'm serious and for the record, I am happy."

Dayana said, "Well, I would say you're a work in progress. Alright."

Garrett replied, "Yup."

Garrett didn't think about what Dayana was trying to do, ease him, relax his mind, it was all new to him. All this relationship stuff was unusual to him. It bothered him to have another person giving him attention. Garrett thought about Jake. Maybe he could help him out. Whatever happened in Houston could have something to do with Pablo since his ex-girlfriends were the ones who got shot. Garrett would rely on the truth. He practiced what he would say if Agusto questioned him. He would say, "Yes, Pablo's my friend, but I know nothing nor had I ever heard him say anything about shooting anyone in Texas."

Garrett shook it off. It was silly of him to be a person of interest. He decided to give Pablo a call. This time, Pablo answered, "Garrett, before we have words, I need to know if you're with me or you're not."

Garrett said to him, "What are you talking about? I'm my own man so are you, living the dream, remember? C'mon, man, we could take racing to a whole new level just—"

Pablo interrupted him and said, "Still wide asleep. El Diablo owns you, everything you do he built, and whenever he wants to, he will take it back. Join me. Let's rise above him and show everyone to be his equal or even greater!"

Garrett said, "Aww, man I don't think Agusto is such a bad guy. He did—"

Pablo hung up.

Garrett held the phone to his head and said, "Hello? Hello? Pablo?"

Garrett tried to dial him back, but his phone said, "Unknown-Number blocked."

The seed had always been in Garrett's mind. He felt bad vibrations from Agusto but due to the good favors happening, he was willing to look past it all in good esteem. Pablo wasn't the first person who had warned him to stay away from Agusto. This time, his friendship with Agusto was costing him. Another lesson from a guy who usually was a loner, he lost a friend. Garrett treated everyone nicely (innocent until proven guilty). Garrett had not been betrayed nor felt unwelcomed by Agusto but for some reason, he couldn't keep all his friends and Agusto on the same side. He was being forced to pick sides. Garrett couldn't even fathom the idea of picking favorites. He decided to choose and appreciate everybody. Jake came to mind. Garrett thought about Dayana wanting him to have friends. He knew he would have to break bread with Jake sooner or later. It was now 6 PM. His shift was over. Time to go.

At Menard Correction Facility, Warren was walking in a single file line to have dinner with a group of 50 guys from his and a neighboring cell block. It was an odd dinner where several people who normally didn't cross paths were all in the dining area together. El Bambino and several of the high-ranking Chicago Outfit members would be attending dinner in the same room with Cruz and several members of the 75s along with Motors and Loro. It was unknown as to how the event was orchestrated. Perhaps the staff wanted all the fellas to settle their differences or give in to foolishness and shake hands. El Bambino could have had enough pull with staff suggesting such a notion to smooth things out with Warren or to press him into acting. There was a thought by Warren that El Bambino had gotten tender ears from hearing about what Warren plans to do but he also believed this was how the Outfit was planning to kill him. Regardless, there was a lot of tension in the room. El Loro had acquired money from Motors for the stabbing weapon. In turn, there was an agreement with a member of the 75s who had made it certain that they wanted it back after the deed was done. The weapon was a foreign metal blade that someone snuck in by gluing to the bottom sole of their foot, possibly a guard. Then a handle was made for it using several wet pages from books then pressing them together and carefully weaving dry joined pages around it, exhibiting true craftsmanship, a true thing of beauty. Someone named it "butter." Occasionally, guys who were in the know would say, "You got that butter?" "Naw, I don't have butter. I don't want the butter. That kind of stuff would get you killed."

Cruz was always in the know. He had to do with the unusual dinner arrangement. He claimed it to be a way just to get to know our neighbors. He also wanted to see his scheme unravel right in front of him with front-row seats. What better way than to be there when everything was working as planned? The guards were seated amongst the inmates during the dining hour at Menard, but it was concluded Motors and 75s were waiting to see if they could leave the dining room. Some of the guards stepped into the hallway. There were now only 6 guards in the eating area, but 3 veteran guys were seated and joking alongside the inmates. Things were working out as if tailored. 50 guys were slowly finishing pasta noodles in tomato juice with a light ham sandwich, a few leaves of lettuce, a cup of water, a cup of orange juice, and an apple. Loro was seating close to Warren. He lightly asked him, "So, you want some butter?" Warren knew what he meant. He looked toward El Bambino who was no more than 20 feet away from him. He thought about Warren, then answered back, "Yeah, give me butter!" 75s heard the sign. They were ready to keep the guards from reaching Warren too soon. Loro asked a guard if he could empty his tray. The guard was seated in the opposite direction. The guard said, "Make it snappy!"

Loro got up and walked over toward the garbage can. He placed 2 fingers near his chin signaling to the members of the 75s it was on. He wanted to carry the "butter." The 75s looked toward Cruz who nodded up and down in approval and also placed 2 fingers on his chin. Next, a third guy slid the blade away from his pants and reached around a big guy to allow for an easy grab from Loro as he walked by. Loro made the grab as he shuffled back to his table unnoticed then transferring "butter" into the palm of Warren over the table.

One of the guards noticed his hands. He glanced around to pick up on anything suspicious, not seen. Warren's eyes were wide open. This was it! Go time, everyone in the room knew that something was about to go down. The buildup was felt throughout the room. All the anger came back to him. It made Warren's blood boil and his spine shiver. He clenched his fists, his body now empowered. The guys from the Chicago Outfit began to notice what was going on. Another one of the guards caught on and yelled, "Motors! Is everything alright?"

He thought about what the alternative would be, bottling up his feeling and sucking it all, never to be free. Always thought of as a coward in his own eyes to have never ventured and done something unusual when the option presented itself, that would bother him. The Outfit could not torment him or his son any further. He believed they sabotaged his parole. Warren was determined. If he was going to remain in his prison, his son would be safe from their reach "forever." He was doing this for Garrett, for himself, and for anyone who may have been trapped by the Outfit. The instrument to his freedom was in his hand. There was only one thing he could do, one thing he wanted to do. Motors caught himself. He stood up and said, "I've never been better."

The guard saw the blade in his hand before he could grab his radio to call an alert code for the dining room. Members of the 75s grabbed him and pressed his face into the steel table. Other members grabbed the other guards in the room and covered them as well. Motors took his note. He lunged toward the table where the Chicago Outfit was seated. A friend of El Bambino tried to interfere and hold Motors from reaching his leader, but Warren clobbered him with a fierce left hand that caught him square in the mouth dropping him immediately. With his right hand, Motors held the "butter" firmly, his index finger following the metal as if his index finger made the tip. El Bambino was seated there ever so still, giving him his right side. Warren hit another guy then pulled him over his shoulder, throwing him rear hard. Warren growled as loudly as he could then he thrusted the "butter" into El Bambino's ribcage below his right shoulder. He pulled his hand out then pressed the "butter" into him one more time, then another and another. Motors had done it. He had gone mad.

Immediately, the other members of the Outfit knocked Warren down before he could get any more stabs. They began to beat him profusely. Warren took several closed fists straight to his face and feet stomped all over his body. His head was beaten against the floor repeatedly. He passed out. The "butter" was stolen from his hand. A small riot broke out in the dining room between the Outfit and the 75s mostly over recovering the instrument of destruction, "butter." Warren and El Bambino laid gushing blood onto the floor. More guards assaulted everyone inside the room. Pepper spray and rubber bullets were flung into the air. Warren was still alive when the guards took control of the situation but he had sustained a lot of damage throughout his body. Both of his hands and legs were broken. He had broken ribs, massive bumps, and hemorrhage on his head. They called for the medic. It was hard to believe Warren was still alive. El Bambino was helped from his stool onto the floor. He held his side gasping for air. It was too late. His friends were around him as life slowly left his body right there on the floor. He was twitchy but managed to mutter out some words to his friends. He said, "Dammit, I forgot to do my bed this morning." Then he passed away. He was known for being an example person as he was always educating those who followed him.

Warren was rushed to the nearest hospital. He was in a critical state. The ambulance sped past the prison gate with the beautiful glow of a red sunset visible ahead of them. It was just past 7 PM.

Garrett pulled into Gene's high-performance shop in West Chicago. There was a trailer that had "BMS Performance" on the side of it. It would be the first time Garrett sees the car he will be driving on Saturday night. As soon as he entered the building, he laid his eyes on the car. Agusto was trusting him with a brand-new Type R NSX. It was a beautiful screaming canary yellow color with several custom-molded carbon fiber panels. On the front, there were vents formed around the hood which fed aluminum intercoolers mounted in the front much larger than factory equipment. The front bumper was not the one that came with the car. It was squarer looking instead of wide pointy, the headlamps had been disassembled, and they had painted the background accents to match the car. The emblem was gone but the car had an air splitter mounted beneath the front bumper cover with the words airbrushed on it in lime green. It read "*Type R.*" The wheels were slightly bigger in the rear. The dishes were polished aluminum with the center painted chrome smoke 19 inches in the front and 20 in the rear. The car had no badging. A thin strip on the rear windshield as if it were engraved in white paint read, **"BMS PERFORMANCE."** The adjustable suspension was given some tweaking then programmed to go lower when at higher speeds. The engine is mounted behind the driver. A twin-turbo V6 engine working with electric motors up front all synced together to put down nearly 900 horsepower to the floor. The exhaust was hand-built and tuned for this particular setup by Gene himself. The chrome pipes with the blue, faded tips looked like cannon barrels from out of either side from the lower bumper cover. There were rubberized, painted panels closest to the exhaust followed by some carbon fiber inserts, but the paint just popped on the rear bumper like a highly polished canary yellow lollipop inviting you to take a lick.

Garrett said, "Wow."

Garrett walked all around then stood beside it. He asked, "How do you open the door?"

Gene went over. The door was mostly yellow but there was a spot to the rear of the glass which was black in color. He pressed the triangle area and the door opened in a diagonal pattern out and up. It sounded as if the door was spring-loaded. There were 2 strikers for the door visible to the rear of the body and another small one to the bottom along with the kick plate. Garrett sat inside. The seat was modified with a thick seat belt harness. The steering wheel was removable. However, it was currently mounted on the column. The instrument panel was the factory. There was no obvious change other than the programming to the ECM. Hector opened the passenger side door then dropped into the passenger seat then he said, "It's all wireless now. Here, download this app onto your phone then I'll show you how to use our upgraded track settings interfacing with the factory ECU."

Garrett was in complete awe and said, "Whoa."

Hector began going over the basic operations of the car with Garrett. After a while, Gene went over and said, "Make sure he learns it. He only has a single day to get familiar with this beast."

Garrett said, "Oh, I'm keeping this!"

Gene said, "Tell you what? If you trash it, it's definitely yours. Driving this thing in town, you'd be lucky to come back with half."

Garrett said, "What if I win?"

Gene said, "Maybe I'll loan it to you on the weekends."

Both of them had a good laugh. Garrett stepped out of the car all smiles. Garrett stood there just admiring the car in front of him. Agusto walked into the shop and in a deep voice, he said, "Get familiar with this car and don't lose tomorrow. I have a lot riding on you to win."

Garrett said, "Are you kidding me? This thing is a rocket ship. I can't lose."

Agusto said, "When was the last time you spoke with your father?"

Garrett said, "Last week? His parole got canceled. I'll be down there this Sunday."

Agusto answered, "Maybe you should start accepting the fact he may never be released. I'm just saying."

Garrett said, "Don't ever say that again!"

Agusto said, "Your father is not in a place where society releases those with dark hearts. It's where they chose to be. Trust me."

Garrett said, "What do you know? You don't know anything about my father."

Agusto said, "You're right. I know nothing, Garrett, but I can teach you how to have the world at your feet. Maybe you will?"

Garrett said, "I got to go."

Agusto said, "Remember, don't lose tomorrow. You will live to regret it."

Garrett was taking the NSX. From now until tomorrow night, he was instructed to get familiar with it. Garrett secured his harness then started up the NSX in the shop. *Heaven,* he thought. Garrett drove by Gene, Hector, and Agusto. Gene told him he would call him in a few minutes. If he needed to be towed back, they would be ready. Garrett nodded. Garrett drove the car very aggressively. It was crisp. It felt like it could cut through the air, a very nimble and safe feeling. He trusted he had picked the right car. Garrett got his phone call from Gene. They talked about tune and comfort as well as safety and performance. Everything he said was congratulatory toward BMS. Garrett stopped in a grocery parking lot to examine the outside of the car and to play with the adjustment settings on it when he received a phone call from his mother. She told him "his father was in critical condition after a fight at Menard." She was very sad. She told him everything she learned from the person who called her. She said, "He attacked the Outfit and lost. He was taken to a hospital in St. Louis."

Garrett was saddened and angry. Gene texted him to get a good feel for the car and that's exactly what he had in mind. He turned on the radio. Gene had been listening to the classical rock station. The song was just starting and very fit for the moment. Garrett set it to track mode. The song was Ram Jam "Black Betty." Garrett cranked up the volume and drove the NSX hard! He pushed the car hard at every turn and pressed the accelerator pedal as deep as he could on the straightaways. He fishtailed onto the expressway ramp then immersed himself into cautious traffic, just what he was looking for, test his handling even if it looked like a reason to injure himself. He quickly weaved by everyone leaving them behind. The instrument cluster said 148MPH, then 158MPH, then 159MPH, 160. He saw the flashing lights of patrol cars behind him, but they were so far back they stood no chance of getting him. He received a text message from Agusto that very same minute, "Don't break it before you buy it."

Garrett screamed at the top of his lungs, "Aaahhh!"

Then he hit the brakes very hard. The NSX spun out of control doing perfect circles in the middle of the expressway. Out of his own luck, he did not hit any other car on the road. When he came to a stop, he was inches away from hitting the median. Garrett felt powerless as if he lived in a cage and there was nothing left for him to do but to conform, yet it wasn't what he wanted. He wanted out of the cage! He wanted to drive forever and that's what he did. He left the city driving fast into corn country. In his thoughts, Garrett started pointing fingers at his father's situation, first at himself, then at Agusto. How dare he! Who the fuck does he think he was to even talk about his father's behavior! Then it hit him. Agusto really was el Diablo. Everything from how spiritual Agusto spoke to how people never wanted to cross him—they all feared him. How did he know all the stuff he does? How does he manipulate everyone? Garrett knew he was not strong enough to confront Agusto but as he kept driving, he said to himself, "One day, I will be." Garrett kept driving the car, enjoyed his little sprint, and idled at stops inviting for more. Garrett changed the radio station. He found a song he enjoyed that also fit the occasion. It was Yellow "Lost Again." His fists were tight, clenching with the steering wheel as hard as he could squeeze it. He decided to return to Black Door and see Dayana but he was now a different person. He was fierce and angry driven by hate. When Garrett arrived, the place was packed. He drove all the way to a handicapped spot next to the door and parked the NSX there. He went inside and as soon as he did, Dayana could tell there was something wrong with him. He broke and told her about his father being critically injured after a fight in prison. She gave him a hug then said, "It's a good thing your friend Jake is here. Maybe he can help you?"

Garrett said, "Jake?"

Sure enough, Jake was seated at the end of the bar. He tipped his left index finger from his eyebrow toward where Garrett was standing to acknowledge him. Garrett walked over in heavy strides. He grabbed Jake by his leather jacket then raised his right arm ready to strike him. Dayana saw him and stopped dead in her tracks, "Garrett!" She gulped as hard as she could in fear of what she was seeing. Then Jake said, "Is this who you are now? Do it. Go on."

Garrett caught himself. He thought about how he looked to the world. He stared around the room at the people who were staring back at him, Dayana included. Garrett held his arm. He refused to do it, then a guy in the chair next to Jake got up and walked away quickly. Garrett let go of his jacket. He was still breathing heavily then Jake said, "Everyone has a choice, your father, and heck, even you. I can choose to beat you blind right here in front of your little girlfriend but I'm going to be the bigger man and see if you would join me for a beer."

Garrett nodded and said, "Sure."

Jake took a long drink from his beer, then he said, "Life sucks, huh?"

Garrett corralled himself in the chair next to Jake then he exclaimed, "uh-huh."

Dayana backed off a bit and went into the back, crying. Garrett frightened her. Everything Garrett was doing recently was nothing like the guy she had worked with for such a long time nor the guy she had grown to like. It bothered her. Dayana definitely knew she does not want that in a guy. It's a huge turnoff.

Back at the bar area, Garrett asked Jake, "How did you hear about my dad?"

Jake said, "No sorry about that grab? Or anything, huh?"

Garrett said, "Did you find out because El Bambino is dead? My dad killed him?"

Jake knew everything that had happened a few hours ago, but as a regular tough guy, he would never admit to anything, He said, "How do you know who that is?"

Garret said, "C'mon, bro, I would see him at Menard all the time. I googled him."

Jake said, "Ever googled your pal Agusto Reyes?"

Garrett said, "Yeah, but only good things come up."

Jake said, "Do you still believe in Santa Claus? It's all bullshit!"

Garrett said, "No, bro, I don't. I actually want to hurt him, but I don't know how."

Jake said, "Look, man, vengeance is really quick to a cold steel slate. You don't want that, bruh. Don't even think of it. Cause your thoughts can mess you up."

Garrett said, "Well, fuck bro! I live inside a fucking cage; this guy is playing me! Everyone is. I got to do something for me or, or this will never go away!"

Jake said, "Did you not hear the words you just said, Merlin."

Garrett said, "What the fuck are you talking about?"

Jake said, "You just laid down a big curse. Your thinking that he's playing you makes him play you, but he's not what you just think he is because somehow, his aura, his reputation made it so. And you and all the silly people following him make it so. In reality, he's just like you and me. It's simple. Don't fear him."

Garrett said, "What? That's some kind of Stonemason, Illuminati type of stuff?" Garrett turned his head and glared his eyes at Jake, then he said, "How do you know about this?"

Jake said, "All men have a heart to think with and a mind to love with. Don't ever confuse who you are."

Garrett said, "And who am I?"

Jake said, "The person you want to be."

Garrett said, "The Outfit taught you all this?"

Jake said, "Your father actually."

Jake stuffed his face with a handful of French fries then threw his shoulders up while flipping his eyebrows next to Garrett, watching. When he finished chewing, he took several gulps from his beer then instructed for another beer. Jake turned to face Garrett then he said, "The myth hurts you, not him. You must see past the words and see him for who he really is, a cold-hearted criminal. Trust me. There are a lot of people who have fallen due to him then praised him for getting them back to where they started. Do you owe him anything? Does he have you pinned with any crimes?"

Garrett had a long stare into a glass in front of him then slowly said, "If he did, why would I tell you?"

Jake gave Garrett a pat on the back then he said, "Don't."

Jake came forward and said, "Look, man, if he's your friend, that's cool. You guys made some money together, fine, whatever. This racing thing, I'm sure he's got other plans. Maybe one of these days, he's going to blackmail you or turn you in, I don't know. There have always been guys doing this, probably since the beginning of time, and I'm sure there'll be someone doing this after he leaves this world. As long as people are afraid or gullible, it'll always go on."

Garrett said, "Well I'm not going to stand for it anymore! I never signed up for this! I'm going to stop racing for good!"

Jake said, "Dude, chill, that may be your true calling. I've seen you in action, you got talent. Well, second to me (of course). Look, man, just behave and don't think like you live in a cage and you won't. Who cares? That's why you should think with your heart. It's pure. When you pick with your mind defensively, eventually, you'll lose it to what your heart wants. Push comes to shove and you'll leave things thinking like, 'I don't even know this guy,' but if your heart's in it, they would have to prey it away from your cold, stiff fingertips before you give something up. The problem is heart and mind are loyal to the host. If he's strong enough, he can control them both. If the host is hardworking, there may be multiple ambitions in his heart and the will to get them all done. Supporting the host with that kind of intensity is hard. Nobody can live like that forever. Eventually, you have to pick one."

Garrett said, "Fine, I'm going to keep racing. I love it, but what does El Diablo love?"

Jake said, "I have no idea. I don't know if there is a God. I don't know if aliens are watching us or maybe we are all gods. Whatever our will desires usually gets done. This sounds like gods to me. Look, man, I can say that certain things always repeat themselves as if by code over and over and over again until we get it right. If you stop the thugs from taking your money overall, they have less. If enough people stop giving them reasons to, they could eventually go broke, then maybe even get a regular job like you or something. Every single act counts. You have a future in driving. Leave Agusto alone. It'll hurt him in the long run. Trust me!"

Garrett stood up from his seat angered and said, "Forget this! It's all gibberish If you won't help me. I can do this on my own!"

Garrett stormed out the door in such a hurry. He didn't even say goodbye to Dayana. She saw him leave and then she saw Jake motion a squeeze of his thumb and index finger signaling he would be right back as he exited after him. Jake caught up to Garrett in the parking lot and yelled, "Hey, wait up!"

Jake looked at the bright yellow NSX. Garrett was about to open the door. Jake said, "Whoa! You're driving this tomorrow, nice! Look, man, I'm on your side. Whatever you want, I'll help you out."

Garrett said, "Get me a gun."

Jake said, "Why does this not surprise me? Nobody can be told what the matrix is. They need to see it. Okay."

Jake flapped his hand wanting Garret to follow him to his Mach1. He opened the driver's door, sat in the chair reaching under the passenger seat, then pulled out a snub-nosed revolver. At the exact moment that Jake handed the gun over to Garrett, Dayana was exiting the building to say goodbye to Garrett. She saw him taking it then putting it under his shirt. Her heart sunk inside her chest. She was heartbroken.

Jake said, "If your mind is made up, I want you to know who helped you."

Garrett said, "Thanks, man, I won't forget this."

Jake said, "This is the worst thing a friend can do for another friend."

Garrett said, "Naw, that would be giving each other a bullet. These have Agusto's name on them."

Garrett climbed into the NSX then stored it in between his racing seat and the center console. He turned the car on and sped away.

Jake stood there watching him and the car. He said, "You're about to do the same thing your father did. On the same day, huh. Brother, we are worlds apart."

Jake turned and caught Dayana near the door wiping clear her tears. When she noticed Jake was looking at her, she walked away. Jake went back inside just to pay his tab, then he decided to leave. He got inside his car and drove away. Jake caught himself in thought then grinned and said, "Wow, now I'm the devil, encouraging destruction."

CHAPTER 12

"All my friends are heathens. Take it slow."

Elsewhere in town, a convoy of SUVs and Lowriders were invading the parking lot of a motel on the near west side of Chicago. All the vehicles had license plates that said "TEXAS" on them. Pablo's STI shortly showed up along with his own convoy of 3 Suburbans and a total of 15 guys with him. 30 guys from Texas were waiting for him to arrive. Pablo was showing leadership qualities appearing as if the events of yesterday had hardened him instead of made him weak. What happened earlier today gave him a new lease on life. He wanted to destroy El Diablo and conquer everything he has before his final breath of air comes for real. Pablo walked to the center of all these hardened people. He stopped then he said, "Thank you for coming out here. We're going to take everything El Diablo has! No one messes with us! Nobody! Today, we become the rulers! Today, we become the generals! Let's take it!"

Pablo's voice cracked a bit at the end of his speech. The guys were too hard to yell "hoorah" or clap or salute. They did however nod in approval at that time. Some gave each other slight pats on the back. Pablo was wearing a jacket with a collar on it flipped up to avoid showing the fabric burns on his neck. He cleared his throat, looked back at his main bodyguards who were immediately behind him, then he spoke again, "In order to take the kingdom, we need to slay the king! There is no better time than tonight! He expects to lure us to an attack tomorrow but that ain't going to happen. No more taking orders or having things on his terms. We move on El Diablo tonight. I have eyes on him that says he is working late in his shop as we speak. I am the new king of Chicago. You are my Angels. We are the righteous hand of the sky. Now, let's bring death and darkness to El Diablo! Let's go!"

This time, there was a heroic cheer. They threw up their arms and said, "Yeah!"

Pablo said, "When we get back, we'll feast, and there will be a hundred females waiting for us!"

An even louder roar came out from the group. Fists were pumping skyward. Pablo grew a smile on his face. Then one of them said, "This is for Chula's!"

A younger guy poked a question to Pablo, asking, "Pablo, what happened at Chula's? Why'd it go down like that?"

Pablo looked toward the sky and took a deep breath. His eyes started getting watery, but he managed to say, "It was El Diablo trying to hit me right in the chest and it worked. But I assure you, I won't return tonight until he or I am dead. Now, vamonos!"

All the guys boarded their respective vehicles and dispersed in all different directions. Pablo was confident he would succeed. He had everything going for him in his favor. Above all, he had no fear he would do what is necessary. All rules were thrown out. He knew he would justify the events of last night. He played some Tupac music to keep himself pumped up. With an edge, he drove his STI with conviction the entire way there. Nearing Agusto's warehouse, there were members from his hit squad visible to those who had just arrived. It was nearly 10:30 PM on an eerie Friday night. Light fog masked the far end of the street. Most houses had their front lights on. Once all the men who were at the motel arrived, little was said. Everyone was holding their best firearm, bulletproof vests were strapped on, and rosaries were kissed and tucked in under their shirts. Then, the bandanas and Halloween masks came on to conceal their faces. Pablo led the group forward for a march a block away. Anger kept Pablo and the rest of the guys focused. Pablo had a firearm mounted on his side. In his hand, he held a small automatic machine gun with the extended stock humped against his right armpit. A message came into Pablo's phone. It said, "He's still there."

Pablo's pace grew faster. All of their shoes could be heard shuffling along the asphalt road. When they reached the front gate, Pablo looked further down the block to see if his Aurora lookout could join them, but the guy he saw standing at the corner where he ordered his guys was not the same person. He signaled everyone to stop. They did. They laid there in silence for a few seconds. They could hear light Mexican music playing from the inside of the warehouse. It looked as if there were only 2 guys standing at Pablo's lookout post and no one could be seen inside. It looked easy. Pablo signaled to apprehend the 2 guys at the corner and surround the warehouse. The Texas hit squad did just that. A team of 3 with their rifles drawn went for the 2 guys on the corner but before they reached them, one of them went for a gun. The other took off running. Both of them were immediately shot dead. That was when the gunfire broke out. Teams of men were hiding on top of semi-trucks and inside neighboring homes, Pablo and his men took cover wherever they could find and returned gunfire. Pablo's men were skilled shooters. They held their ground and began entering the property from various points. They overwhelmed Diablo's guys who were part of his ambush, took their positions, then began trying to enter the warehouse. Pablo proved to also be a skilled fighter. He knocked one out with a hard-right-handed fist. The team enjoyed a moment to scavenge and reload before entering the building, only to be suppressed by more gunfire from inside the warehouse. Pablo yelled out, "Take cover!"

The word was out. Diablo had summoned reinforcements as well as the local police force. Agusto began retreating deeper and deeper inside the warehouse trying to avoid being shot before they arrived. Pablo was pinched against a wall inside along with a group of his guys. He could make out Agusto's voice nearby and based on the different sounds of gunfire, there may have been 2 or 3 guys remaining with him. Pablo went around the outside of the building to a window where he could peer inside the room. As soon as he did, somebody shot toward him barely missing him. Pablo fell to the floor just avoiding getting shot bullets burst through the wall where he would have been standing had he been standing. When the glass broke, small pieces lightly cut Pablo on his face. He began bleeding. He did catch sight of Agusto in the room, then he heard them leaving the room to the rear of the corridor. His guys shot one of them. Pablo went to a further window. He had a clear shot of Agusto and one other guy. He aimed his automatic but no bullets came out. It just went "click, click." The guys noticed him in the window but instead, went through across the corridor through a small conference room and into the warehouse area. Pablo went back to the front of the building and entered it. All of his guys had eyes pointed in every direction. One of them said to Pablo, "They're in the warehouse."

Pablo said, "Let's go. You guys cut them off from entering the corridor. Let's corner them in the warehouse."

A steel barrel rolled next to Pablo. He pushed it away from where he was standing and dove behind it. A second guy ran behind him to another safety spot. They were both taking a lot of gunfire. The barrel illuminated from so much gunfire ricocheting off the drum. Pablo asked his fearless backup shooter, "What's your name?"

The guy said, "Homero Beltran."

Pablo said, "As soon as they go for the recharge, we open fire!"

The guy nodded yes in agreement. Pablo went for his second pistol holding one in every hand. They heard the click then took no thought about it. They both raised to their knees and opened fire. They hit both men who fell to the floor. Pablo surveyed the warehouse searching for any other shooters. None were found. The rest of the guys entered the room, but sirens were clearly audible, getting close very fast. Agusto was nowhere to be seen. Most of the men started retreating and disbursing as fast as they could. Agusto slowly got to his side and sat up against the wall. There was a rear door that exited the building to a fire escape platform that went down 2 stories into a wooded area leading to train tracks behind Dearborn. Pablo took notice he was headed there. Pablo found him wounded. Reaching for the door handle, he said, "Stop!"

Agusto stopped in his slow crawl and drag then slowly got to his feet before turning to face Pablo and said, "I didn't think you could be strong after the blow your heart took. I underestimated you. I'm sorry. You're more resourceful than I give you credit for."

Pablo said, "What was meant to happen, happened."

Agusto said, "Not yet. It hasn't."

Agusto was within 2 feet from the fire escape. He used his last strength to throw himself at it, flipping it open and lunging off the platform outside. Pablo unloaded multiple times along with Homero next to him. Pablo ran to the fire escape and peered over the rail but could not see him. Homero said, "Only the real Diablo could survive that. He's dead, man, c'mon, let's go."

The two men hurried out the front of the building running full speed the entire length for 2 blocks to their cars. The first squad car arrived on the scene from the opposite direction. At that very moment, they could see Agusto's supporters just stood idle watching. They knew what had happened. Some of the young guys waved at Pablo. Pablo raised his right hand and waved back. He had won. He wanted everyone to know it. The kingdom was now his! The cars started up and left without erratic movements. Neighbors by now had taken to the streets and a few caught a brief glance at the flashy STI leaving the area. Nobody wanted to put the pieces together even though everyone rightfully knew what had happened on their block.

Before the hit squad had made it back to Chicago, a wounded Agusto made it 4 blocks crawling to a house of one of his most faithful friends. He knocked on the door. When they saw him, they picked him up and carried him off to the basement. Agusto asked to have all the lights turned off. They obliged.

An Aurora investigator questioned a wounded guy who said he heard them say they were from Texas. The investigator made the call to a sergeant already working on a similar case, Sgt. Juan Vega. It was now 11:15 PM, Friday, when Sgt. Vega called Julissa, he said, "Hey, it's me. Something happened and it's about your uncle. It seems like a bunch of Texas boys came down to stop him. I'm heading out there right now. I can pick you up in 10 minutes."

Julissa replied, "Ok."

As the hit squad reached the motel on the west side, the area was blocked off to normal traffic restricted to only Pablo and his people. Taqueros were called to cook for the team's private party. The area smelled delicious. Several women from all over northern Illinois came to hang out with the victors. Businesses gave them entire tubs of beer for them to enjoy their feast. Pablo had done it. He was on top of the world! With the deep smell of Barbacoa and Arracherras in the air, the new king of Chicago had delivered as he had promised. Everyone was having a good time. His men suffered only two casualties which they would take with them back to Texas. There would be no sleep for any of them that night. Several women approached Pablo and gave him hugs and kisses but one caught his eye. He walked over to where she was sitting down and introduced himself. He said, "Hi, my name is Pablo."

She said, "Natasha, so is there room for a new queen in your kingdom?"

Pablo took a deep breath and said, "Absolutely."

In an Aurora basement, Agusto was near death when the lights turned on after they brought a man to operate on his bullet wounds. He still had bullets in his body and had lost a lot of blood. He looked pale and his eyes were bloodshot red. They put towels over the windows to cover up any light from leaving the room. The doctor injected Agusto with morphine. He began losing consciousness. Agusto muttered, "Please let me die."

The doctor looked over at the owner of the house. Further allegiance to Agusto depended on whether Agusto survived or not.

The guy looked down on the body of Agusto Reyes, then he told the doctor, "Patch him up."

Sgt. Vega arrived at Julissa's condominium building. He sent her a text message and waited for her to come out. Julissa eventually came out taking the passenger front seat of the black police-owned Blazer. Once she entered, she said, "Can you stop for coffee?"

Sgt. Vega said, "Aren't you worried for your uncle? There's a chance something bad happened to him."

Julissa answered, "So, now you care for him?"

Sgt. Vega replied, "Innocent until proven guilty. Why are we falling behind on these Texas guys that were your lead?"

Julissa replied, "Because all I have are shadows. They know somehow. Ugh, all I want to do is put a bullet in these guys."

Sgt. Vega said, "Is all this too personal for you? Did I make a mistake giving you this case?"

Julissa replied, "No, Sir."

After some silence, he said, "I have to fuel up. It's quite some way out to Aurora."

He pulled into a gas station, exited, then asked Julissa, "Decaf 2 creams?"

Julissa said, "You know it."

They drove out there the rest of the way pretty quietly, but Sgt. Vega said, "There's more to your uncle, Juli. Do you now believe your uncle is the big crime boss some officers believe him to be? Don't you think these Texas boys are here for payback from Thursday night?"

Julissa said, "What do you mean?"

Sgt. Vega continued, "You can't see it, can you? For a while, things in town have been running smoothly. The underworld, if it's in your uncle's hands, has been somewhat steady, but the rate remains high. The ones paying the price are bad 'hombres.' But if you ask me, something changed. This Pablo guy must've stepped on your uncle's shoes and is retaliating hard which in turn Pablo had ties with these Texas boys and they all went to Aurora to take your uncle out."

She looked at Sgt. Vega in shock then said, "I don't believe any of that!"

Sgt. Vega said, "It's hard, I know, but you must learn everybody can change, even you. If you want to remain who you are, then practice staying within your willpower. Approach everything neutral and assume nothing. I have been betrayed or pressured into looking the other way, but I have refused to. Looking back, I realized those people betrayed me. They betrayed this shield. Betrayed their family. Betrayed themselves. Remember, assume nothing. I feel blessed every day I leave my house, appreciate every single day, cherish the small things like when my wife makes meat casserole. Whatever happens tonight or tomorrow, I can say it's been a great life."

Julissa smiled, "Has she made the one with tuna and chorizo again? You're favorite."

Sgt. Vega said, "Don't remind me."

Julissa laughed because she had some on a visit to his house. His wife was trying a recipe she saw on late-night television. The following day, they joked about how awful it was and how much they cringed while they ate it. Sgt. Vega replied, "Like I said, she was experimenting that night. Just happened you came over, jeez. Damn."

They approached the warehouse shortly after midnight. Before he exited the truck, Sgt. Vega saw a flashy yellow sports car drive in the opposite direction. Sgt. Vega told her, "That guy might be lost. Watch your back. These Texas guys could still be around. And don't say too much. We don't know if these Aurora cops stand in relation to anybody. Don't mention he's your uncle. They might think we're working with him."

She nodded. They exited the vehicle and walked toward the warehouse. Sgt. Vega introduced himself then referred to Julissa only by her first name, then he said, "What do we get here?"

The Aurora commanding officer began to go over how they suspected the scene took place. They went over most of the vehicles on the lot pointing out bullet holes. All of them owned by Agusto

Reyes, Julissa made her way to the office where her uncle conducted his business. It was empty. There was no visible blood anywhere, a small relief. Technicians were analyzing the surveillance video. Sgt. Vega asked where Agusto Reyes was. They sped forward to reach that part when Pablo shot Agusto from behind the steel barrel. The fire escape door opened and Agusto flung himself outside. She asked the technician to find an outside camera. They did but it showed Agusto plunging to his death. Her face grew frightened. She looked over at Sgt. Vega then rushed over to the rear of the warehouse where there were other officers already at the bottom investigating where Agusto landed. Julissa went around the building asking some officers with dogs to assist in tracking Agusto from behind the building. They agreed and joined her. There was a path that had drips of blood. She always assumed she would find his body over the next patch of tall grass, but the dogs just kept going. They made their way to the rear of a house. It was the house where Agusto had gone to for help. The officers used their flashlights to look inside the basement windows. They could see nothing due to it being so dark and vast. The owner of the house opened the door and said, "Can I help you?"

Julissa said, "We need to take a look at your basement now!"

The guy said, "Sure"

He opened the door and turned on the lights leading to the basement. The officers hurried down the stairs. Julissa was the third person to go down. She held her hand on her sidearm but when they reached the bottom and saw what was there, there was nothing, no sign of Agusto ever having been there. The scent from the dogs grew cold. There was nowhere else for them to go.

Saturday morning, Garrett awoke with a bitter taste in his mouth. He hated that when he finally made the drive to Aurora last night with a gun in hand, he arrived late to the shootout. He returned home and found comfort in a bottle of Jim Beam with about 25 ounces left. He drank the entire thing himself while crying in silence in his room. He felt like a coward. He walked over to his bathroom and washed up. It was 7:15 AM. He had 45minutes to get to work.

Remembering he was driving an Acura NSX lifted his spirit. He buried the events from last night like they never happened. Garrett was no longer happy where he was. He thought about quitting, leaving town, and hoped Agusto was dead. Was Jake really his friend or was he being set up by someone he never really knew? He decided to do what he had always done, be himself, trust himself, and things would sort themselves out. He made it to work with plenty of time. Garrett stepped out of the car and turned back to look at it. At work, no one asked anything about where he got the car. Several people went up to it to admire and take selfies with it, but not a word as to why he was driving it.

Pablo awoke in a room at the motel with 2 naked women at the top of him. He smiled saying to himself, "It's good to be king."

Julissa stayed up all night going over the warehouse, looking for evidence or clues as to where her uncle could have possibly gone to, hoping she could find it before the local authorities do. Julissa was in pain thinking that maybe the worst had happened to her uncle. There was an APB issued for Agusto Reyes. 6 Northern Illinois counties had patrolmen on the lookout. To no avail, she left frustrated and disappointed. Julissa gathered the information recovered and left the crime scene in the morning with another officer from her precinct. Sgt. Vega left home around 2 AM. Julissa took her gathered intel then asked to get dropped off at her office Saturday morning. She claimed to take a cab home. The officer agreed. She did not want to accept it, but she always knew there might have been something illegal about her uncle's dealings. To her, he will always be her sweet uncle August. Yes, she knew of his problematic past, but she was too young back then to compare him next to a criminal. The man she knew was an accomplished scholar. A determined entrepreneur, he was the guy who never says "I quit" and never gives up on anybody. She realized she was too vested emotionally to keep working on the case. It was a strain on her emotional well-being. She looked at the clock. It said 10 AM. A fellow detective came in, walked up next to her desk, and said, "You look beat. Go home."

She plainly agreed with him. She stood up, placed her jacket over her shoulders, and said, "Thank you. Keep me posted, will you?"

Julissa exclaimed, "Will do."

She was mentally and physically exhausted. She called a cab and fell asleep in the back seat. The driver had to wake her once they had reached her building. The guy was repeating, "Officer, we're here! Officer, Officer, we are here!"

She uncurled herself, placed her hand above her face, then raised her head squinting her eyes. She paid the driver then exited the cab saying, "Thank you." She went inside and immediately fell asleep.

On route 30 heading west past Hinkley, in an empty semi-truck parking lot, there was a white cargo van parked in a spot with newspaper taped to the rear windows to keep anyone from seeing what was inside. The van may have been used for polishing laminated or hard surface flooring. There were brushing machines and several types of fabric pads and brushes everywhere along with rolls of hoses. In the center, there were stacks of towels and blankets. Some of them illuminated red with the stain of blood on them. It was Agusto's blood. It was his body lying under the towels and wrapped in a blanket. The blanket had a roll of duct tape which had been spun around his ankles, then around his knees, his shoulders were still free to move. They left the top part of him uncovered to check if he was still breathing. His face was partially covered. He opened his eyes and took in his surroundings noticing a pair of shovels near him. There was a heavy number of bandages wrapped around his middle torso. El Diablo was still alive. A guy opened the door to check on him. The sun was at its clearest. The inside of the van was the warmest it had been all night. The guy who opened the door may have been 17-20 years old. Once he pulled open the door, Agusto's eyes closed in pain. It was too bright for his eyes. Agusto said in a battered voice, "Where am I?"

The guy did not answer. He just stood there, then he looked down as if to wonder what his next move should be. Agusto repeated his question this time in Spanish, "Donde estoy?"

The guy said in Spanish, "Vine a checquar te. Aver como estavas."

Agusto looked toward the shovel and said, "Y eso?"

The guy replied so cool and casual, "Por si te avias muerto."

Agusto answered in English to himself saying, "Hurray, I'm still alive."

Agusto took grace in hearing himself, slightly chuckled, then he replied, "Ya ves que no. Llerva mala nunca muere, quien los castigara?"

The guy didn't know what to say or what to do. He just stood there again and looked to the floor. Agusto helped himself to sit up then said, "Mi ropa. Anda, y me llevo la van también."

The guy said, "Es que acá de hacer las pases Don Braulio con el Nuevo Rey y me mandaron desaserme de usted."

The guy's boss had made a deal with Pablo and was sent to ensure Agusto did not return to Chicago ever again. They had pleaded mercy to the new crime lord Pablo. This poor guy had probably been out here all morning waiting for orders and when he finally gets them, Agusto woke up. Unknown to Agusto, there was a .45 caliber revolver tucked in the back of this guy's pants, but he suspected it. Something deep inside of Agusto gave him that level of wisdom. He leaned forward acting to be coughing clinching with his left hand while reaching for a glass bottle with the right. He got it and in one quick motion, arched back and slung the bottle forward hitting the guy, but he managed to put his arm up to shield himself. The bottle did not break. It ricocheted and flew high into the sky. The guy was shaken but not unconscious. Agusto taped legs and all, flung himself forward from the van, then on top of the young man. He was wearing nothing but his boxers. Agusto overpowered the guy, dropping him to the ground. The guy went for the gun but just managed to fling it 5 feet to one side. Agusto slammed the guy's head against the gravel floor. His punches were weak, but he still pounded at the guy several times. Unable to entirely defeat the guy, he made a play for the gun. Agusto got it, but the guy held his hand, keeping him from getting a clear shot. Agusto squeezed the trigger firing a bullet into the sky, but it damaged the hearing of both men momentarily. They were both in pain. Agusto's wounds began bleeding. A thin bead of blood ran down the front of him. The guy punched Agusto in the ribs which left him breathless. Agusto took the pain then sharply head-butted the guy square in the nose. He began bleeding profusely spilling all over his face. Agusto used his body weight to undo the guy's grip on the gun away from him. He did it. He had possession of the weapon. Then using the butt end of the grip, Agusto repeatedly hit the guy on his face with it, over and over and over again. The guy laid there dead. Agusto fell over to one side and looked skyward. He was hurt but still alive, free again. A few moments went by. Agusto had thoughts of leaving town, leaving everything, and starting a new life somewhere else. He had accomplished everything he wanted to do in Chicago. He believed the city was in a better place now that he had organized its people through fear. He exclaimed, "Only the strong survive."

Agusto undid the duct tape seizing his legs, then he slowly got up and walked toward the van. He found his clothes on the front seat. They were damaged and bloody. He traded some items with the guy who he had just killed. Agusto took some moments to catch his breath but he needed to dispose of his guardian and leave town. Things seemed to be pointing in that direction. Agusto loaded the guy in the van then drove westbound until he stumbled upon an old small cemetery, perfect to conceal the guy. Agusto got out of the truck and looked around, nothing but flat green fields, not another soul for miles. He looked skyward and said, "This is your work. I am but a messenger."

Agusto pulled out a shovel and began to dig a grave for the poor guy. He was weaker than normal but still sturdy enough to manage the task at hand. It took him nearly 4 hours to get to about 5 1/2 feet deep. To get out, he had to lock his legs on the opposite side then push himself upward until he could get a good grip and pull himself out. He was so exhausted he rolled out of the hole and just lied there on the grass for several moments. The sun would go down soon. It had been a beautiful Saturday afternoon. He brought out the guy. He burned anything that could link back to him inside the hole. Agusto felt bad for the guy, but he convinced himself that this is what God would have wanted for him. He believed everything always happened at exactly the right time, always and forever. Today was no different. He just happened to be too loyal to the wrong guy, perhaps deserving his fate.

Agusto gave the body a slight push. The guy came to a resting place exactly how he was meant to, longways with his hand on his chest facing upward. Agusto looked at him for a moment. The guy looked as if he was praying, wrapped like a sarcophagus. Agusto caught his breath then gazed again skyward. He yelled, "If you had given him to me, he'd still be alive!"

Agusto began raking the loose dirt he had pulled out next to the tomb into the grave. His mind was racing because he was serious about leaving town but kept wondering if he really was making a difference. Had he helped anybody back in Chicago? If he really would have saved the guy, had he been instructed to teach him the ropes about life? When he was almost done, his strength gave out. Agusto fell to his knees then he yelled, saying, "Pablo, yeah, what about him? Oh. You're right. I made him! Too good of a man? Maybe, I can't save them all. Just as you did with me!"

Agusto began crying. He could see this monopoly ripple effect playing out in his mind, the yin and yang taking on a pyramid 3D effect, which trickled down to every single person he had ever come in contact with. He yelled, "Fine! I will not walk away! I will not leave you! You will not leave me! You hear that! I want this. I will continue down my path and destroy what I have created hoping you can do the same!".

A crack of lightning went off in the distance. Agusto rose to his feet, the strength of him now returning to him. His muscles seemed to radiate in intensity. He was hit with the last of the sun before it hid behind the horizon. His body swelled in fulfillment as more oxygen rushed into his veins. It renewed his face and the dark rings around his eyes. Agusto said, "I will worship your will. You may have my strength for I am your messenger. I will spread your message. This I pledge."

Agusto's mind was racing. He could see the events of the next 12 hours but in multiple options. The chosen path had not yet been taken. He finished burying the young man then noticed the guy's wallet was in his pants. He opened it, saw his name, then took a knife and carved his name on the surface of a block of wood which he pressed into the ground above him, "Orlando Puga." Agusto then gave the guy a moment of silence before driving back into Chicago. It was now 7 PM. Everyone would be in for the retaliation of El Diablo. He had no plan. He would just ride it out. He trusted in his options. He just had to not want it too much and believe it will happen.

Julissa was now back at work. She wanted to arrest Pablo. She had a patrolman stationed a few houses away to look for him, but he wasn't there. It was now dark and still, there was no sign for him or anyone leaving or entering his home. Julissa decided to investigate some leads on her own, then she went by to check in on the patrolman. She pulled up alongside the squad car and said, "Anything?"

The patrolmen said, "Nothing."

Julissa wanted to take over his shift. She said to him, "I'm 1811. I can take it from here."

The patrolman agreed then drove away. She took the same spot where he had been and made herself comfortable. Shortly thereafter, she received a text message from Sgt. Vega. It read, "No heroes. Keep me posted."

Julissa texted back, "Ok."

Julissa sat there for a while. She had a delivery service bring her a sandwich and a large cup of coffee. Around 10 PM, she saw something, a dark Tahoe with Texas license plates pulled up to the house's driveway, then a group of people stepped out. The person from the passenger side front was Pablo. A full entourage of 4 guys walked along with him. They also entered the home. One of the guys stayed outside near the front of the house and looked around. He caught sight of Julissa's car. He began walking toward it when another guy called to him saying, "C'mon, get on inside."

She was grateful he turned around. She was outnumbered. Julissa decided to move to a different spot on the other side of the block. When she found a spot, she had no time to call it in. The group of men soon turned off all of the lights, entered their vehicles, and left. The Tahoe drove toward them. She was very visible to them. The guy who noticed her earlier said, "Hey, that chick's trailing us." Pablo took note of the MK5 as he passed. He also noticed Julissa from when he saw her at NTB. He began thinking that she was a police officer. Julissa turned her car on, went down to the intersection, and made a U-turn.

One of Pablo's guards said, "Hey, I know that broad."

Pablo said, "You know all the women?"

Another guy said, "I think that's Dona Chita's granddaughter. She lives next door."

Pablo said, "She's a cop. I can feel it."

His driver said, "She's going to follow us."

Pablo answered, "Let her. This is too big for CPD. The only thing they can do is follow us."

The vehicle continued on its course. His friends from Texas had already left. All monies were already paid and even if they did arrest Pablo, they had nothing on him. The race was about to begin but he didn't even have to be there. Everything was set. Julissa had to keep a very far distance to avoid being noticed. Pablo didn't even mind. Deep inside, he liked her. She was very attractive to him and presumed he would get a chance to charm her. He knew his path and Julissa's would intertwine. Pablo headed to a location halfway between where the drivers were to meet. He waited for the green MK5 to come behind it, but it didn't. He figured she had lost him or given up, but she was being cautious and stopped off to a side avoiding being seen. The guys switched vehicles then headed to an area near the starting line of the race. He would personally greet the underworld's most famed figures and driving enthusiasts before the race. Pablo knew of the events that took place in Menard Correction Facility and he knew Garrett would be there, but he would tell him the truth if confronted. Pablo had no interest in carrying out any plan to have Motors kill El Bambino. It was Cruz and El Diablo's work. Pablo remembered when Garrett denied to automatically side with him, but he was in such a good mood he would offer his friendship to Garrett again. Pablo liked Garrett's chances in the race. He might actually win the whole thing. It would look bad if Pablo arrived aggressively toward any race car driver. This night, Pablo would be assuming Garrett had pledged his loyalty to him. If not, he would kill him in the morning along with Cruz Santiago and any other person who were still partial to El Diablo.

Most of the racers were part of the criminal underworld from around the country. Some were celebrity amateur drivers who had always lived like bosses in their own right. They all had big attitudes and big egos, people who enjoyed taking risks and raising the bar in life, along with a passion for driving fast cars. Jake and his GT were a late entry, but he agreed to plead himself and his crew loyal to Pablo, assuring him the guys from the Franklin Park area would now side with him. Pablo agreed and accepted the late entry. Jake was the kind of guy who always survived. He did not have a dumb bone on his whole body. They would begin at I-90 and Touhy Road then race into downtown while all surveillance cameras would be hacked to feed Pablo and his spectators all the action. They had high-powered cameras atop buildings and drones which would aid the video production. All drivers had been sent a link to open a virtual map as they drove highlighting the route. Pablo would set himself up near the end of the race. Everything would happen quickly. He mustn't spend too much time at the start so he may nestle himself inside Agusto's very own penthouse as he would have wanted to do, then party with the drivers after they arrived.

At the same time, Agusto had made it back to Aurora. There were police everywhere still on high alert from the acts of the night before. Not only that, but he did not know who he could count on and who he couldn't. Agusto snuck into his home, cleaned up, and decided to make noise against the newly crowned king. He suspected he would find him near his condo in Greektown. Agusto took his own race car from his garage, a rare Vantage Austin Martin he cherished greatly. He ignited the ferocious V8 and sped off out of his garage.

CHAPTER 13

"She's out of sight and I'm out of my mind."

The race car drivers met at a gasoline station near Touhy. They all began arriving shortly after 11 PM. Among the first to arrive was a Porsche GTR2, a beautiful 720S, then a pair of guys showed up with Missouri license plates, driving Focus RS's both with a metallic blue wrap and racing number on the sides. Jake arrived in a dark matte grey wrapped Mercedes Benz GT R along with a following of cars which included the driver of the RX7 from 2 weeks ago. He too was in the race. Jake's car had smoke color wheels and bright yellow brake calipers all around. The car looked fierce and sounded like an Indy race car, high revving. There were 2 other Chicago guys driving along his side. One of them drove a white Nissan R35. The other was driving an MK5 Supra. Both cars were amazing to look at. A driver with Ohio license plates showed up in a brand-new Cadillac CTS-V3 carbon edition that sounded like a stroked big block with a deep throaty rumble, which resonated through the floor. The driver was an older gentleman, maybe in his late 50s, a bit of a Walter White character wearing a fedora, but his age did not deter from his game. There was a Lexus SUV following him with 4 beautiful blondes driving it. They all climbed out and hugged their esteemed boyfriend caressing him profusely while everyone watched. The women said to him, "You're going to win." "Oh, you got this."

A modified Mustang GT350 showed up. The guy looked familiar like he was a professional basketball player. The bass from his speaker system drowned the noise from his exhaust. The bass could be felt standing 20 feet away. A young woman pulled up driving a Z06 Corvette, then immediately following her, Garrett showed up in the NSX. Garret drove right down the center of the drivers. They had aligned themselves in a set of 2 rows facing the center. He went to the far end and parked the woman in the Z06 and said, "Hey, nice car."

Garret replied, "Thanks."

Most of the people were keeping to themselves but Garrett stepped out and began trying to mingle with the other drivers nodding his head to everyone, waving. Jake was standing with his crew next to his car watching Garrett thinking to himself, "Please don't come up to me. Please don't come up to me."

Garrett walked over admiring Jake's car then said, "Hey."

Jake did not know if Garrett had made amends with Pablo. He needed to be sure. Jake might need to stand up for the guy if Pablo got hostile, but why would he? He thought being seen talking with the guy could be hazardous to his freedom. Jake nodded and said, "Hey."

A silent car snuck up behind them and took the next position in line. The driver was an Asian guy with no license plates on the rear of the vehicle. The car itself a rare piece of beauty. It was a brand new fully electric, Lotus Evija. The next car that came in was a Tesla roadster, and the driver may have been a good friend with the driver of the Evija since they were joking and teasing one another from the moment they parked. That driver of the Roadster was a big man in a little with a flamboyant attitude to match he said, "I know we haven't started because I haven't won yet. Where's the host with my prize money?"

A bright copper color Ferrari eased to a stop on the street next to the parking lot far from the gathering of drivers. A serious-looking woman was driving it. The rear license plate said Minnesota. They were all there at the meeting point. Everyone was gathered who was scheduled to be in the race then a motorcade of SUVs arrived at the gas station. It was Pablo along with a small army. Julissa kept a lot of distance between the SUVs, but from afar, could see what was happening. Immediately, she called Sgt. Vega and notified him saying, "It looks like another race is underway."

Sgt. Vega said, "Where? Juli, do not engage. These guys are dangerous."

Julissa said, "I'm staying on Pablo Gutierrez."

Pablo made his way around the lot from one driver to the next. They exchanged contact information and Pablo agreed to do business with them. He also promised to give each one a better deal. Pablo was a bit silent when he approached Garrett, just saying, "Thank you for coming."

Pablo completed his round then walked to the center of all the cars and said, "Ladies and gentlemen, again, thank you for coming here tonight. I will leave shortly and meet everyone at the finish line. Everything will be made electronically. You'll receive the course at a link. All winners will be paid then there will be a party downtown. All night long!"

People cheered, then Pablo began again, "Everyone of your moves will be monitored, all traffic and streetlamps will be cleared in your favor. This is what you get when you work with me, the world bending itself to suit us. $10 million for first place, $8 million for second, and $2 million for third place, just enough to spice up the night. In a few moments, follow your device to the start line and get ready to race!"

Garrett was excited. He smiled and looked over at Jake who had some words for him, "Glad you didn't do anything stupid last night. Don't do anything dumb now. If you see me, just let me go first."

Garrett said, "Yeah, right, that money is going home with me!"

Garrett went over and mounted the NSX to wait for the link to appear on his phone. Pablo and the people who were not racing left to greet their contenders at the finish line. Garrett sat there strapped up in his harness engine off. Some of the other racers had neck support braces and very nice helmets placed on their heads. Suddenly, the link came in simultaneously to all the drivers. It was now after midnight. All the cars turned on. The sudden burst of noise coming from the cars shook the ground like thunder. Garrett set his phone inside a cup holder. The link showed him a set of arrows to reach the starting line, then he began to make his way there. Garrett had an icon of his yellow car in the lower center of the screen. It followed every move he made to his exact location as if peering down from a satellite. Once he approached the starting line, a red icon stop sign told him to stop where he was. He was behind a red light in a staggered formation with the other drivers.

Once all the cars were in place, their phones began a count down from 20 seconds. The pressure was building. All of the cars were revving their engines waiting for the final seconds to count down. At 5 seconds, all the streetlamps stopped flashing and remained solid red. Then, the display on their phone changed and showed the following street in a 3D bird's eye view slightly ahead of them. They were to turn right into a long circular onramp and head south on 294. The streetlamps all went green at the same time. All of the drivers dashed insanely forward trying to get ahead of one another before the first turn. The starting line was next to the Chippewa Woods reserve. The loud noise was tremendous and earthshaking. The ground trembled as the race cars drove by. The Cadillac had a lot of straight-line power. It nearly made it to first place ahead of the pack. Garrett was somewhere near 7th. Jake was in 3rd. He started in the second row from the start. The Lotus Evija was firmly in 1st place. As the cars began to make the first turn onto the ramp, the streetlight was flashing green. The other 3 directions were held with red, stopping oncoming traffic. This gave the drivers the confidence to push their vehicles as hard as they could. Jake passed the Cadillac in the long round turn on the onramp taking 2nd, while the 4th and 5th cars bumped into each other. The Mustang was on the inside of a Ford Focus RS which was pushed off the ramp by the Mustang and landed on the grass area where it got stuck unable to keep going. Garrett now took 6th.

Julissa had continued following Pablo from afar. Pablo was now arriving at Des Plaines St under the 290-expressway bridge. Julissa declined to tell Sgt. Vega where Pablo was. She assumed he would leave soon. Besides, she wanted to be subtle and look for strays she could manipulate for information. She wanted to get answers for herself on her own. Pablo now had a group of spectators around him, all of them watching the race on their phones or tablets. She was too far to pinpoint people. She got out of her car and walked closer to a bus stop bench then used the zoom feature on her phone to get a better look. Meanwhile, the same one of the guys who spotted the Supra earlier again saw it parked down the way on Des Plaines certain it was the same car that was parked near Pablo's house. He began to make his way toward it.

The race cars were flying down I-94. They switched positions and pressured one another. They approached their next merging highway, a narrow ramp to I-90 East into the loop. The view of the Chicago skyscrapers was phenomenal. Garrett pressed the NSX even harder just to keep pace with these crazy drivers. They were fearless and reckless but showed some skill. Garrett had his work cut out for him. He had a feeling of guilt coming from breaking the law. This was not a closed course. He could die. The car did not belong to him; he had to be cautious, but cautious is not what racing is about. Garrett had fallen back to 10th then the Ferrari squeezed by him, dropping Garrett into 11th. Some of the lead cars were reaching 150 MPH and swerving in between traffic. Garrett accepted to be deliberately breaking the law, then he began to press the NSX forward. Some of the cars were tuned for low torque, others for turning or high-end power, yet the more exclusive cars could do everything. Well, for them, their position laid entirely with the driver. An Audi RS 5 was doing well above 120 MPH, was ahead of Garrett in 10th place, but he passed him, then it began fading away in his rear-view mirror. In 9th, a Mazda MX-5 Miata RF was screaming down the road with its turbo glowing beneath the carbon fiber hood but soon, it too was taken by Garrett's NSX, fading to the rear pack. In front of Garrett, the Evija proved to be an exceptional road machine. It was in 1st place, followed by a McLaren 720S in 2nd, and Jake in the Mercedes GT 3rd. A Nissan GTR followed in 4th then the copper Ferrari in 5th, a Porsche 911 6th, the Mustang was in 7th, and the Cadillac 8th. They rounded out the top positions in front of Garrett. Garrett could see the Lotus Evija, but he didn't know if he could catch up to 1st. Garrett adopted a different strategy. He would not use the brake at all. Instead, he would just be downshifting and accelerating in the curves, testing the suspension to the brink. They were now deep in the loop passing Western Ave.

Back over on Des Plaines, Pablo's guard was taking strides reaching closer and closer to where Julissa had parked her car. He verified the car to be hers. She did her best to hide near the bus stop. Just then, the roar of a throaty V8 could be heard. It was Agusto in his Vantage Aston Martin. There were guards and cars blocking a direct shot to Pablo, so the Aston Martin stopped near the intersection. The pitch-black power window scrolled down. Agusto stretched out his arm with the tip of a handgun peering outside before it fired. The guard fell struck by a bullet. The Aston Martin accelerated away. Pablo's guards boarded a pair of SUVs in hot pursuit, tires began squealing. One of the guards yelled out, "That was Agusto!"

Another guy said, "But he's dead!"

Pablo reached upward then pulled himself from where he ducked avoiding gunfire. Then he yelled, "Let's get him!"

Julissa realized it was Agusto in the Aston Martin, so she ran to her car to aid her uncle in the pursuit. Agusto hurried around the Chicago Downtown area attempting to evade the group of SUVs behind him. He maneuvered around narrow streets to avoid giving them a clear shot at him. The SUVs eventually caught up to him.

They began shooting, extending themselves outside the window to get a better shot at him. Several bullets hit the car. Then, a new shooter joined in on the chase. It was Julissa in her MK5 Supra. She drove and put pressure on the SUVs from behind the convoy. They raced through streets littered with skyscrapers on either side. The Aston Martin took substantial damage, but most of her functionality was still there. The echoes from the exhaust came off the glass buildings perfectly. Julissa got a clear shot on the driver to the last SUV and took it, disabling the vehicle, sending it crashing into parked vehicles on the side of the street. There were 3 more SUVs in between her and her uncle's. She hurried to the next one. When she caught up to the third SUV, she sacrificed the beautiful exterior on her MK5 pressing the front fender into the rear tire area of the SUV then turning into it quickly. This sent the vehicle sideways where its front end caught a parked vehicle and spun out uncontrollably. Julissa struggled to recover control of the MK5 coming to a complete stop before crashing into a steep curb. She put the car in reverse, regained traction, and hurried to catch the other 2 SUVs who were right behind the Aston Martin.

On the expressway, Garrett now in 7th, he noticed his phone indicated they would be leaving the expressway and heading east on Fullerton. The Avija slowed down due to the abrupt exit which he was unfamiliar with. He thought how if he stayed at a higher gear for longer, he may be able to come closer to the first 5 cars that were now within reach. Garrett did not use the brakes going down the ramp. It was a very dangerous play. He swung out far and then cut the steering wheel early and wide without hitting any of the other vehicles. He passed a car. He was now in 6th. He accelerated before the apex of the turn. Even with all-wheel drive, he worried the rear end could swing out, but he managed to make the turn work. The car was screaming. He had gone into a lower gear. Garrett upshifted, then the car pulled forward. The racers approached an urban intersection. One of the drivers slowed down and checked the traffic. Garrett thought, *Big mistake.*

Garrett passed the number 5 car there, taking 5th for himself near Damen. He kept his aggressive pursuit in full force. The NSX and Garrett were in sync with one another. The cars in front of him were the Lotus Evija still in 1st place followed now by Jake in the Mercedes GT in 2nd. Then, the McLaren 720S in 3rd with the Porsche now directly in front of Garrett in 4th. They kept a high speed above 80 MPH. As all vehicles hurried through the urban area, there would be a stretch where the street would narrow significantly with a lot of people walking nearby. Members of the 75s were attempting to keep people off the street, but just then, the race cars flew by, at speeds nearing 100 MPH intimidating pedestrians. Garrett could not afford to be cautious. He had to push his car, but he recalled the area and remembered it was troublesome with potholes. The Porsche caught a pothole. The front rim shattered. The car cross-steered in the opposite direction across the path of the NSX slamming into parked vehicles. Garrett quickly reacted taking the lane the Porsche was in, then he took his spot in 4th. The racing convoy continued past Racine and Sheffield. After Halsted, the route became silent and eerie. The racers coasted on the small and narrow street one after another with no space to spare. It ended into a spur that fed into Lake Shore Drive just after the block. All the cars slowed down forming a tight single line formation to head South on Lakeshore. The Evija was fully electric and slowed a considerable amount on a bridge with a steel floor approaching the wider road. Jake made a bold move and passed the Evija. The driver may have gotten caught sightseeing or looking at his screen for the next turn, but he lost the lead. He mishandled the Evija accelerating which made it lose traction. He slowed down to catch it again but the 720S and the NSX showed no mercy. They passed the Evija on the bridge with the steel wire mesh floor. Jake looked back and noticed the NSX in 3rd. He reached out the window and gave Garrett a fist pump. He was happy for he was in the lead. Garrett wanted to pass Jake. He maintained his killer instinct. He knew the road very well. Garrett would have to find a spot where he could pass the McLaren and position himself to take the lead.

The three cars raced in a tight formation. As they passed Navy pier then approached the first intersection, it was when Garrett noticed the Lotus Evija was hot on his trail and closing in fast. He couldn't stop him nor was he willing to be fearless and try to block him from advancing. Garrett decided all he could do is drive his best race and if the guy passed him, he passed him. Garrett was focused forward and avoiding making any mistakes. Now the four cars were closely together. Garrett pressed on hard. A few citizens made it difficult to maneuver. The Evija fell further back and Garrett narrowed the space with the 720S. There was a lot of traffic near Buckingham Fountain when the racers passed by. The 720S took a poor route which let Garrett pass him and now take 2nd. Jake and Garrett, the 2 local boys, were confident about being in their backyard. Garrett was still pressing on. He believed he could get in line to make a push and take the Mercedes. He peered back into his rearview and noticed the 720S and the Evija had taken some damage to their front end.

Meanwhile, Agusto was losing speed in his Aston Martin. The car was sputtering, and he was wounded along his left leg and his bicep. He was also still bleeding beneath the bandages from the night before. Agusto struggled to control the car with only one hand. He took a ramp last minute to lower Wacker Drive then the front SUV crashed into the rear of his Aston Martin sending the sports car spinning out of control. The SUV came to a stop and all of its passengers stepped out, then walked over to the mutilated car ready to finish off the deed. Agusto checked his sidearm. It was empty. They stood there watching the car for a moment, then when he did not return fire, they slowly made their way up to the car. The second SUV came down the ramp. Pablo exited the vehicle but as he walked toward the Aston Martin, the MK5 came down the ramp. Julissa stopped her car sideways, allowing it to protect her as she opened the door then took cover as they sprayed her car heavily with gunfire.

Julissa reached the rear of her car then opened the rear hatch. Once open, she reached over and found a duffel bag. She pulled the heavy object toward her. She opened the duffel bag revealing a G36C assault rifle. She inspected the magazines then attached them and prepared for firing using the scope which was dual optics equipped. She peeked forward then quickly picked off 2 guys using a pair of subtle bursts, the nozzle humming a steady beat line as she pulled the trigger. The remainder of the guys now took a shielding position behind their trucks. Julissa walked around her car then hurried behind nearby columns. She crouched slightly to anticipate their gunfire, then after they shot, she moved to shoot the guys who had shot at her. She killed 2 more. Pablo was heard boarding an SUV then squealing the tires leaving very quickly. She came out from behind a column only to have 2 guys shooting at her from nearby. Pablo would get away. She caught a glimpse of one of them, then she switched from burst to single shot. She slowly peeked with the barrel of the gun around the large pillar and when she saw him, squeezed off a single round that caught the guy on the top of his head. He fell over forward. The last guy decided to make a run for it. He tried to evade her running up the next ramp. The guy could go behind a wall which would put him out of her sight, so she aimed for him at about a foot before the guy would be covered by the edge of the wall. She needed to pull the trigger at precisely the right time to hit him. She pulled the trigger and heard the thud of the guy falling face first in full stride. She had killed him. Julissa went up to the mangled Aston Martin and said, "Hey, bet you're glad to see me."

Agusto said, "Thank you, but you should've let that guy complete his destiny."

Julissa said, "What do you mean?"

Agusto was gathering himself and said, "Don't change. Call your boss and go home."

Agusto slowly got out of the car and said, "You're hurt!"

Agusto said, "I got to go."

Julissa said, "I can get an ambulance coming."

Agusto said, "No, there's a guy in Pilsen that can stitch me up. If I don't make it, just take care of yourself."

Julissa said, "I can go with you."

Truthfully, Agusto suspected Pablo was going to take his place as the new Diablo in the Midwest. Agusto would have to rebuild and take it back by force much the same way Pablo had, but tonight is not the night. He had endured some of the worst pains known to man in the last 24 hours and didn't know if he could overcome it, but he didn't want to worry her. She had to come away as the best detective in town. Agusto answered, "I can manage. I'll take the first SUV. There's a race going on. The finish line is in Greektown."

Julissa said, "Wait, how do you know Pablo Gutierrez?"

Agusto answered, "Because he is El Diablo. Now go and arrest as much as you can."

Julissa nodded agreeing. She helped Agusto into the first SUV. She closed the door then returned to her car. It still worked. It was clear to her Pablo was the real underworld kingpin. She called Sgt. Vega. As soon as he answered, he said, "Hey, where are you?"

Julissa replied, "There's a major street race ending in Greektown. Get all units to the area right now!"

Julissa sped off in that direction. Nothing was going to stand in her way. She wanted to kill Pablo and rid Chicago of evil forever.

Inside Garrett's NSX, the map interface showed they would turn west on Roosevelt Rd. Garrett feared the end of the race was nearing and he wouldn't be able to win the race. Garrett was performing well. Getting through the night without damaging the car should be enough of a win for him. The fact of receiving money is just icing on the cake. They made the turn, then flew past Michigan Ave. speeding over 100 MPH, then they quickly passed Clark St. speeding across the bridge. Up ahead, there was a pair of semi-trucks making a turn north from Roosevelt to Canal. They were facing the direction of the race cars eastwards and turning northbound would mean the lead truck would cross in front of them. It had begun to make its turn. The cars were still half a block away but approaching fast. The race cars weaved around the slower-moving vehicles as they approached the intersection, then Jake made a maneuver to cut in front of the moving truck to beat it before crossing the westbound lanes. Garrett went into the oncoming traffic. The map said they were to continue west until Halsted. The McLaren 720S driver tried to get too fancy and squeeze beneath the 53-foot trailer. The 720S came in hot and executed a hard right to cross beneath the trailer at an "X" angle, but the car got clipped by one of the rear tires sending it spinning out then slamming into the front of a commercial building. Garrett and Jake remained at the forefront. They stared each other down then continued accelerating forward. They flew past Clinton and Jefferson neck and neck in a virtual tie. They had to slow down as they approached Halsted. Neither one of them wanted to give in to the other, but after making the turn, Jake held the inside lane. He remained in 1st place.

Garrett attempted to hold the RPMs of the engine higher for a longer time, but he just couldn't slingshot around Jake. The turn was too narrow. He had to avoid hitting the back of Jake's Mercedes. There was a good amount of traffic still on the road making it harder to attempt passing. Garrett had the faster car but couldn't find a good spot to attempt it. The cars flew past U.I.C., then rushed over the 290-expressway bridge. On their map, a checkered flag icon could be seen nearby. They were going to go as far north as Madison then turn east. They made the small, short turn keeping in file a small number of cars who were also in the race that was now close behind them. Garrett saw they were going to head south on Des Plaines Rd. He guesstimated the checkered flag to be close. If he was to come in the first place, now was the time to take the lead. He would not decelerate but take a lower gear and accelerate again going wide at a high speed. Garrett noticed a parking lot to his right, but the random placement of cars ruled it out as an option. The terrain was rough as well, not good. He had a split-second decision to make and he took it. He sped around the corner as if the NSX was stuck on rails, controlling his speed and steering. He was continuously accelerating while pulling the steering wheel with not too much oversteer and not too much understeer. He looked over and saw Jake had executed a much sharper turn. Maybe he thought Garrett would settle for a second. Garrett added a lot of speed. The momentum threw him to the far-left side of the street and he slowly inched by Jake until he passed them. All the buildings rumbled with the noise from the car's exhaust. They could all see the finish line on the screen. It was on the intersection before reaching the 290 overpass. Garrett and Jake pushed their vehicles hard. Neither wanted to let off any pressure from the accelerator, then Garrett crossed the intersection. The display on his screen replied, "1st place" "1st place" "1st place."

Pablo reached Greektown after the drivers had finished the race. They were already parked in a reserved area ahead of the finish line. Pablo arrived but was wary as to if he should stay. He warned the drivers the police were on their way so several of them decided to leave. He approached Garrett and since several bosses were still present, he congratulated him and assured him his payment would go through this exact moment. Jake and the driver of the Evija were also still present. Pablo bumped Garrett's fist and said, "Congratulations, you're now 10 million dollars richer."

Garrett verified the payment on his phone, then said, "Thanks."

Pablo saw the pistol tucked in between the seat and center console and said, "Is that what you were going to do if you lost?"

Garrett winked then said, "Just for protection, you know."

Pablo began calling his close friends who he left on Wacker Drive. None of them answered. Jake had friends in Pilsen. At that very moment, he was told Agusto had been seen entering a tire shop. Jake went over to the NSX to talk with Garrett. Jake told him, "Hey, you still want Agusto? I know where he's at right now."

Garrett said, "Where?"

Jake answered, "A tire shop in Pilsen named Santos Tires. I can go with you."

Police sirens were heard getting close to Greektown. The few people who were still there began to leave the parking lot. The old man driving the Cadillac yelled at Pablo saying, "I thought you had the cops covered! Amateur!"

Garrett responded to Jake. He said, "No, I might not be coming back. This one is for my old man."

He turned on the NSX then hurried off Southbound. Jake received a call. He answered it. It was Agusto. He said, "Is he coming?"

Jake replied, "Just as you said he would."

Agusto said, "Even with all that money, evil does not hide. Let's see what he does."

Jake hung up. Over in Pilsen, Agusto was being worked on by an old man wrapping up his thigh. Agusto kept drawing a circle with his index finger in the air thinking of the events that were unfolding. Suddenly, he caught himself then made an urgent phone call, apparently to a police officer who worked alongside Sgt. Vega and Julissa. When the person answered, he quickly asked, "Is she with the sarge?"

The voice on the other end said, "Negative."

Agusto hung up the call. Something was wrong. He could sense it as if he had been outwitted by himself. Agusto wanted to leave and go find Julissa, so she did not confront Pablo. He was worried he would kill her. Agusto looked at his clothes then told the old man, "Let me borrow your pants."

Back in Greektown, the guys could hear sirens getting closer. Pablo was embarrassed they had ruined his coming-out party to the other crime bosses. It was time for him to leave but before he boarded the SUV, he saw Julissa's MK5 appear. He held himself from getting into the truck and instead, went to the tailgate and retrieved a large Carbine rifle with a grenade launcher attachment on it. Pablo pounded his chest yelling, "This is my town! I'm not going anywhere!"

Pablo's guards did not leave Pablo by himself. He had conquered a lot of stuff against incredible odds this week. They believed they would celebrate more victories alongside him. Julissa saw him taking aim with the assault rifle. She stopped and exited her car just before

Pablo hit it directly with a grenade. It exploded behind her. A pair of squad cars could be seen from the north end of Des Plaines. Pablo and his men annihilated those officers inside. Pablo for the moment had the upper hand. Then, another group approached from the east which was also dealt with by Pablo and his gang. The Chicago Police Department would think twice before advancing toward him again. Pablo and his guys had neutralized all of them. There was no further noise from Julissa, so they began to make their exit. Julissa had retreated to assist some of the officers who had come to the scene from the east. She assisted them and used their radio to report on the scene. Then, she drove a squad car around the block to seal Pablo's SUV from getting too far. She saw the SUV slowly pulling forward with Pablo on the 2nd-row seat. She accelerated and rammed into the side of it. Pablo's friend in the passenger side front seat immediately died. The driver was injured and slowly moving. Pablo had been beaten in the back but exited the SUV on the driver's side. He was stunned. He dropped his pistol and fell onto the floor. Julissa came around the side and pointed her own sidearm at him saying, "Don't move!"

Pablo raised his hands then said, "Hey, calm down, sweetie. Do you know who I am? I can make you a very happy woman."

Julissa said, "Save it! Keep your hands where I can see them."

Pablo had a grin on his face. He was happy to see she was by herself, not because he meant to overpower her but because he felt comfortable around women. He took his chances on seducing her. He believed he could casually ease her by sweet-talking to her, telling her the things all women would want to hear. Pablo said, "Wow, I knew it, I knew it, you are that hot woman I saw at NTB the other day. I must be the luckiest guy in the world to have run into you twice in a single lifetime."

Julissa said, "Maybe I'll arrest you in the next life too?"

Pablo said, "I would like that. Do you feel the same thing I do? Like we were meant to meet each other? Do you?"

Julissa didn't say anything. He felt it inside. He could charm her because she hadn't shot him yet. He went on saying, "Please, officer, you are an officer, aren't you? Aren't you going to read me my Miranda rights? Go on. Take me away, c'mon."

Julissa said, "I should kill you right now. You killed all those people in Texas. You are El Diablo."

Pablo chuckled and said, "Babe, you must not be as good a cop as you look. Agusto Reyes is El Diablo."

Julissa yelled, "That's a lie!"

Pablo said, "Where are you from? The moon. I am the one giving back the freedom to all of the people of Chicago. I am the one, avenging the death of my ex-girlfriend Karina and Patricia, and yeah, I'll take that to trial. Agusto plays everyone. Especially you."

Julissa's eyes got wet. She said, "Shut up!"

Pablo said, "Calm down, baby, we can get him. Together. Join me."

Julissa's breathing increased. She had been aiming at him staring at him, but now she noticed his handsome gaze. He was overpowering her. The sound of his voice, the bare confidence, and arrogance he had, was exactly what she considered a man would be like. It is what she imagined the man that she would fall in love with would say to her. Throughout her whole life, she yearned to have somebody say these things to her, and here he was, grinning right in front of her, and yes, she was frozen and confused because before being an officer, she was a woman.

At the same time in downtown Chicago, Sgt. Vega stormed outside the building then saw a working truck had parked directly behind his police vehicle blocking him in. He said "Dammit!"

A patrolman who caught sight of Sgt. Vega pulled up alongside and said, "Hey, can I give you a ride, sir?"

Sgt. Vega said, "Sure, let's go."

The patrolman looked uneven. If he were not driving a squad car in front of the precinct, it would be very hard to believe the guy was an officer. He was scruffy-looking, possibly a Hispanic guy in his late 20s. The guy's shirt was untucked, and as he drove, he was playing with his left shoe partially taking it off so he could grace the vehicle with the odor of his feet. Sgt. Vega said, "Des Plaines and Harrison, step on it!"

At the tire shop in Pilsen, Agusto finished getting himself dressed and cleaned up. He wore his friend's pants while his shirt was stained and had holes in it. There was hair gel in a small shop bathroom in the back where Agusto freshened up and restyled his hair. He thought to himself, *If this is the last time I dress myself, might as well be in style.* The sound of the NSX pulling up to the front door was heard, followed by the noise of the engine being shut off. Garrett walked in the front door. The gun he took from Jake was clenched in his right hand. Rodrigo, the old man, was frightened. The old man lifted his hands then pointed to the office in the back corner of the shop where a faucet could be heard closing. Agusto's shoes were now heard hitting the floor. Garrett signaled the old man in his briefs with a wave meaning he could "leave," then Agusto emerged from behind the thin tall doorway. He stepped forward and said, "Hey, kid, I heard you won big tonight. Taco's on you?"

Garrett said, "I raced my ass off. You had my dad nearly killed. You sit back and manipulate people. El Diablo, huh. What a joke! What is this place anyway?"

Agusto said, "Let me tell you a story. When the owner of this tire shop started it, the shop was called Lucifer's Tires, the hottest deals in town. Hmm, the place went bankrupt. The guy asked me to buy it from him at a very discounted price just so he and his family could afford to eat for a few days. I told him he was a good man, but his mind was in the gutter. He needed to see the light. I told him to change the name to Santos Tires and I would gladly invest in his shop, even bring him customers."

Garrett said, "So what?"

Agusto said, "Well, the owner wasn't convinced either. He said he was done. He said he had suffered too much and gotten nowhere. Besides, his name wasn't Santos."

Agusto laughed, "It wasn't Lucifer either." Agusto took a step but Garrett flinched the gun in his direction. Agusto went on saying, "I told him it doesn't matter what the name of his business was. It's how he and his business acted that mattered. He was being selfish and negative from the start. It was his mindset that was beating him. I fixed him. I told him to smile more, participate in local events, not to be selfish, and always be honest. The bottom line is it doesn't matter where you live or what your past was like. Anyone can walk a straight line so long as you bury the mistakes and move forward. Obey your heart and you will be successful."

Garrett said, "So, they run drugs for you now or something?"

Agusto said, "No."

Agusto took a foldup chair from between a toolbox, placed it beneath a light bulb in the center of the room, then carried on saying, "Pretty exciting. 3 weeks, huh? A lot of people would call you a hoodlum, yet many people have written all about how good of a race car driver you are."

Garrett took a step forward again, clinching the pistol but not shooting. Garrett said, "I don't care about gossip. Forget 'em."

Agusto went back to trying to tempt Garrett into shooting him, committing a sin even if it would be against himself. He had tried to bring him to the light, but he didn't want to. His hatred toward Agusto may have been too great at this point. Agusto said, "I fixed these last 3 weeks of your life. I played you and your father to get to the leader of the Outfit and it worked. The Outfit is no more!"

Garrett said, "Fuck the Outfit! This is for my dad!"

Agusto opened his arms accepting his fate but no bullet was shot. Agusto pushed on by saying, "You know why that girl at the bar started dating you? Because of me! You gained something you never had before, a backbone."

Agusto raised his voice saying, "That I gave you! You should be thankful. Heck, I bet even to her you're ungrateful, too consumed by this vengeance to enjoy what has been given to you! Well, go on! Be a man! I pay my debts."

Agusto composed himself. He leaned back in the chair then calmly said, "What's it going to be?"

In a hospital room on the outskirts of St. Louis, a beaten and bandaged Warren Lee was asleep recovering from his wounds. However, as by mystical form, his vitals began to spike, accelerating for no apparent reason. Warren Lee was having complications breathing. Nurses rushed into his room. His muscles were cramping, his body arched at his spine, then he began shaking. The nurses scrambled to assist in keeping him alive. They began using a hand air pump to assist in his breathing. One of the nurses touched him and said, "This man is burning up with fever!"

A second nurse said, "Something isn't right. I'm going to the doctor."

Nearing Harrison Ave., the patrolman who was driving Sgt. Vega had to stop at an intersection where an ambulance was loading a person from an automobile accident and the street was clogged with cars. Even with the lights flashing, the traffic was being shuffled through but very slowly. They were within blocks of where Julissa was. Sgt. Vega sighed then went through his phone to call her. The patrolman said, "When we get there, I can wait for you if you want."

Sgt. Vega said, "No, that's fine, I'm calling my team. Some of them should be there already."

The guy said, "You're Sergeant Juan Vega, right?"

Sgt. Vega said, "That's right, what's your name, sir?"

The patrolman said, "Felipe Martinez, sir, at your order. You know when I was 17, me and my twin brother were out joyriding. One night, me and my brother were driving my parent's car, this big old Caprice Wagon with the chrome grill. Well, around midnight, you pulled us over. We had both been smoking weed and we both thought we were going to the can for sure. But you let us go."

Sgt. Vega didn't raise his eyes from his phone. He said, "Maybe I saw some potential Officer Martinez and I was right."

Felipe said, "Yeah, and my brother, the guy turned his life around after that. He went clean, signed up in the army, made a lot of money, married a beautiful girl, became a CIA Agent."

Sgt. Vega said, "Like I said, I saw some potential. I'd love to meet the guy."

Felipe got a little choked up, then he said, "Well, you can't, he's dead. I do this kind of to honor him. I was probably the one who needed the can to set me right."

Sgt. Vega stopped what he was doing. He faced him and said, "You are an amazing person. It's not a mistake you're here. There's a plan for everyone."

Felipe said, "Thank you, sir, let's get going already, damn."

Julissa was still holding Pablo in the same manner she had for the last few minutes. Pablo was telling her all about the criminals Agusto still held acquaintances with and how he baited people into misery for his own amusement. She was even considering of letting the guy go. She did not have any handcuffs on her but there were wounded officers, maybe 50 feet behind her paying attention to every word Pablo said. Julissa's lips were shaking. Her eyes began to get watery. How could this perfect man be standing in front of her for all the wrong reasons? She was also believing it to be true. Her uncle could indeed be El Diablo; Pablo may be the first person who really told her "how things were." She could learn from the guy. She wished they could have more time, but they didn't. Pablo continued talking, "You know what? It's decision time, let me go. I can be your inside guy and together, we can fix Chicago. Why stop at Chicago? We can fix the country then maybe even the world. Here, lower that gun and take my hand. Let's talk."

There was the sound of patrol cars nearing the scene. Pablo reached toward her. He touched her forearm, lowered the barrel of her handgun, then caressed her arm near her elbow and up her arm. She welcomed it. She began thinking about what people would think. Could she ever really stand a chance at being happy with this guy? Would it be worth it? Then, the way organized crime works rushed through her head, prying on the weaknesses of people, blackmailing and controlling them forever. Julissa had lowered her gun. Pablo was clearly blessed in the art of seducing women and she thought that she was just another number. She believed this was his way of blackmail, using love. She didn't believe he was truly interested in her, but he was. Pablo said, "I hope to be the one who puts a ring on this hand. I just can't believe how beautiful you are. The things me and you are—"

A gunshot interrupted his speech, then another one. Pablo widened his eyes. The officers witnessed the whole thing. Pablo fell to his knees with 2 wounds in his abdomen. Julissa squeezed off 1 more piercing him in his chest. The impact thrusted her back to the pavement. The officers approached with their weapons drawn not knowing the situation. One of them inspected Pablo then in a low tone said, "He's gone." The squad car with Sgt. Vega was nearing Des Plaines.

At Santos Tire Shop in Pilsen, Garrett remained holding the revolver keeping it pointed at Agusto. He always knew that somebody deserving would one day kill him. Just as Agusto trusted in the events that gave him his glory, he had to trust his demise was coming. He was prepared for whatever happened next. Garrett had his willpower, all of it. His decisions would affect the outcome of the entire Midwest and beyond. Agusto closed his eyes and took in a very deep breath enjoying every single moment as if it were his last. Then Garrett thrusted himself back, threw his arms back, and said, "I won't! I won't do it! I'm not like you."

"Making plans. Manipulating events. Even if the whole world tells me to kill you, it won't help my dad! It's not the answer, not my fate because I choose not to. This isn't me."

Agusto said, "What?"

Garrett said, "I'm leaving. For good. You can have your cut. I'm done."

Agusto said, "Don't worry about the money. Do you like the car? The NSX?"

Garrett nodded then Agusto said to him, "You gave me new life. I will give yours a boost. The car is yours. I'll cover it with Gene. I'm sure he would see it the same way. Oh, you do know I told Jake to tell you where I was. All beef die right now and if you ever mention retaliation in my direction, I will kill you! And it will be self-defense, trust me. You needed to know what it is and make your decisions accordingly because now, you're old enough. There is no "I didn't know" after this. Now, get the hell out of here before something bad happens."

In the hospital outside St. Louis, the doctor rushed into the room where Warren was being held. Even the guards from the prison went inside to assist the nurses in holding his body down. The doctor didn't know what to make of it. There was no reason for him to be awake, yet his body had been very active then suddenly, he stopped. Warren was immediately stabilized. His vitals returned to those of a healthy person. There was no explanation for what just happened.

When Sgt. Vega and Officer Martinez reached the scene, an officer informed them they witnessed one of his detectives commit murder in cold blood. It was Julissa Reyes. Sgt. Vega ran down toward her then he said, "Julissa, what's going on, what happened?"

She was depressed. Just staring forward blankly, she said, "Do you think he was El Diablo? Or someone made to look like El Diablo that I killed?"

Sgt. Vega was confused. He asked, "Pablo Gutierrez? Look, Julissa, no one knows why things happen. This guy got to you, huh. I'm sure you had your reasons. You felt like shooting him was the best thing to do for your safety, whether he was El Diablo or not. We're on the side of good. If he's bad, we'll get him."

Julissa said, "Screw you. Why don't you ever tell me what you know about El Diablo? About the Outfit, maybe we're evil, Juan. Maybe we're all just fucked up."

Sgt. Vega shook his head and said, "Julissa, you don't mean that. Look, know who you are and never stray from it."

Julissa said, "Then tell me!"

Sgt. Vega said, "I hadn't trusted you enough. Besides, sometimes, talking about evil makes it rear up its ugly head. I couldn't risk it."

Julissa got angrier and said, "Dammit, so just keep me in the dark! I'm done! I don't care about you, Juan!"

Sgt. Vega's heart was broken. He said, "I failed you, Julie. I'm a lousy mentor."

A single tear rolled down his eye.

Elsewhere in town, Garrett stopped in the NSX at a gas station. He was very emotional, a new millionaire. He thought about Dayana as he stood there. It was near 2 AM. Her shift was almost over. He reached for his phone and he called her. She answered then he said, "Hey, babe, how are you?"

Dayana said, "Well, not as good as you. I saw that you won. Congratulations."

Garrett said, "Thanks, hey, I really want to see you. I love you. Look, I'm a new man. We can get a room tonight, downtown? What do you say?"

Dayana answered him as plainly and sincerely as she could, "Garrett I feel like I don't even know you. I got you all wrong. You're here one day, gone the next. You need to fix yourself. Your dad is in prison fighting people, your friend Jake gave you a gun . . . yeah . . . I saw it. You call me at 2 in the morning looking for sex. Who are you? This is not what I want."

Garrett responded saying, "You're right. I haven't been the best to you. I've been caught up in all these personal things. I'm sorry. But let's start over. I can buy you things. Let's do this?"

Dayana answered, "I'm sorry, Garrett, but I don't date gangsters."

She hung up on him. He threw his head back and closed his eyes realizing all his actions had driven her away. Agusto was right. He had veered off too far to get back. He did the only thing he could. He deleted her phone number, drove home, and got a good night's sleep. Garrett didn't know what was going to happen, but he was confident in himself he would figure it out. It helps to have 10 million dollars in your back pocket.

Garrett woke up early on Sunday morning. He had about $10,000 in cash stashed in his room and left it for his mom on a plate inside the refrigerator. She called him around 9 AM. Garrett had just begun driving on the interstate. He answered his phone and said, "Yeah, mom?"

His mother said, "Garrett, are you ok? And how did you get all this money?"

Garrett said, "I'm good, mom, never been better. I won that money racing 'n there's more where that came from."

His mom asked him, "Where are you?"

Garrett answered, "I'm going to be with pops for a while then after that, I might go to Dallas for a few days. I'll let you know. I feel like I love racing. Maybe there's a career in it for me."

His mom said, "Well, stay safe, son, and thank you. I'll talk to you later."

Garrett answered, "Goodbye, Mom, talk to you later."